DUTCH POINT

——————Kareem R. Muhammad

iUniverse, Inc.
New York   Bloomington

Dutch Point

This is a work of fiction. All of the characters, names, incidents, organizations, and dialogue in this novel are either the products of the author's imagination or are used fictitiously.

iUniverse books may be ordered through booksellers or by contacting:

iUniverse
1663 Liberty Drive
Bloomington, IN 47403
www.iuniverse.com
1-800-Authors (1-800-288-4677)

ISBN: 978-1-4502-6703-8 (pbk)
ISBN: 978-1-4502-6704-5 (ebk)

Printed in the United States of America

iUniverse rev. date: 11/8/2010

This book is for my Carla, Maitê, and Tainá.
Rio de Janeiro, Brazil, is in our future. This book is
also for my brother Steven Khalif Arnold Bright-Wynn,
November 28, 1977–February 27, 2010. Rest in peace.

Acknowledgments

I would like to thank Allah (God) for blessing me with all the challenges, accomplishments, and gifts in this lifetime. To my Carla, Maitê, and Tainá: this is my effort to get us to Rio. To the entire Muhammad family: thank you for that extra push and support. To my DCF family: special thanks to Rose Furmanek, Joseph Guion, Eduardo Rivera, Dr. Mark Horwitz, Bonnie Resnick, Tina W. Jefferson, Michael Williams, Maritza Velez, Orlando Cuadrado, Felix Rodriguez, and Dr. Michael Schultz. To the Hartford Police Department's Juvenile Investigative Division: thank you for the support. To Jim Solomon: those book reports were great. To Hall High School, Mississippi Valley State University, and Eastern Connecticut State University: thank you for the education. To Colin Poitras and Dr. Anna Salter: thank you for your time and honesty. To my parents and grandmother Elizabeth Edwards: thank you for being such great role models. To everyone that has supported me over the years: thank you.

CONTENTS

PART I
Sorted Confusion

Chapter 1   ANDREW

The glare of the sun shines through my eyelashes as my body lies limp and numb. The sound of my heart beats through my ears like a samba drum as purple, red, and orange circles and squares dart across the inside of my eyelids. A tug and pull to my right, another to my left. Voices echo. The smell of cigarette smoke mixed with the strong scent of spices and urine lingers in the air.

"This guy is bleeding badly. Give me some more gauze!" a male voice says with a slight Spanish accent.

"What was he thinking coming near Dutch Point without the police? This is a crazy neighborhood," a second voice says.

The two voices speak to each other as the audio in my head fades in and out. I try to see what's going on, but everything is black. The voices fade as I hear the footsteps of others who gather around me. In the distance a woman is speaking on a portable radio. I try to pick up pieces of her conversation over the constant ringing sound in my ear.

"Is that the police? Um, what was that?" I say.

A mellow feeling comes over me.

The man with the accent says to me, "I gave you a shot to help ease the pain a little."

I swallow and sigh deeply.

"Sergeant, we have two down: one critical and one fatal. We also have the shooter in custody," the female voice says, now much closer than before.

"You ID this guy?" the woman asks.

I try to open my mouth to let them know he ran inside the apartment to the girl.

3

"The name on the badge is Andrew Edwards, DCF Hartford," one of the voices says.

That's me! What's going on? Hey! Hey!

"He's shaking. Give him a little more morphine."

The voices become distorted and out of tune.

Chapter 2 MADELINE

Madeline Williams, a petite African American woman with a medium complexion, walks out of the labor and delivery department of St. Francis Hospital. She takes one final look behind her to see if the nurse is following her and then hurries onto the empty elevator. Inside the elevator she presses the button for the main lobby. She leans her right shoulder and head against the wall while her left hand rubs her basketball-sized belly. The last thing she wants to do is leave the hospital, but she knows what her body needs, and there is no way she can find it inside the hospital. She zips up the oversized jacket over her hospital gown and walks out of the elevator toward the main entrance.

Madeline heads down Collins Street toward Sigourney Square Park in Hartford's Asylum Hill neighborhood, unaware that she is walking into history. Her footsteps overlap the likes of Mark Twain and Harriet Beecher Stowe, both of whom lived in Lords Hill as it was called in their time. Asylum Hill was the name given to the neighborhood in the 1800s after Dr. Thomas Hopkins Gallaudet and Laurent Clerc established the first American School for the Deaf. The steeples of Asylum Hill Congregational Church and St. Joseph's Cathedral shoot high into the clouds and watch over the forever-changing Lords Hill. The ravages of drugs and violence obscure the beauty of the neighborhood.

Hours from delivery, Madeline craves one last taste of heroin before the baby's arrival. She enters the park and heads toward a sitting area in the far right corner where a group of men are socializing. In the distance a little girl no more than four years old is climbing high on the monkey bars, no adult within a twenty-yard radius.

A tall, athletically built black male detaches from the group in the corner of the park and heads toward Madeline. She watches him cover his smooth-shaven bald head with the black hood of his sweatshirt and then light up a cigarette. When he is five yards away, they make eye contact.

As he passes her he whispers, "Smoke, smoke."

She turns with a look of desperation as he strides by. "You got smack?" Madeline asks.

"Follow me," he says.

He heads toward the monkey bars and screams, "Alizè, let's go."

Alizè cautiously makes her way to the ground by herself and runs behind the bald-headed guy and Madeline.

They walk down the driveway of what appears to be a condemned Victorian home. The paint is chipping off its textured masonry, the original stained glass windows are broken out, and the beautiful ornamental shingles are falling off the roof.

"Go inside with your mother," the bald-headed guy tells Alizè.

Madeline follows him into the dark basement of the building. The floor is wet, and there is a very damp and stale smell. The man directs Madeline to a room and tells her to hang tight as he closes the door behind her. She hears a click and turns to see that the door is locked from the outside.

Madeline stands in the middle of the room. It is furnished with only a stained twin mattress with no sheets and a milk crate next to the bed serving as a side table. The walls have water damage, and the drywall is sagging and breaking apart. She slowly guides herself down to the bed, twitching with excitement, knowing that her chase of the dragon will soon continue. She lies there with her hand rubbing her belly and begins to think of her first date with smack.

With her eyes closed she is taken back to the summer of her thirteenth birthday. It was her last day of school and her second time repeating the fifth grade. On her way home from school, her aunt Hattie picked her up and drove her directly to Union Station in downtown Hartford. She was handed a packed bag of clothes, one hundred dollars, and a one-way ticket to Meridian, Mississippi. She really didn't understand what was going on or why she was going to stay with her grandmother.

What happened to my mother? Where is my little brother, Michael?

She could tell from the tone of her aunt's voice that something wasn't right. She was only told that something bad happened and that she had to leave and stay with her grandmother for a while.

It was a long, hot summer that year. Madeline remembers trying to call her mother in Hartford but not getting through. She knew her mother was into bad things, but it still didn't make sense why she was sent so far away and why her brother wasn't with her. The days and weeks in the South seemed to pass so slowly. In the mornings, she would clean the house and run errands for her grandmother, and in the afternoons, she played with her cousins and friends in the neighborhood. It started as a visit for a summer but turned into several years.

Sugar, flour, and peaches were on the list Madeline's grandmother gave her for the grocery store one morning. Her grandmother planned to make her famous peach cobbler. When she reached the market, Madeline ran into her sixteen-year-old cousin, Derek, who was hanging out with some friends. Derek looked taller and skinnier since the last time she saw him. He was her aunt Hattie's middle son. He was sent down to live with some of his father's family the previous year after being released from Long Lane Juvenile Detention Center in Connecticut. Back home in Hartford, he was always getting into a lot of trouble in the neighborhood. On their walk home, he asked if she wanted to take a shortcut. She agreed, and they walked down the train tracks.

"This bag is getting heavy," she said.

They sat for a minute and spent the time conversing about the old neighborhood. Derek took some cigarette rolling papers from his pocket and brownish powder from a little bag.

"What's that?" she asked.

"You don't want to fuck with this, Maddy. It's a new type of cigarette," he said.

Madeline was already experienced with marijuana and had been drinking since she was ten years old from her mother's leftover stash. She grabbed the cigarette from him almost before he could finish lighting it.

"Slow down, slow down, girl," he laughed as the paper hit her lips.

She took a long drag, and her eyes rolled to the back of her head. A euphoric rush flashed through her body as the smoke hit her lungs.

"Oh, what was that? What kind of shit is this?" Madeline asked as she closed her eyes and tilted her head to the sky.

Derek sat next to her smiling. "You will chase this dragon for the rest of your life," he said.

*   *   *

A sudden jolt of pain passes through her back and heads to her stomach.

"Oh, another contraction," Madeline says, gripping her stomach in pain.

Through her squinting eyes, Madeline can see the bald-headed guy enter the room. She sighs deeply as the contraction passes. She feels that her contractions are getting much closer now and that the baby could come any time. She begins to sit up, but he tells her to lie back down.

"Oh shit, my boys wouldn't believe your ass is pregnant," he says laughing. "Anyways, I got your shit," he says, picking up the forty-ounce bottle of liquor from the floor and taking a quick gulp.

Heroin is Madeline's drug of choice. Over the years her beautiful looks have given her a pass to many things, including copping drugs. She knows that she left the hospital against the doctor's orders and also knows that she didn't have a red cent on her. She looks up at him and says in a desperate tone, "I need this, man, I need this."

Madeline can see him smiling as he tosses the bag on the bed and walks toward her. He pulls the hood off his head, revealing a fairly handsome young man with an eight-ball tattoo on the right side of his neck. Madeline finally sits up as he stands directly in front of her. He places the forty-ounce bottle on top of the box. Madeline looks at him with disgust as his fingers slide down the right side of her face, outlining her high cheekbones and sunken cheeks.

"You know what you got to do," he says smiling.

Madeline remains sitting on the edge of the bed as his pants and underwear drop to his ankles. He then pulls the string to the ceiling light hanging above him. The neon glow of the clock radio illuminates the room. He pulls her head toward his torso with his hands. She looks up at him and sees that his eyes are closed.

This will be a brief moment of ecstasy, she thinks.

With her right hand on his hip, the other reaches for the bag of heroin. She places the bag in her jacket pocket next to a dull knife that she took from one of the hospital trays. As his grip tightens on her hair, her hand wraps firmly around the knife hidden in her pocket. Almost simultaneous with his ejaculation, she thrusts the butter knife into his abdomen.

Madeline feels his hands release her hair. He lets out a loud squeal, and she imagines him feeling a fusion of pain and pleasure flashing through his body. As he falls backward, she can see him grabbing at the knife fixed into his abdomen. He looks disoriented and shocked about what has happened to him.

A burst of adrenalin pushes Madeline to her feet as she heads to the door.

Chapter 3   ANDREW

The arm of the clock ticks the minutes away as the session comes closer to the end. There's a long pause marking another block in my thoughts.

"You give perfect detail and description, but then you stop at the same place," Dr. Sol says and slides his mug onto the side table.

I've been seeing Dr. Sol for several years now. He's a fit middle-aged Caucasian male with short salt-and-pepper hair. Over the years I have grown to trust him. He has played a strong role in my life, helping me sort through some of my confusion.

Dr. Sol shares his office space with one other colleague in an office building in downtown Hartford. His office is modestly furnished with two leather armchairs in the middle of the floor. I usually spend the time pacing back and forth while he sits taking notes and asking questions when necessary. The walls of the office are painted in a soft cream tone, and dimmed lights give the space a nice ambience. There is a small wooden table with a bonsai tree on it next to a window that extends the full length of the wall. Behind his desk he has a bookshelf, his academic credentials from Stanford University, and a large photo of the Golden Gate Bridge.

I was referred to Dr. Sol after attending several sessions at the Employee Assistance Program. I've been trying to work through some of the stress and anxiety in my life.

"My mind doesn't seem to want to go forward. It's like it's stuck or can't find the ending," I say, sitting in the leather armchair in the center of the room.

"Traumatic events can have significant effects on the memory," Dr. Sol says as he stands and then moves behind his desk.

I get up and walk toward the window as the blood rushes to my feet. "I'm much more relaxed, not so anxious. It's still hard to sleep through the night," I say, looking out the window.

Dr. Sol places a couple of files into a locked wooden cabinet next to his desk. "How are you coping with the job?" he asks as he sits in his large black leather chair.

"On my return it was difficult to go out in the field. I was looking over my shoulder every chance I got. Every client, every person that I came across, it felt like they were either after me or reading my mind. It was like they knew what I was going through. I tried to rationalize my thoughts, telling myself that there were certain benefits to living in the city. People know you in the community. Every once in a while I may bump into old clients in the grocery store or at the park. I thank God I wasn't mean to them during my investigations. The thing is, they know who I am. They know what I do for a living. Some even know where I live," I say with my hands in my pockets while I stare out the window.

"Andrew, I can see how all that can be stressful. Are you still considering moving out of the city like we discussed before?" he asks, cleaning his glasses with his tie.

This thought has come across my mind many times since the incident. I haven't had too much energy to think about it lately, never mind pack my bags.

"Either way, you can't isolate yourself. You have to put yourself out there again, Andrew," Dr. Sol says as he gets up and walks toward me.

I know he is here to help me, especially with giving me direction and some closure.

"Sometimes the best thing is being around other people. It can help you move past some of the fears and confusion. It can help you fill in certain voids. We have much more work to do before things will start to feel better for you," he says, standing next to me and looking out the window at the traffic below.

I know if anything comes up, I can call him.

"Andrew, excuse me for a couple of minutes. I have to speak with my

11

secretary. You can stay in my office if you like. I have twenty minutes until my next session," he says and then exits the office.

Looking out the nineteenth-floor window, I see the cars and people rushing down Main Street and making their way to work. A pigeon walks along the side of the window sill with the wind blowing its feathers. I can remember many times feeding the pigeons at Bushnell Park with her and enjoying Monday night jazz concerts in the summer. The pigeon looks back and ruffles its wings. I blink, he jumps. I close my eyes and follow. I fall with my arms spread for flight. The wind passes through my hair and fingers as the speed accelerates. The thoughts of escaping the pressures of this life can all end with my face implanted in the sidewalk. I have been here many times before.

"Andrew!" Dr. Sol calls out.

Surprised by his voice, I lift my forehead and hands from the window. A moist impression is left behind.

Dr. Sol walks toward me with a file in his hand. "Here's the next assignment and the address of the group I mentioned." He hands me a file and a folded piece of paper. "At least try to check out the group," he says, putting his hand on my shoulder.

I nod and take a deep breath.

"Let me walk you to the elevator," he says as I exhale.

*   *   *

Only a couple of hours into the workday, the investigations floor is already busy. The Hartford regional office is located in the Parkville area of the city. In the nineteenth century this section of the city was mostly farmland. Railroads were later built bringing many industries, from Royal Typewriter to bicycle and brick manufacturers. Parkville manufacturers also built thirty-seven-millimeter cannons for fighter planes during World War II. Over the past two hundred years the ethnic populations of the city have gone from French, Irish, and German to Portuguese, Brazilian, and Hispanic. Many of the old industrial buildings have been converted into small businesses and office space. One of the largest buildings in the area houses the office of the Department of Children and Families, or DCF.

There are over three hundred social workers in the Hartford office, making it the largest regional office in the state. We have units for treatment services, adolescent services, mental health, foster care, and investigations. The Hartford investigations units receive reports that cover the entire city of Hartford and the outer suburbs of West Hartford, Windsor, and Bloomfield. The five investigations units are housed on second floor, with a little over thirty investigators, six per unit. The fifteen-foot-high windows cover an entire wall, spanning the length of the building. The old red brick walls are all painted white. The carpeted floor is sectioned off with over fifty six-by-six cubicle workstations.

Many investigators are whisking past me heading out into the field on new cases or following up on reports in progress. Others are at their desks inputting narratives on their most recent activity on their cases. I can also see that one of my colleagues has an emergency on one of her cases.

"Does anyone have a car?" she yells out to anyone who will listen.

Searching for a car or a car seat is a daily occurrence in the office. The need always seems to arise at the time of an emergency.

A report is waiting on my chair with a note from my supervisor asking to see me in her office. I begin to take my jacket off, but instead I throw my hat on the stack of cases piled on my desk and grab the report.

"Andrew, what's up, guy?" a voice from behind me says.

I turn to see David Carol, a short, chubby Caucasian male, walking toward me. David and I were both hired eight years ago and went through the DCF training academy together.

"Hey, man! When did you transfer to Hartford?" I ask while shaking his hand.

"I got here last week. I had to get out of Manchester and treatment services, man. My supervisor was a pain in the ass. Plus I hated working out in the sticks. I was next on the transfer list, so I took the opening in investigations here in Hartford," David explains.

I smile and think about my transition into investigations from treatment services years ago. I remember shadowing a veteran worker named Randy at the time. While out on a case, he yelled at his client throughout his entire interview.

"You know, you can tell if the allegations are true or false by reading the report thoroughly," Randy said.

I came to find out that the client Randy was yelling at didn't speak much English and that was the reason she wasn't speaking during the interview.

"We are the first line of defense for the children out there. We have to let these parents know how serious we are," Randy preached.

I knew that wasn't an approach I would take with my investigations. Randy was mysteriously put on administrative leave by administration a couple of weeks later.

"In investigations the pace is different. The majority of the cases are crisis oriented and some aren't so big," I tell David.

"How's the family? You still with what's her name?" David asks.

I cut him off with a big smile. "You know what, guy? I'll have to catch up with you later. I have to meet with my supervisor," I say as I start to walk in the opposite direction.

He obviously doesn't know.

"Let's do lunch soon," David says, walking backward.

"Sure, I'll let you know," I say.

*　　　*　　　*

Stephanie, a petite Caucasian female with long blonde hair, sits behind her desk typing in a narrative as I enter the office. Stephanie is a complete multitasker, answering a call and motioning for me to sit down as she continues to type a case conference note.

Above her computer hangs a sign that says, "Verily after every hardship there comes ease." I gave it to her as a gift on her birthday a couple of years earlier. When I was younger, my mother recited that saying whenever we were going through a tough time. I seem to utter it every day now.

Stephanie hangs up the phone and then spins her chair around to face me. "Sorry about that, Andrew. I had to put a note into Link before I forgot," she says as she sifts through some of the cases on her desk. Link is our internal system that allows us to input information about our cases and search for history on others.

Stephanie seems to always have her mind going a hundred miles per hour.

"Oh, give me a quick second," she says and then quickly stands up and walks out her office.

I turn around and see her speaking with Kim, the investigations screener. Kim receives the reports from our hotline and then assigns them to the individual units on the floor.

"You gave me four cases already, and I have only two workers available to take cases today. You know Jane had a removal and can't receive any new cases," Stephanie complains.

"Stephanie, everyone is getting hit today. Sorry, but you're gonna have to keep it," Kim says, holding a handful of unassigned cases.

"When I get done with Andrew, I'm going to meet with Tracey," Stephanie says and turns to walk back into her office.

"I already met with her," Kim says as she walks back to her desk.

"Sorry about that, Andrew," Stephanie says as she sits back down in her chair, still focusing on the paperwork on her desk.

"I was going to try to catch up on some work, but I see that I have another report," I say, holding up the report that was on my desk.

"Things have been very busy as you just heard, Andrew. I was trying to get one of the cases assigned to our unit pulled back and assigned to another unit," Stephanie says, picking up and reading one of the reports on her desk. "This morning we had two high-risk newborn reports come in. One is from Hartford Hospital and the other from St. Francis Hospital. I assigned the Hartford Hospital one to Jessica."

"What are the details on this report?" I asked as I held up the report that was on my chair.

"Well, that one is a seventy-two-hour response. You have three days. This is the one I need you to go out to this morning." Stephanie slides the new report across her desk to me.

The case name on the new report is Madeline Williams.

"I already called the hospital and let the nurse know you were going to be on your way. The baby is in the Neonatal Intensive Care Unit and will not be discharged for at least seven to ten days or possibly longer." Stephanie stands and heads to the printer outside her office to pick up the directives for the case.

15

Before leaving the office, I pass my desk to grab my hat and notice that it knocked over one of my picture frames. I return the frame face up, and I'm hit by her beautiful smile. That smile sends waves through my body today, the same as it did the first time I met her. My happiness now lies in the shadows and contrasts of my many black-and-white photos of her.

With the state car keys in hand, I make my way to the parking lot. The morning is cool. The sun sits above the clouds, searching for space to break through. As I cross Hamilton Street, I see a colleague arguing with one of the security guards at the main gate to the parking lot.

"You see me every day. You know that I work here and have done so for ten years mind you, and yet you still ask me for a pass to get into the lot. Write me up," Kristy says, annoyed as the guard trails behind her.

I show my pass as I walk by.

"I'm sorry, but you can't leave the lot without a signed pass. These are your administration's rules," the security guard says, trying to rationalize with Kristy.

"Robo-Cop." That's what they call him. Some of my female colleagues say that his approach is intimidating. Sometimes he stands behind a car with both hands on his hips and doesn't let the driver leave unless he sees a pass. It's a little extreme, but he is doing his job.

Over the past few months, some state cars have been reported as missing. No one had an explanation for where the cars were or who last used them. They were usually taken after hours and parked in one spot in the morning and another in the evening. So in order to keep track of the hundred cars in the fleet, our administration came up with a plan. In order to leave the lot, an employee has to show a pass that is signed by a supervisor with the car's license plate number, date, and time of departure. With all the complaints that the procedure is a waste of time, we'll see how long it will last. I'm sure we will come up with a different way to get the cars if this problem continues.

Chapter 4 GORDO

The door to the third-floor unit is shut. A stream of light from under the door shines onto the stairs below. Voices are heard from inside.

"Lie like that! Oh yeah! Hold your head up a little more," Gordo says as the strobe lights flash into a young girl's dark brown eyes.

Several years earlier Gordo had been released from prison. The convicted felon and lifelong criminal served two years of a four-year sentence for possession of narcotics, intent to sell narcotics, and possession of a deadly weapon. His rap sheet is five pages long with charges ranging the long spectrum of criminal activity. Like so many from Dutch Point and the lower income areas in the city, he became associated with the drug trade and the gang lifestyle as a boy. While he was serving his time, he befriended his cellmate, Tyrone Fisher. Tyrone was in prison on similar drug charges with arrests out of New Britain, Connecticut. Many criminals go into prison only to come out more efficient and complete felons.

One night while in their cell, Tyrone explained a criminal trade to Gordo that he promised would put more money into his pockets than he would ever achieve as a street level drug dealer.

"Yo, Gordo, how much money you pull in when you were selling back in Hartford?" Tyrone asked as he sat on the toilet in their cell.

Gordo lay on the bottom bunk with both hands behind his head. He responded after several seconds. "There were some nights I would bring in a G. During a good week I could pull in five to eight grand for the family. The family would then give their soldiers a cut. That included all the ass, clothes, cars, and weed we wanted," Gordo said with a smirk on his face.

"What was your cut of the profits though?" Tyrone asked as he stood from the toilet and pulled his pants up.

"About a G a week," Gordo replied as Tyrone stood next to the bed looking at him.

"That's it? That ain't real money, brother," Tyrone said as he raised his eyebrows. "What if I told you there was a way you can make unlimited money, brother, with no middle man and with you in full control of your own trade?"

"What you talking about, some pyramid scheme, son?" Gordo chuckled as he looked over to Tyrone who shuffled through some letters he had received from home.

"Far from it. My cousin from home sent me a letter last week. He told me he made three G's in a matter of minutes. That wasn't selling drugs. It was selling pictures, son," Tyrone said, making Gordo curious. "Yeah, I knew that would get your attention. Listen to this, son. He was taking pictures and recording some video of naked girls from the neighborhood. He then traded his product over the Internet to clients all over the world. He's making real money. And check this shit out. He's taking these pictures from a spare bedroom in his sister's apartment. Plus there is an extra bonus. The younger the girl, the more money you can make. That's some genius shit, man," Tyrone explained as he laughed and tossed the letter to Gordo.

The conversation with Tyrone took place a couple of months before Gordo's release from prison. Gordo thought for the remainder of his sentence how he could make this new trade work when he got out. He knew Tyrone was not stupid and would want something for the information that was shared. So Gordo agreed to deliver one thousand dollars to Tyrone's baby mama in exchange for the contact information for Tyrone's cousin in New Britain. Less than a week after Gordo's release, he had his first and only meeting with Tyrone's cousin. He was amazed at how easy it was going to be to start his own trade. That same day, Gordo went to Walmart and bought a cheap digital camera.

Gordo does the majority of his work in a spare bedroom in his sister Persephone's apartment. Gordo convinced Persephone to rent a larger apartment on Norwich Street across the street from the Dutch Point housing project where they both had lived the majority of their lives. The room is fairly large. It has a queen-size bed in the middle of the room and two professional photography strobe lights with umbrellas attached in front of the bed. On one side of the bed is a large plastic container full of costumes and toys. On the other side of the bed is a bowl with an assortment of candy. In the far corner near one of the two windows, Gordo has several colorful studio backdrops. Near the window facing the front of the building, he has his desk and a laptop positioned so he can see all the people coming and going from the building. Black sheets cover both windows.

After Gordo explained to Persephone how easy it was going to be to make tons of money in a short period of time, she joined his team with no questions. Gordo already knew she was running an illegal daycare in her unit for some of the mothers in the neighborhood. He sold drugs to many of these mothers before being incarcerated. While Persephone provided the product in girls, he expanded their network of clients.

Gordo slowly maneuvers his short, round, sweaty body around the bed. He cautiously steps onto the wooden chair next to the bed in order to get a better angle. He sets his newly purchased Canon 20D digital SLR on rapid shot so he won't lose a single frame.

"Put your head to the side and stick your chest out a little more," Gordo directs the six-year-old Hispanic girl as she sits on her knees in the center of the bed.

"Gordo, am I going to get my strawberry ice cream after this?" she asks, smiling into the camera and throwing several locks of her curly brown hair from her face.

"Yeah, you'll get two scoops and the dollar I promised. But first take off your shirt and put on the gown next to the bed," Gordo directs her, pointing to the plastic container full of costumes and toys.

Three more shots fire off while she is pulling her shirt over her head, exposing her flat, pale chest.

"Now listen, Claudia. The pictures look better when you don't speak, okay? Now take off your pants. You are going to look beautiful in the tiara and princess gown I bought you," Gordo says while trying to keep his balance on the chair.

19

The girl pauses for a second looking confused by his request. She begins to smirk. "My name is not Claudia, silly. It's Caroline."

Gordo recognizes his slip with the names. "Yeah, yeah I know. I just wanted to make you smile. You are Princess Caroline, remember? Now slowly put on the gown," he says annoyed and takes several more shots.

"You think I'm a princess? Wow, I can't wait to tell my mommy," Caroline says happily while she bounces on her knees in the center of the bed.

"No, no. Remember we agreed that you wouldn't tell your mommy if I gave you the ice cream she said you couldn't have. Plus we wouldn't be able to take pictures anymore if you told," Gordo says, thinking to himself what would happen if his work were exposed.

"We wouldn't be able to take pictures? Why?" Caroline asks.

"Because we wouldn't, okay?" Gordo says angrily and walks to his laptop.

With her shirt still off, Caroline picks up a doll from the container and begins to play with its hair. Gordo sits behind the desk, takes the memory card out of his camera, and begins to download the pictures to his MacBook. It takes a minute for the download to finish. He takes a CD from his desk to make a copy of the shots from the day's session.

"Can I have my ice cream in a cone this time?" Caroline asks from across the room, still playing with the doll's hair.

Gordo ignores her and then attaches a couple of JPEG files to a network of e-mails. The subject line reads, "New Princesses Shots." From the window in front of him, he moves the black sheet to the side to get a better view of the street. Caroline's mother is parking her gold Nissan Altima in front of the building.

She's early.

"Put on your clothes and get off the bed!" Gordo nervously commands Caroline as he quickly locks his computer screen. He then turns and moves his oversized body fairly quickly from behind the desk toward Caroline.

Caroline pulls back the sheets and throws the pillows to the side of the bed looking for her clothes. She quickly finds her pants and struggles to get into them.

"Hurry, girl!" Gordo yells as he moves toward the bed, picking the shirt from the floor and throwing it at her face. The stairs squeak from behind the door. Gordo looks at the door, then to the computer, and finally to Caroline who now has her shirt on. He strides on his pudgy legs to the door.

Chapter 5 ANDREW

My job consists of going in and out of people's homes, to schools, and to police stations. This day it's a trip to St. Francis Hospital's Neonatal Intensive Care Unit or NICU. Some of my worst cases come to me here. When I think about it, it depends on what qualifies as a bad case. Is it sexual abuse? Serious physical abuse or neglect? Or maybe some mom who decided to get high throughout her pregnancy. Today it's a heroin-exposed baby. I have the nurse page NICU social worker Renee Tisdale.

My cell vibrates in my pocket. *What does Peter want?*

Peter, my older brother and only sibling, shouts over the phone with his normal enthusiastic tone. His energy surges through the line as he invites me out to lunch. I let him know that I am working on a case and will not be able to connect today. He insists that I accompany him to an art exhibition at Real Art Ways on Arbor Street that weekend.

"There will be a lot of women there, man. That's where they hang out," he says.

Out the corner of my eye I can see Renee approaching. I tell Peter I will think about it and hang up.

"Andrew Edwards, how are you?" Renee, tall, lean, and sporting a low-cut hairstyle says as she hands the folder to an assistant behind the nurses' station.

"I thought my eyes were deceiving me when I saw your name on the report."

We give each other a quick embrace and walk toward the nursery. Renee used to be an investigator in the Hartford office a couple of years back. For many years she worked in the same specialty unit I'm currently in. I shadowed her on some of my first cases in the field. After putting in a little over ten years with the department, she left looking for a new start. It was rumored that she messed up on one of her cases, but she says that she left because of the bureaucracy and that she had enough of snatching babies and disrupting families.

After leaving she took a year off to raise her first child. She did some part-time work as a therapist, and now, as of two weeks ago, she's working in the NICU, looking much healthier and less stressed and wearing a big rock on her finger that I immediately notice.

"Yeah, Thomas finally asked the big question after five years and a kid," she says with a smile. "I heard about Kay. How are you doing?" she asks sympathetically.

"I have my days," I say as we enter the nursery.

As we stand over the crib, a tiny baby sleeps, twitching every couple of seconds. She strokes her finger on his stomach.

"This is baby Williams. He's displaying the typical symptoms of a heroin-exposed baby with constant tremors. He's not eating much, so no diarrhea."

I see that there are several babies in the nursery today, many crying.

"Madeline was very reluctant to provide much social history. She mentioned her own mother briefly and said she had a brother but didn't provide any details. Madeline also had little to no prenatal care," Renee says as she reviews Madeline's file. "I followed up with Community Health Services, the health center on Albany Avenue, and they said she tested positive for marijuana at her first and only appointment during her first trimester," she says as she hands me the file.

Renee met with her prior to the delivery and says she didn't look right. "I mean she was just so paranoid, Andrew. She came in complaining of some abdominal pain, so we admitted her thinking the baby would come any minute. She was pacing the room and wouldn't sit down," she explains.

A little after their initial conversation, Madeline disappeared for several hours and then came through the emergency department high and contracting fast.

"She almost had the baby out on the street, Andrew. It was bad. Soon after the delivery she disappeared again."

Looking at the report I check to see if Madeline has a history with us, but it seems to be her first involvement as a parent, and I'm not sure if she had one as a child. The report lists her as living on Barbour Street.

Renee says, "She lived with a friend in Hartford and was moving possibly down South with family. The address on the report is the same one that was in the hospital file."

"Did anyone visit her while she was in the hospital, or did she say who the father is?" I ask.

"She wasn't here long enough for anyone to visit her. And she was real hesitant in giving the father's name, but I found the paperwork for the birth certificate next to her bed. It's in the file," Renee says.

Flipping through the file pages, I find the application for the birth certificate. She named the baby Trevan Williams and has the father as Buford Donnelly.

Handing the file back to Renee, I let her know that I will get back to her about the department's plan after following up with my supervisor.

"My experience tells me that you have a removal coming. I'll prepare the nurses with the possibility. The baby won't be discharged for a while, so it gives you some time to try to locate Madeline and Buford," she says while walking with me out of the NICU.

"Yeah, it doesn't look good," I say as I pull my cell phone out to call Stephanie. "I'll be in touch, and in the meantime, please contact me if Madeline or anyone else comes to the hospital asking about the baby."

In the hallway I give Stephanie an update on the case over the phone and let her know that I'm heading to the address on the report. I give her Buford's name and ask for her to do a check in Link on our internal computer system to see if he shows up, but there is nothing. She says she will review the case with administration and wants me to at least attempt to locate Madeline and speak with Buford to see if he has a plan for his son or if he is even aware that Madeline gave birth. I hang up and make my way to my car.

*　　　*　　　*

I park the state car in front of the Collins Bennett low-income housing apartment complex at the corner of Cleveland and Barbour streets. Throughout the city there are many low-income or subsidized housing programs. Many of my clients have some sort of state assistance in the form of food stamps, cash assistance, or section 8 housing, if not all three. One client told me last week that she paid twenty dollars for her three-bedroom unit at Mary Shepard's Place, which is one of the city's subsidized housing projects. A good deal by any standard, but she told me she wasn't sure how long she would be able to live there with the drug dealers terrorizing and controlling daily life and the outside landscape of discarded Philly blunt tobacco, drug dealers, and prostitutes as her children's reality show. That scene is common across Hartford and many of the country's inner cities.

The opening of Adrian's Landing is the first step in the big plan for downtown to be revitalized with luxury condos and housing over the next ten years. Many in the outside neighborhoods, such as this one in Hartford's North End, which is filled with West Indian immigrants and African Americans, feel that the revitalization will lead to the isolation of the city's blacks and Hispanics and to a possible displacement of these communities or, the worst case scenario, urban gentrification.

"Will we lose our neighborhoods? After they get done, the rent and cost of living will be so high we probably won't be able to live here," one community activist says in an interview run in the *North End Agent*, Connecticut's largest African American newspaper.

Will the people in the city change like the buildings developers plan to tear down and luxury apartments they plan to construct in their place? Most people have no hope for the city. They come to work at the insurance companies and businesses downtown and then leave for the security of their overpriced homes in the suburbs.

A rock or something hard hits the back of my car. Looking through the rearview mirror, I see a couple of little boys playing at the corner. I get out of the car and walk to the back. A ball is stuck under the muffler. After pulling it out, I hand it to the freckle-faced boy who yelled out, "Nigga, give me my ball!" The boys then run in the opposite direction.

BET and MTV are raising our children today. Will they turn out to be like the group of guys across the street in front of the bodega or the ones on the stairs ahead, some of whom should be in school? A dog sniffs around some garbage on the side of the building, and a couple of people sit on cars parked in front.

"Yo, yo, Troy, pass that shit to me, nigga," one of the guys says as I walk up the stairs to the front door through a dense cloud of marijuana smoke.

The door is locked, and there is no telephone or apartment number on the report. I begin to press the doorbells randomly starting with the top floors.

"Who you looking for?" Troy, the tall dark-skinned guy asks as he takes a hit from the blunt and then takes off his sunglasses, staring me up and down.

I let him know that I can't share that information with him. The guy standing next to him nudges him and points to the state car. It's not like the state-issued Ford Taurus is unmarked. Every investigations unit is issued two. They all have a huge circular emblem on the side door with the state seal, which allows us to be seen a mile away. I turn back to the door and try to see if there are any names on the mailbox, but many are scratched out.

"Who's that?" a girl from the window on the top floor asks with an attitude in her voice.

I tell her that I am just trying to get in the building.

She pauses and then yells out to the guys behind me, "Don't touch the car today."

From behind me Troy shouts up to her, "Open the door, nappy."

"You a busta, Troy," she says and then pulls her head back into the window.

Through the glass door I see an old bearded man walking toward the front. The door buzzes before he reaches it.

"Grandpa, I told you I would help you down the stairs," a young girl, maybe fifteen years old, says as she jumps out of the car in the front of the building.

The guys begin to scatter and make their way toward Cleveland Street. Troy is the last to get up. He stands in the middle of the stairs watching his boys walk away.

Holding the front door open, I let the man pass.

With his face down and hand on his cane, he says in a low-toned voice, "Good luck. The police were here again last night."

The young girl grabs her grandfather's arm and helps him to the car. Troy stands in the middle of the stairs with his back to the door.

"Excuse me, Troy," the girl says politely.

Troy turns around and looks up to me. He puts his sunglasses over his hazel eyes and walks to catch up with his friends.

*   *   *

I decide to start with the third-floor apartment. Graffiti and holes decorate the walls throughout the building. That old guy was bold to speak with me without knowing who I am. I must have DCF written on my forehead or something. I make it to the third floor and then knock on the only apartment door on that level. Almost immediately the door opens. A skinny teenage African American female stands at the door popping a piece of gum through her teeth. She is the same girl that was yelling from the front window.

"What you want?" she asks with an attitude and a little swing in the neck.

"I'm from DCF. I need to speak with your mother if she is home," I say.

Before I can complete my sentence, she rolls her eyes and struts back down the hallway in a long weave, swinging side to side.

"Ma! Some dude from DCF is at the door for you," she yells.

From where I'm standing, the apartment looks clean and in order.

Several minutes later a heavyset African American woman in her mid-forties, wearing a short pink robe and hair curlers, stops in the living room and yells at the girl, who I assume is her daughter. "Tanisha, what you calling me for? You knew I was in the shower, girl."

Unsure if she noticed me at the door, I continue looking down at the report, trying to save her from the embarrassment of her appearance.

From inside I can hear Tanisha say, " Ma, uh."

The woman notices me and walks to the door. "And how can I help you?" she asks with the same attitude and swing of the neck as her daughter. She looks me up and down almost like she is undressing me with her eyes.

I try to stay focused and look her in the eyes, not letting my eyes go any lower than her lips. "My name is Andrew Edwards. I'm an investigator from Hartford DCF," I say.

"What did the school call for this time?" she asks, clearly annoyed.

"No, Mrs.—," I pause waiting for her to give her name.

"Mrs. Towanda Jenkins," she replies.

"Your address was on some paperwork at the hospital. Do you know anyone named Madeline Williams?" I ask.

"Come inside," she says and walks back down the hallway.

"Would you like me to wait outside until you get dressed?" I ask.

She suddenly turns. One of her rollers falls to the ground, and an elongated and deflated breast flies out of her robe. My first reaction is to cover my eyes, like when I was a kid watching a horror film and trying to escape the scary part. This one I can't escape. It is only a couple of seconds before she realizes that she showed me her breast. The image is already stamped in my mind, playing back over and over.

"You acting like you never seen a woman. Come in and have a seat in the living room," she says smiling as she tucks her breast back in her robe. She disappears to a back room.

I know the brain can hold millions of memories. I just hope that is one I can erase in time.

The room is outfitted with Sammy's Discount Furniture's finest. There is a matching black pleather sofa and love seat, side tables, and lamps, and a three-foot black porcelain panther in the corner. Sammy's advertises all of this for less than $399. Crazy. Taking up almost half of the room is a huge television screen tuned to BET, playing *106 & Park*. They can barely pay their portion of the rent, but the families we serve almost always have the same big screen television from the local Rent-N-Go. These rental places are a scam, feeding on the country's poor by offering low weekly payments with extremely high interest rates.

Usually I am nervous to sit in a client's apartment not knowing what will crawl into my sleeve or bag. This one is fairly clean. A couple of years back, I had a client that had one of the worst roach infestations I have ever seen. I remember watching her sit on the sofa and the roaches crawl on and around her like water from a sponge. I ended up standing for the entire interview. When I returned home that night, I took off my clothes in the garage and even thought about throwing them out.

Wearing a pair of jogging pants, T-shirt, and pink slippers, the woman returns to the room. She apologizes for her appearance at the door, which to me is no better now.

"So who you say you were looking for?" she asks as she sits on the pleather sofa.

I know she heard me the first time.

"Madeline Williams left her address on some paperwork at the hospital," I say.

"Oh, Maddy? She in some kind of trouble or something?" she asks, nodding her head to the music video.

"Mrs. Jenkins, I really can't go into the details as to why I need to speak with Mrs. Williams, but I thought you could get a message to her that I need to speak with her as soon as possible," I say.

"Well, I'm not stupid. I know she just had a baby and that is the reason you're here," she says, turning off the television and facing me.

So why ask me then?

I feel like she is gauging me and acting like she doesn't know where Madeline is. For all I know, the girl that answered the door could have been Madeline.

"Maddy would stay here with me and my two kids, Troy and Tanisha. The last time she was here was two weeks ago, but that was just to say hello," she says, pulling the rollers out of her hair.

"Do you know anyone named Buford Donnelly?" I ask.

"Never heard of him," she replies.

I begin to feel like I'm getting the runaround. "Mrs. Jenkins, thank you for your time. If Mrs. Williams happens to return to visit, would you give her my business card?" I ask and hand her a card. I turn and walk back toward the front door.

"So, you guys gonna take her baby, huh?" she asks, holding the front door open for me.

"You know I can't answer that, but we are always looking for resources for the children that come into DCF care," I say.

"I always wanted to be a foster parent but have my hands tied with my own two. You know how teenagers can be," she says.

"Yeah, I'm sure it's tough. Thanks again," I say and then head to the stairs.

Chapter 6 GORDO

Gordo opens the door, but there is no one behind it. He has done this too many times to get caught at this point, but he knows who was hiding in the shadows. He pulls Caroline down the stairs and closes the door behind him. He kneels down to face her at her eye level.

"Now, here's the four quarters I owe you, and you'll get four more next time for your piggy bank. Remember, you are Princess Caroline, and I don't want you to tell anyone about our little game. Okay?"

"Okay," she says, putting the coins in her back pocket.

She hears her mother's voice and begins to run down the stairs.

Gordo turns around and walks into the bedroom behind him. The walls are decorated with pictures of the latest heartthrob and many sketches. The dresser has a huge boom box, and the bed is covered with stuffed animals. He locks the door behind him and then pulls the shade down.

In complete darkness behind the closet door, Cassandra can sense his presence on the other side and smells his aftershave.

He stands in front of the door and begins to speak in a low, taunting whisper. "Cassandra, Cassandra, Cassandra, I know you were there at the door. I thought I told you to stay downstairs to keep watch for me?"

His hand begins to turn the doorknob and pull it toward him. With her eyes wide and grip firm, Cassandra pulls the door in the opposite direction with all her strength. Gordo feels the pull of the door and gives a strong yank. She flies out to the floor, but before she can react, he is on top of her in one swift motion.

She tries to wrestle him off, but she is weighed down by his pure strength. He lost an enormous amount of weight while in prison. He's been in and out of the correctional system most of his life and still has affiliations with the Latin King street gang.

He puts his hand over her mouth and comes face-to-face. "I don't need a camera for this. I have enough pictures of you. If you scream, I'll cut you," he whispers in her ear and then licks the tear falling down her face.

He takes his four-inch pocketknife out and lays it next to her head. He pulls her pants and underwear down and unzips his own. She looks up to her glow-in-the-dark constellation on her ceiling, and then she closes her eyes. She knows not to struggle and lies there prepared, with her body relaxed.

Chapter 7 ANDREW

Back at the office, I sit and relax for the first time that day. Some children must have been removed from their homes because I see Lindsey, the worker who was looking for a car earlier, sitting with an infant in one arm and two other children in the playroom. I open my desk drawer and pull out a sleeve of Ritz crackers, which will serve as my breakfast and lunch for the day. With my chair as low as it can go and the back reclined, I stretch my legs.

The little boy that was sitting with Lindsey runs out of the playroom past my desk screaming. "I want my mommy. I want to go home," he yells.

Lindsey rushes out of the room, calling for him to stop running and for someone to get him. Several other investigators catch him before he makes his way to the back steps.

I'm working on-call, so I prepare my field notebook and grab an extra set of car keys. I turn on my computer and sift through some of my e-mails. I see that Peter sent one with the subject line "Real Art Ways." Under that message is one from Stephanie.

She let the unit know that she had to leave because of a family emergency. She also wrote that she reviewed the Williams case with administration. They made the decision that if we cannot locate the father or any other family member when Trevan is ready to be discharged, the department will invoke an administrative hold, which allows us to remove a child from a dangerous situation without any legal intervention for ninety-six hours.

I spend the remainder of the day updating some of my cases by inputting narratives, which is a never-ending task. At DCF, when one thing is finished, another immediately comes up: a telephone call, meeting, or the assignment of a new case.

With a couple of minutes to spare, I shut down my computer and prepare to leave. I take a couple of cases from my desk and the folder that Dr. Sol gave me and put them in my bag, thinking that I'll work at home. I exit out the back door through which the little boy tried to escape.

Let's see what the night brings.

Chapter 8 — DETECTIVE DUPRI

From a couple of blocks away, Detective Sandy Dupri can see that the crime scene is taped off. The local news stations are already lined up getting their story ready for the morning block. A steady drizzle falls on her broad shoulders and her dirty blond hair. She reaches into the middle console of her unmarked vehicle and grabs her coffee. Her watch shows 2:30 am. The grass is wet, and branches lay on the street and sidewalk from the strong winds and rain earlier in the night.

"Detective, is there any connection between this murder and the one last night?" Janet Fierra, crime reporter from the *Hartford Courant*, asks.

Completely ignoring her, Detective Dupri, a fifteen-year veteran of the Hartford Police Department, walks under the police tape. She towers over the patrol officer. She is taller than most of the guys in the department, standing nearly six feet. Single and in her mid-forties, she spends a lot of time racking up the hours working private jobs and trying to build a nest egg for retirement. The officer points her in the direction of the body lying under a tree. Detective J. T. Wright approaches her after wrapping up his interview with the only witness.

Detective Dupri looks down at him as she sips her brew of Dunkin' Donuts' finest. "What we got tonight?" she asks.

"The victim is a forty- to forty-five-year-old Caucasian male with multiple stab wounds and no identification on him," he says.

"White guy on this side of town? Does it look drug related?" she asks.

"I don't think so. More like a robbery if anything. We have no wallet and no vehicle at the location. Donna's the witness. She's been booked on solicitation and assault in the past. She found the body up here near the tree," Detective Wright says, pointing to the detectives processing the scene for evidence.

Detective Dupri looks over at Donna and senses something very odd about her but can't pick up on it yet.

"Donna says she was walking eastbound after a friend dropped her off on the corner of Love Lane and Vine Street. She said she saw a dark-colored sedan driving away at a high speed in the opposite direction. When she got closer, she saw the body up here next to the tree," Detective Wright explains.

The body is about ten yards from the street. Detective Dupri pulls out her flashlight and shines it on the ground around the body. From the curb where Donna said she saw the car leave, the street is smeared with blood, and there are two parallel lines that lead to the feet of the victim.

"The Crime Scene Division is processing the scene. Over a half dozen detectives are out searching the grass and the street for evidence. They have taken many photos of the scene and the victim. They have also taken some blood samples from the body of the victim and from the blood that was on the street," Detective Wright reports.

Detective Dupri kneels and lifts the sheet to take a look at the victim. The victim's pants are down, and her eyes instantly move to the genital area. *Now that was different.* The victim's body and clothes are covered with a large amount of blood. Detective Dupri shines the light on the victim's hands and sees what appear to be defense wounds. She observes multiple stab wounds about four inches in length to the upper chest, shoulder, and abdomen.

"This looks personal," Detective Dupri says as she places the sheet back over the victim's body. "I want to speak with Donna. Have an officer bring her to the station."

Chapter 9   ANDREW

The room is silent. The door suddenly opens and the floor squeaks. I lie still in the bed, trying not to move. Shielded in my cocoon, I feel my heart racing. I cautiously peek out of a hole and see a shadow on the wall. Its snakelike facial features and four long tentacles slowly stretch along the walls in the room, moving in and out of darkness. I attempt to follow the head of the creature but sense that it is getting closer. I recoil into the shelter of the cocoon. I lie with my eyes closed and my body curled tightly, praying that the creature won't resurface. I feel cold air on my back. The cocoon is broken. It's behind me.

*   *   *

"No! No!" I yell out loudly, waving my hands in the air.

My body is soaked with sweat. My heart is pounding in my chest. I turn to my side and move the empty liquor bottle from in front of the clock.

It's another night with no sleep.

I sit up against the headboard of the bed and look around the room. There are clothes scattered on the floor, several empty pizza boxes, and at least two empty liquor bottles next to the bed.

I'm alone.

My hands mask my face. Tears seep through the spaces between my fingers.

*   *   *

Sitting in the passenger seat has always given me a headache. The pill I took earlier begins to take effect, helping to relax my mind and body and keep the voices in my head filtered. This morning I'm accompanying one of my fellow investigators, Steve Winfield, on a case. Steve is an African American male in his mid-twenties. He has been at the department for five years and recently transferred into investigations from a mental health unit.

"Do you believe this shit? I got a same day and a twenty-four-hour response yesterday. How is that shit possible? Good thing the cases didn't turn into a removal," he says very animated, making hand gestures as he drives the state car down Vine Street. "Then check this out. I helped Emily by responding to one of her cases. Now her supervisor thinks I should be stuck with it since I interviewed everyone." He continues complaining like this for another ten minutes.

"Yeah, it doesn't sound fair. We are all in the same boat," I say, exhausted from the past night.

The pill I took earlier seems to be working fast. His voice plays in the background as I lean back in the passenger seat.

I constantly hear complaints from investigators in the field. Why don't they hire new social workers? Why not open up more investigations positions? The current freeze on hiring for any state job makes it unlikely that we will find any relief from our caseloads. When we are interviewed to come into investigations, the supervisors explain to the candidates that the pace of the work in investigations is different from any other unit within DCF. They explain that emergencies can come in at any time. I mean, it's the frontline first response. What do you expect?

"So how did you say you cut your hand?" Steve asks unexpectedly.

I look down at the two fresh linear marks on the back of my left hand for several seconds, not remembering myself how I sustained the injury. "I was changing my room around last night. I scratched my hand on the brick wall as I was moving the bed to the other side of the room," I say, coming up with a quick excuse.

Look up.

"Hey, it looks like they got something going on up there," Steve says, pointing to a spot ahead of us.

The police have a roadblock on the corner of Vine Street and Love Lane in the city's North End. I pull my seat up to sit erect. We are directed to turn right onto Westland Street.

"I thought the house we are going to was on Main Street?" I ask, now more alert.

"It is. I told you that I had to drop off a clothing voucher at a foster home first. You all right, man?" he asks, looking over to me with his eyebrows raised.

"Oh, yeah. I remember. It was just a long night," I say as I try to regain my focus, rolling down the window for some fresh air.

"I'll be real quick," he says. He gets out of the car and heads into the foster mother's home to drop off the voucher.

What was I thinking? Am I all right? Maybe I wasn't ready to return to work. I look down at my hand, passing my fingers across the cuts.

Steve returns to the car. We now respond to his new case to interview the household members.

"Mrs. Loody says there was a murder down the street last night," he reports while strapping on his seatbelt.

This is the second murder in the last two days in Hartford and about the twelfth for the year.

"No wonder the HPD can't solve any murders in the city. They begin working on one case and then another body turns up. Probably another gang shooting," he says, complaining about the violence in the city.

"Yeah, maybe that's all it was," I say, looking out the window and wondering how long we will have to wait for next murder.

Steve's client lives on the second floor of a multiunit apartment building. A short African American female in her mid-thirties with a black silk scarf covering her hair answers the door. The door opens several inches. A short metal chain secures the top of the door as the woman peeks through.

"Hi, Mrs. Cuttley?" Steve asks.

"Yes, I'm Mrs. Cuttley."

"My name is Steven Winfield, and this is my colleague Andrew Edwards. We're from DCF. There was a report called into DCF that I would like to speak with you about. Do you mind if we come inside to review the report with you?" he politely asks as she stares through the cracked door.

"What report? Who the hell called in a report on me? You can review it with me right here," she demands.

"Mrs. Cuttley, I would love to review the entire report and answer any questions that you may have. It is not appropriate for me to review a report with you in the hallway. Everyone deserves to have privacy when DCF responds to their homes," he explains.

I forgot to ask him what the case was about before we arrived. Steve called the school before we left the office. Mrs. Cuttley's daughter wasn't in class today.

After several minutes Mrs. Cuttley agrees to allow us to enter. She can barely open the door all the way because of the enormous amount of boxes, clothing, and toys in the apartment hallway. We squeeze ourselves into the narrow hallway and follow her toward what appears to be the living room.

"You gotta excuse the mess. I was just getting around to cleaning up the place," she says, almost tripping on a plastic bat on the floor.

It seems like every empty spot in the apartment is occupied with miscellaneous items. I've never seen this much clutter in my life. I take a quick glimpse into the small galley kitchen. The sink is overflowing with at least a week's worth of dirty dishes. Roaches are crawling on the floor and countertop.

"I know my neighbor called this shit in. I'm gonna get that bitch. Her apartment is dirty too. That's how I got these damn roaches. Fuck her. You know what? It was probably my mother who called you guys. Dumb crackhead bitch was mad I wouldn't give her money. She said it was for groceries. She thinks I'm stupid," Mrs. Cuttley says, gesturing with her hands and speaking fast and very loud.

"Mrs. Cuttley, slow down. I understand your anger, but hear me out first," Steve says as he holds up both hands for her to stop talking.

"Have a seat," she says, pointing to the two chairs at the dining room table with books and papers piled up on them.

Steve takes the items and places them on top of a stack of clothes and boxes already on the table.

Steve hands me a copy of the report as we sit. The case name is Darleen Cuttley. The report is from a teacher who wished to remain anonymous. The condition of the house was not even mentioned in the report. The allegations are against a guy named Glen, last name unknown. The victim is Mrs.

Cuttley's eight-year-old daughter, Benita Reynolds. A peer reported to the teacher that Benita disclosed that a guy named Glen allegedly fondled Benita's private parts on multiple occasions. The report had very little detail and did not say when or where the abuse occurred. *The report was a twenty-four-hour response and should have been dealt with yesterday,* I think as I read through it.

Steve continues having a hard time taking control of the interview.

"Mrs. Cuttley, let's make this simple. We have a report with allegations of sexual abuse toward your daughter Benita. The condition of your apartment is secondary at this time," I say firmly, interrupting her rant.

She suddenly stops and turns toward me. Steve also turns with a look of relief. Now that I have her attention, I take the lead with the interview.

"Sexual abuse? Benita ain't been sexually abused. Who the hell called it in?" she asks angrily.

It always amazes me how some parents defend the perpetrators instead of the victims. She didn't ask who allegedly sexually abused her daughter. She didn't ask when or where the abuse occurred. She didn't say she was going to kill the person that did it. At this point in the investigation, it is unknown if Mrs. Cuttley is already aware of the abuse toward Benita or the disclosure that Benita made to the school.

"The reporter wished to remain anonymous," I say before she starts up again.

"Well, ain't that convenient? Someone can call and make up some silly shit like this, and you guys come out believing everything," she says, with her left hand on her hip and right index finger waving in the air.

Shut this crazy-ass lady up. Do it now.

"Who is Glen?" I ask, cutting her off.

"Glen? Why you want to know about Glen?" she asks as her voice begins to rise again.

"The report notes that Glen fondled Benita on multiple occasions. We have very little detail in regard to the alleged abuse. The purpose of our visit is to review the report with you and also request to interview Benita about the abuse," I calmly explain to her. "So who is Glen, and how can I contact him so I can speak with him about the allegations?" I ask.

"I know this is bullshit, but since you asked, Glen was a guy I was seeing a couple of months back. We were fucking. He was never alone with Benita. So I can't see how he could have, as you guys say, sexually abused her. He changed his number, so I can't reach him," she says with a smirk on her face.

From the corner of my eye I can see movement from the cluttered narrow hallway. A young African American female, wearing a pair of black jogging pants and a white T-shirt, stands with her back to the wall listening.

"Well, you heard them talking about you. Come in and introduce yourself," Mrs. Cuttley yells out as she spots Benita.

Benita enters the room with her long braids covering her face and walks to the cluttered sofa where her mother sits.

"Hi, Benita, my name is Andrew Edwards, and this is my colleague Steve Winfield. We are from DCF and are here to speak with you and your mother," I say.

Benita is standing next to her mother and begins to cry. Mrs. Cuttley does nothing to comfort her. She sits on the sofa and rolls her eyes.

"Benita, you don't have to cry. You didn't do anything wrong," I say in an attempt to comfort her. "If you don't mind, Mrs. Cuttley, I would like to speak with Benita one on one?" I ask.

"So you can put some shit in her head? No, speak with her in front of me," she says, staring in my eyes and challenging my patience.

"Well, Mrs. Cuttley, there are some other things I would like to speak with you about. By allowing Mr. Edwards to speak with Benita, we can get through with the interviews faster," Steve explains.

Mrs. Cuttley appears to calm down as her shoulders relax and she sits back on the sofa. She looks at me and then to Benita. "Benita, you don't have to answer shit, okay?" Mrs. Cuttley says with a very sharp tone as she looks at Benita, who appears very nervous and barely looks up.

"If she doesn't want to speak, I will end my interview. This is not an interrogation," I say, regaining some of my composure.

I stand up and hold my hand out for Benita. She shuffles forward and takes my hand.

"Can you show me to your room, Benita?" I ask in a soft voice, bending down to her eye level.

We walk down the hallway and into her room. Her room is an extension of the clutter. There are piles of clothes on the bed and on the floor along with empty potato chip bags and candy wrappers. Benita sits on one of the two beds in the room. There is a cage on the dresser for some type of animal.

"What did you have in that?" I ask, pointing to the empty cage.

"My gerbil Hercules was in there. He escaped somehow a couple of weeks ago," she says softly with her head down.

"I had a pet gerbil when I was a boy. He just got too old and died. He was brown and had white spots. How about yours? What color was Hercules?" I ask.

"Hercules was all black. He was fat and ate a lot," she says smiling and looking up at me very briefly.

I wonder if Hercules is hiding under some of the piles of junk in the apartment.

"So what is your favorite class at school? What do you like to do when you get home?" I ask, trying to build some rapport.

"In gym my friends and I jump rope and play tag. Mrs. Applebee's art class is fun too," she says.

"Benita, the most important thing to remember when you speak with me is I want you to tell me the truth. If I ask you a question that you don't understand, please let me know. I can always try to ask it a different way. Okay?"

"Okay," she mumbles under her breath.

"How does your mother discipline or punish you? Does she send you to time out? Does she use physical discipline or something different?" I ask.

"She usually yells at me. I get hit only when she drinks. Sometimes she calls me names and tells me that I remind her too much of my father. She doesn't like him very much. She says he is good for nothing and stays in jail. I never met him," she replies, finally looking at me with her hands crossed on her lap.

"Did you learn about drugs in school? Does anyone in the home use any drugs?" I ask.

"My mother smokes cigarettes in the house. She goes outside on the porch and smokes with some of her friends and tells me to stay inside. I heard her talking about smoking something called weed," she says.

"Does your mother have a husband, boyfriend, or partner?"

"She broke up with my father before I was born. After that she had a lot of boyfriends. The only one I really remember is her last boyfriend named Glen. His friends call him 'Eight Ball.' "

"Have you ever seen Glen or any of your mother's past boyfriends push, punch, or hit her?" I ask.

Benita pauses for several seconds. "Glen would yell at her all the time and call her crazy. Glen told her that our apartment was too dirty and that was why he wouldn't visit her. He smacked my mother in the face a couple of times during an argument about her not wanting him to leave her. My mom cries a lot in her room. I try to enter, but she tells me to leave her alone. My aunt Trina says my mother is depressed. I think that must mean that she is sad."

"How does it make you feel when your mother is sad?" I ask.

"It makes me sad. I try to make her smile, but she doesn't have time for me. I try to tell her things, but sometimes I feel that she isn't listening to me. So I keep everything to myself."

"Do you know why I'm here today, Benita? Did you hear what I was speaking with your mother about in the living room?" I ask cautiously.

Benita's demeanor changes instantly. One second she is engaged in the conversation, and the next she retreats back behind her wall.

"I didn't hear everything," she whispers.

"Has someone ever touched you or tried to touch you on any of your private parts? Or ever try to touch you in a way that was uncomfortable or a way you did not want them to touch you, Benita?"

"No one touched me. Glen never touched me," she says as she looks up at me.

"Well, I didn't say Glen touched you. I asked you if someone has ever touched you on any of your private parts," I say correcting her and sensing she heard the entire conversation I had with her mother.

"Well, whatever the report says, it's not true," she says and turns to look out the window in her room.

At this stage in the interview, I risk that she will completely recant the

43

information that she disclosed to her peer. This is why DCF usually responds to the school in such cases. By going to the school, we could have interviewed Benita and possibly the child she made the initially disclosure to. We would have then called her mother to the school to review the report with her.

Benita is clearly afraid to speak about the allegations in the home. Her mother's influence appears to have played a big role in her daughter's unwillingness to speak during the interview. My gut tells me that something happened. With sexual abuse cases, it's usually difficult for the police to take action without a disclosure of abuse. We can put a safety plan in place with the mother for Glen not to have any contact with Benita. We will also have to attempt to locate Glen to review the report with him.

"Well, Benita, like I said at the beginning of the interview, it is important that when you speak with DCF, you tell the truth. I understand that you may not want to talk right now. You should know that my job is to make sure that parents keep their children safe. And if they can't keep their children safe, it's DCF's job to help the parents. I want to thank you for talking with me today. Here is my business card. If you ever want to speak with me about something, you can call me. Do you have any questions for me before I leave?"

Benita sits motionless on the bed. Tears well up in her eyes as she stares blankly out the window. "No," she says and turns on the television next to the bed.

I stand and leave the bedroom. I navigate through the mess in the hallway. On the wall there are some class photos of Benita and other family photos. One photo shows Benita and her mother posed in their Sunday best. There is another photo with a bald-headed guy. He has an eight ball tattoo on his neck and poses in front of a black Mercedes flashing a grip of money. These are the cases that make my blood boil: when you know that something happened, but you really can't do much. When the secret overpowers the truth, and the truth is the secret.

"So, she didn't tell you anything, did she?" Mrs. Cuttley says with a giggle under her breath as I return to the living room.

Go force it out of this crazy lady.

"I'm all set, Andrew, with my interview with Mrs. Cuttley."

"Let me just say this, Mrs. Cuttley. I believe something happened to your

44

daughter. I think she is just afraid right now to speak. If it comes out later that she was abused and you were aware of it, believe me when I say we'll be back, and you're not going to be very happy then either," I say staring at her. "There was no disclosure today, Steve. I suggest you draft a safety plan with Mrs. Cuttley recommending that Benita have no contact with this Glen guy," I recommend to Steve as he begins to write.

"Well, that won't be hard. I haven't seen Glen in months. And I still don't think it happened," Mrs. Cuttley says.

"I also suggest you recommend a substance abuse screen and evaluation and possibly a mental health assessment. Benita says her mother drinks and possibly smokes weed. Benita also mentioned that her mother is sad a lot," I say. "Have you ever been diagnosed with depression, Mrs. Cuttley."

"First of all, you are a rude-ass worker. Second, Benita doesn't know what she is talking about. Yes, I drink. Everyone does, and that shit ain't illegal. I don't know what you are talking about this weed shit. I ain't taking no substance abuse evaluation, nor am I going to cooperate with a mental health assessment," she says angrily, shaking her finger at me.

"I'll wait for you outside, Steve," I say as I walk to the door.

"Yeah, you should have been outside the entire time. You know, I'm gonna call your supervisor. Get out of my house," she yells as I reach the door.

My head is pounding, and my body is heated as I leave the apartment. I am able to keep the voices in my head under control. Outside, the wind blows a fresh breeze in my face. I lean on the car waiting for Steve.

There will be others we will catch.

Several minutes later Steve walks to the car.

"Hey, guy, never seen that side of you. Thanks for coming out with me. I'll probably go to the school tomorrow to interview her," Steve says as he opens the car door.

There are many sides to all of us. They just need to come out at the right time and for the right reasons.

"No problem. I'm here when you need me," I say as I open the passenger side door.

Chapter 10 DETECTIVE DUPRI

Detective Dupri and Sergeant, Raphael Lindo watch Donna through the one-way mirror at Hartford Police Department Major Crimes Division. Donna touches up her makeup in the small, cramped, soundproof interrogation room. Donna rap sheet shows she is Hispanic, in her mid-twenties and five feet eleven. Detective Dupri watches as Donna puckers her full brown lips in the one-way mirror and slides on bright red lipstick. Donna's long black hair hangs to the center of her back. Her lean and well-proportioned body fits perfectly into her skintight minidress that shows off her round breasts and broad shoulders. Her brown skin glows under the fluorescent lights. Detective Dupri squints her eyes and looks closely at Donna's neck area where she notices what appears to be an Adam's apple not completely covered by the silk scarf Donna is wearing. Detective Dupri looks down to the rap sheet again.

That can't be, she thinks.

"You can't be serious. She gonna try to pick up one of the detectives? Go get this over with," Sergeant Lindo commands.

"Have a seat," Detective Dupri directs Donna as she enters the interrogation room and pulls one of the cushioned leather chairs from behind the table. She places the chair in front of Donna.

"Thanks for cooperating with the investigation. It takes a bold person to call the police like you did," Detective Dupri says in a friendly tone.

"I just wanted to do what was right," Donna replies as she nervously sits and shuffles through her Gucci patterned knockoff purse.

Detective Dupri watches as Donna places a cigarette in her mouth. *She has no idea that she is a person of interest in the Love Lane murder.* She tosses a file on the desk and begins to ask Donna some easy questions, trying to loosen her up by building rapport as they call it in Interviewing and Interrogation 101 at the police academy.

"Now that is a nice bag. You must have paid a lot of money for that?" Detective Dupri asks, noticing a little break in Donna's tension.

"No, not really. I got it down in New York City a couple of months ago for like fifty dollars. Everyone thinks it's the real thing," Donna says anxiously, taking the cigarette out of her mouth and staring at the file.

Detective Dupri puts her arm over the file, picking up on Donna's curiosity. "So, Donna, you from Hartford? You have any family around here?" Detective Dupri asks in order to get a baseline of Donna's normal behavior during nonthreatening questions.

"I was born in Hartford and lived here as a kid. I just moved back to the city in the past couple of years. I have family on Park Street," Donna replies, still staring at the file. Once Donna was comfortable, she wouldn't stop talking. "I always had a dream to study at the Fashion Institute of Technology in New York City. My dream was to have my own clothing line. My friends always told me I had good taste in clothes." Donna goes on like this for ten minutes.

Even prostitutes have ambitions, Detective Dupri thinks. She can't believe Donna has gone on so long with the conversation, but she will do whatever it takes. She decides to change the direction of the interview.

"So, Donna, how did you say you found the dead body?" Detective Dupri abruptly asks.

A little thrown off by the question, Donna leans back in her chair visibly uncomfortable. "Like I said to the other detective, I was dropped off by a friend and was heading home down Love Lane. I saw some guy quickly jump into a dark-colored car and speed off in the opposite direction. When I got to where the car was parked, I saw the body under the tree," Donna explains.

Changing her tone, Detective Dupri firmly says, "I don't think you've been totally honest with us. How do I know this wasn't one of your johns you cut up? How do I know you didn't take his money and wallet before we got there?"

"Cut up? Wallet? I called so it wouldn't be pinned on me," Donna says with her voice changing from a softly spoken falsetto to a deep tenor.

"Now why would you do that? You have a history with us, Donna. What would make us think any different of you at this time?" Detective Dupri asks.

"What should make you think differently? I am telling you I didn't do it," Donna says.

The caffeine is traveling through Detective Dupri's veins. She is getting pissed. "So all of a sudden you're a fucking good Samaritan? You know how many murders happen in this city with eyewitnesses and no one comes forward. Why you? Why out of all people does a prostitute call the police?" Detective Dupri nonchalantly says and then spins the file in Donna's direction.

Donna pauses and then says with her head down, "I was out with a john. He kicked me out of his car on the corner of Love Lane and Vine. We had an argument over pay. There were other people out on the street that could place me where the body was found. I didn't witness the murder, but I think the guy getting into the car next to the body was a tall, medium-complexioned black or Hispanic male. He had dark-colored clothes. The vehicle's license plate was from Connecticut but had some funny design on it. The car then sped off in the opposite direction. I didn't think anything of it until I got closer. That was when I saw the body."

"Wow. That's completely different from what you initially reported. Now you were close enough to see a Connecticut license plate. So an outstanding citizen like yourself calls the Hartford Police Department because you were concerned? Let's get fucking real now," Detective Dupri says.

"I've walked up on many things in my life. This was the first time I saw a dead body. For all I knew the john I was with could have called you guys thinking it was me who killed this guy. So I called," she says.

Growing impatient, Detective Dupri stands and begins to read off Donna's past charges. "The beginning of the month, assault third, possession of a weapon, a knife at that. Three months ago, solicitation twice in the same month. You're a busy girl. Let's not forget the fucking murder charge you're gonna get." Detective Dupri walks behind Donna and leaning toward her ear whispers, "After we get you for this one, you'll be a good piece of ass up at

York Correctional women's prison. Or maybe you think I'm a dumbass and don't know you are a fucking man and only changed your name. You are still a male on paper. You can't hide your secret from me. If the word gets out, you are done. Just like the guy you killed, if you know what I mean."

Donna quickly turns and stares at Detective Dupri with her eyes wide and jaw clenched. "I have nothing to do with this fucking murder. Yeah, I'm a man, but that don't mean shit. You don't have any evidence that I did anything wrong. I was only trying to help you dumb fucks," she says angrily.

Detective Dupri throws a copy of the crime scene photos on the table. "So you sure this isn't the john you cut up? Why did you fucking do it, Donna?" Detective Dupri fires back.

After taking one look at the pictures, Donna pushes away from the table, turns, and then vomits on the floor, barely missing Detective Dupri's shoes.

"I told you I didn't fucking kill this guy. I sure as hell didn't cut his dick off, you sick bitch," Donna says and then leans over in the chair, another stream of vomit coming from her mouth.

Sergeant Lindo knocks on the door. Detective Dupri takes a deep breath and then exits.

"From the looks of that, she may be telling the truth. We'll have to cut her loose for now. A fucking man? Why didn't you tell me that before you went in?" The sergeant smiles.

With her hand on the doorknob, Detective Dupri begins to return to wrap up the interrogation.

"We actually got another shooting while you were inside. I need you to head to Brown Street in the South End. I'll have Detective Wright wrap it up with Donna for you," Sergeant Lindo says.

Chapter II MADELINE

Madeline races down Cleveland Street, looking back every couple of steps. Since the stabbing and leaving her son in the hospital, she's been underground and moving from house to house hiding from the bald-headed guy and DCF. She called Buford Donnelly, one of her sugar daddies, who lives alone on Cleveland Street in Hartford's North End. Noticing the urgency in her voice, he invited her over since she didn't want to speak on the phone.

She walks down the darkened driveway to the back porch and knocks on the door. Waiting for him to answer the door, she paces side to side on the porch. Minutes earlier she left Towanda's apartment, which is down the street. She was able to get a quick shower and fresh clothes. Towanda also gave her the business card from the DCF investigator Andrew Edwards, who visited Towanda's home looking for her. The pain from the delivery made it very difficult to get around, but she knew the bald-headed guy and DCF would be looking for her. Before she could get high, she had an important matter to attend to.

"Maddy baby, how are you?" Buford asks as he opens the door, wiping the sleep out of his eyes.

With the door barely open, Madeline squeezes past him, closing the door and then locking it. "Anyone here with you?" Madeline asks and then walks through the kitchen, into the living room, and down the hall toward the bedrooms.

"What you think, I got another girl here? No, I'm alone," he says smiling.

Buford Donnelly is a tall, obese, African American male in his mid-sixties. He has lived in the same home for over thirty years and has never been married. Madeline watches him as his massive body lumbers to the refrigerator.

"You want a beer?" he asks.

"No, I'm good," Madeline replies as she walks back and forth in front of the window, peeking out the sides to see if she was followed.

Buford straggles into the living room sipping his beer and has a seat on his Lazy Boy recliner in front of the television. On the side table next to him is an empty bucket of KFC chicken, with the bones on the table and the floor, and a half-eaten container of fried rice from the Chinese restaurant.

Madeline anxiously paces in front of him and then says, "Buford, I'm in big trouble. I did something really stupid."

Buford takes another sip from his beer and says, "What you mean you in trouble, baby? Come here. Sit and talk to me."

"No! You don't understand. They could come right now and take me out of here," Madeline yells, waving her hands in the air. She can feel that she is a little on edge and needs the drugs in her system.

"Who is coming here? What are you talking about?" he asks confused.

"I had the baby, Buford." Madeline finally stops and looks Buford in the eyes as she tells him the news about the baby.

Months ago Madeline told Buford that she was pregnant and that she wasn't sure if she was ready to have a baby. When she told him about the pregnancy, he instantly thought the baby was his, so she went along with his assumption. She knew that she didn't have much family around that could support her. He told her in the past that if the baby was his, he would support both of them with the little he gets from social security and his pension from the City of Hartford. He was no rich man but definitely well off from Madeline's point of view, owning his home and always giving her money and a place to stay.

"Had the baby? So where the hell is it?" Buford asks, sitting up in his chair.

Becoming more frustrated as the conversation goes along, she yells out, "I had to leave him at the hospital. They are surely going to take him after they find out I had drugs in my system."

"Take the baby? Who is going to take the baby?" he says now angry and with a more commanding tone.

Madeline senses his anger and backs off a little. She sits on the floor with her head on his knees, forcing the tears out of her eyes. "DCF, Buford. I used right before the delivery, and the baby and I tested positive."

"When DCF start taking babies for someone smoking a little weed?" he asks.

She hears in his voice that he has calmed down, and he begins to caress her head with his hand.

Madeline left out the part of copping the smack and stabbing the bald-headed guy. She also never told him that she was using heroin. Sitting on the floor and sobbing with her hands covering her face, she says, "The hospital social worker told me that they were mandated reporters, whatever that means, and that they had to notify DCF of the delivery."

"Notifying DCF doesn't mean removing the baby," he says.

"You have to help me get the baby, Buford. That's the only way to make it right," she pleads.

"Girl, how am I gonna do that, just walk out with the baby? They probably think I'm the kid's grandfather." He chuckles and then takes a sip of his beer.

She stands in front of him, looking at him intensely, and places her hands on both of his knees. "Buford, if you don't get *our* baby, they will put him in a foster home."

He takes her hands from his knees and holds them softly in his. "I'm sorry, baby. I didn't know you had the baby, that's all," Buford says.

"Your name is on the birth certificate as the father, and all you have to do is go acknowledge yourself and get in contact with the DCF worker," she explains. "Here is the worker's business card," she says as she hands it to him.

Kneeling between his legs, in an instant she turns from a heroin fiend to a seducing sextress. She makes her way from his knees to his pajama bottoms, pulling them down. As she caresses his penis she says, "I need you to make this right, Buford." Looking up at him, she laughs to herself and thinks how she has this old guy wrapped around her fingers in so many ways.

"I'll make it right, baby. I'll make it right," he says.

Madeline pulls his pants off.

"Girl, let me go get one of my pills real quick?" he asks as he tries to get up.

Forcing him back down by squeezing his penis tighter, she asks for him to promise that he will help get their baby. Caught in the heat of the moment, he says yes and falls forward on top of her in the middle of the floor.

Chapter 12   ANDREW

The small waiting room is full with its regulars. The need to release the confusion in my head seems to be an epidemic not only attached to me. My mind constantly races from one thing to the next. My steps move swiftly and precisely. I'm overwhelmed by a whirlpool of emotions when I think. It's no longer about right or wrong. When the glass and pills hit my mouth, a wave of acceleration sweeps over me. The label on the bottle says don't take the pills with alcohol, but I disregard it because liquor gives me that extra edge to walk in the dark. Sometimes I wonder where my mind has gone. Will it all catch up with me?

Dr. Sol says no one will care in the end and that I will be praised. It used to be simple directives at work that I would forget. Now it's so far beyond misplacing the car keys. How much of me did I erase over time? How much of me has been lost or locked in my mind? How long can this go on? My hands can't stay still. I squeeze them to stop but only transfer the shaking to my feet.

I look across the room and catch Mrs. Clemens staring again. Mrs. Clemens is a Caucasian female in her mid-fifties with long gray hair. What's wrong with her? I know she watches me. She speaks to herself, but what does she say? I hear only mumbles, but sometimes I catch some audible gibberish. What's in her purse? She looks in it often and checks the clock on the wall every five minutes.

What about Garry? He's a tall Caucasian male in his forties. He's been coming here longer than me. He seems to know everyone here. He flips through the pages of the magazine in unison with me. Is he reading or just looking at the pictures? There he goes once again to the counter.

"My name is Garry Stein. I have an appointment this afternoon. I have been waiting here for ten minutes. When will the doctor see me? I want to see him now!" Garry demands.

This is his fourth time to the counter since I've been sitting here. The new secretary seems to be getting an introduction to the madness of this office.

"Mr. Stein, can you please have a seat and wait to be called?" she asks politely.

Garry returns to his seat and starts flipping through the magazine rapidly. He looks back to the secretary with a smug look on his face. What's his diagnosis? It's like a game here. Merv Griffin could have come up with a show called *Guess My Diagnosis*. I wonder what they think of me. Do they see me?

The secretary calls me to the counter. Garry looks at me and then gets up to stand beside me.

"I was here before him! I have an appointment. What's taking you guys so long?" Garry asks frustrated.

Now with a little frustration in her own voice but still polite, the secretary stands and meets Garry eye to eye. "I'm sorry, Mr. Stein. Could you please take a seat? It's not your turn. There are other clients here. I will be sure to let you know when the doctor is ready for you," she says and then sits back down in her seat. She looks at me and asks, "Do you have an appointment with Dr. Sol for today?"

"No, I don't have an appointment. I don't think it should be a problem though. I called him earlier so he is expecting me," I say.

The secretary flips through the calendar. "He will be finishing up with a client soon. He will have twenty minutes before his next session. It's up to him if he wishes to meet with you. I'll leave a message on his voicemail," she says.

I always have a feeling of exclusivity with Dr. Sol. I know he only keeps a couple of dozen regular clients.

I can feel Garry staring at me as I walk back to my chair. He pulls the magazine over his face and squints at me. I take a seat on the opposite side of the room. In the chair is a copy of the *Hartford Courant*. The front page has an article with the mayor of Hartford requesting assistance on the streets from state police because of the recent rash of murders.

"The residents of Hartford should not have to live like they are in a war zone," the mayor said to the reporter.

I will definitely have to be more careful on the streets.

"Andrew! How are you?" Dr. Sol calls out from the door.

I stand and walk to the open door. I hand Dr. Sol the newspaper and the folder with the most recent assignment as we walk into his office.

Chapter 13 ANDREW

The end of the workweek is always something to look forward to. My headphones are on, but I play no music and listen instead to the sounds of my colleagues socializing around me. Every once in a while I pick up on the office gossip about who is having sex with whom or the latest worker that was walked out of the building for some sort of misconduct. I even hear whisperings about me.

"Why did he come back so soon?" I heard one girl ask another colleague when she thought I was listening to my iPod.

"He should have taken more time to return to work. He should have just left this place," others have whispered.

They're right in some ways. I have my reasons to stay at DCF. Part of it is my own personal mission to help people. Other reasons may be my own demons that scratch the surface but run back into the closets behind closed doors. My hand is on the mouse as the arrow sits in the middle of a typed page, a strategy to make it appear that I'm working when I'm not. My phone vibrates in my bag. I check to see a text message from Peter labeled urgent.

"Guy, you better be there tonight. Get your head out the dirt. HOLLA," Peter writes.

Peter always seems to make me laugh when I need it. When we were younger, he used to beat me up a lot. He said it was to make me stronger so I wouldn't be a punk, a momma's boy. I guess that's what big brothers are supposed to do. It was just the two of us back then.

Are you sure of that? The way I remember, it was you who was in the dark room hiding. Big brothers are supposed to also protect you. Did he protect you, Andrew, when you needed him the most?

57

Stop. This is not the time, I think, trying to stop the voices in my head.

Maybe Peter's right. Maybe what I need is a good time out. Let me give him a call back. My office line begins to ring with a call from the security desk in the front before my cell connects with Peter. I answer the office line.

"Mr. Edwards, we have a Mr. Donnelly here to see you," the security guard says.

Hmm, just the guy I was looking for.

"I'll be down in a minute," I say and then grab my steno pad and pen.

There are many people in the waiting area this morning. I look at the security guard who points me in the direction of the middle-aged African American male sitting in the far corner of the room.

"Mr. Donnelly?" I call out to get his attention. "You can come this way." I hold the waiting room door open as he stands from his chair.

Buford Donnelly holds out his hand, which is rough and feels like sandpaper, and firmly shakes mine as he passes me in the doorway. "Buford Donnelly the third," he says with a deep bass in his voice.

Mr. Donnelly stands several inches taller than my six feet one. I point him toward one of the unoccupied conference rooms. He walks with an envelope in his hand and a slight limp.

"Have a seat anywhere you like," I say, closing the door behind me.

"I was at the hospital today and was told you were the guy I needed to speak to before I could visit with my son Trevan. Renee, the social worker there, gave me your number and address. She also suggested that I give you this," he says and hands me the envelope he is carrying.

Inside the envelope are copies of Trevan's birth certificate and a signed copy of the voluntary acknowledgment of paternity by Mr. Buford Donnelly.

"What do I need to do to have Trevan come home with me? I already signed acknowledgment and put my name on the proper paperwork at the hospital. I understand Trevan will be at the hospital for a while for further monitoring. I would like to at least visit him," he says as he sits across from me at the conference room's metal table.

"When I initially responded to the hospital, Madeline left only an old address. She left no other contact information. I had no way to reach you. It's good that you came forward because DCF was looking to take legal action if we couldn't find you. There should be no problem scheduling a visit at the hospital with your son. I will have to review this new information with my supervisor to determine DCF's next steps," I explain. "Have you heard from Madeline since the birth of Trevan?" I ask.

"Yeah, Maddy visited me the other night. She told me about the news of the birth. She didn't tell me where she was going or how I could reach her. She only told me to go to the hospital as soon as possible," Mr. Donnelly says, leaning forward with most of his body weight making the table squeak.

"Why weren't you at the hospital at the time of the delivery?" I ask while taking notes on my steno pad.

"I didn't know that she was back in town," he says.

Or were you not sure if this was your baby?

"Are you aware why DCF has an open investigation with Madeline? " I ask.

"Well, that's one reason I'm here. I really don't know much. Maddy told me she was smoking a little weed and DCF would take the baby," he says.

"She didn't tell you everything then. Madeline and your son Trevan tested positive for heroin at the time of delivery," I say as I place my pen down.

Mr. Donnelly is caught off guard with this information. He raises his eyebrows and pushes back in his seat a little. "You know, she was always hanging out with the wrong crowd. I told her she needed to clean up her shit. I thought she left town to get cleaned up and get away from the bad influences. To be honest, I was not aware that she was using heroin," he says.

"Let me be very clear with you, Mr. Donnelly. Your son would surely have been removed if you didn't come forward. Trevan is in the NICU because he is withdrawing from the heroin Madeline was using during the pregnancy. The hospital also believes she used possibly minutes before she came through the emergency room," I explain.

"There's no way I could let DCF remove my son. That is why I am here. I want my son and will do everything to protect him. My oldest daughter, Kendra Donnelly, resides in Bloomfield and will be a support. I can give you all her contact information if needed. I will also have all the necessities for Trevan before he is discharged. You can come to my home anytime to ensure that it is a safe place for him to live," he says with a much stronger tone and sitting more erect in the chair.

"Like I said before, I will review the new information on the case with my supervisor," I say. "I'll call social worker Renee Tisdale at the hospital and inform her that it is okay for you and your daughter Kendra to visit Trevan."

"And what about Maddy? Will she be able to see the baby?" Buford asks.

"I will first need to speak with Madeline in person before she sees the baby. If Madeline contacts you, let her know that I wish to speak with her. What is your address and telephone number? Also, I will put your daughter Kendra down as a family resource," I say, flipping the page of my pad.

My cell vibrates in my pocket. It's Peter.

"Here is my business card. I'll call you after I review the case with my supervisor," I say and get up from my chair.

"Thank you for your time," Buford says as he walks out of the DCF office.

"Peter, what's up, man?" I say when I answer my cell.

Chapter 14   BUFORD

Buford exits the DCF building and crosses the street to his silver 1980s model Cadillac DeVille. In Troy's parked car at the corner, Madeline calls Buford's cell phone. When his phone rings, he doesn't recognize the number. He hesitates in picking it up, still a little thrown back about what he learned about the heroin.

"Hello, Buford speaking."

"Buford baby, it's Maddy."

"Hey, Maddy," he says as he sits in the driver's seat of his car.

"Did you go to the hospital and sign the paperwork like we discussed? Did you speak with the DCF worker?" she knowingly asks as she watches him from a block away.

Buford pauses for a couple of seconds. "Maddy, the guy said you and Trevan tested positive for heroin. Is that true?"

Madeline knows she wouldn't be able to hide this fact from him. Just as long as he signed the paperwork, she is still in the driver's seat with her plan. "You gonna believe everything they tell you, Buford? That's our baby, and you now signed the paperwork that proves it," she yells over the phone, cutting him off.

"But, Maddy, you didn't tell me you were using heroin."

"I told you I was in big trouble. That's why I came to you. Don't try to back out of being a father now. You said you were going to take care of this so they won't take *our* child," Madeline yells.

"But, Maddy," Buford tries to speak over her but can't get a word in.

"Did you sign the paperwork, Buford?"

"Yeah, I signed the paperwork at the hospital. I'm also leaving the DCF

61

office as we speak. Maddy, the worker said he will speak with his supervisor about me getting custody. He also said Kendra and I can visit Trevan at the hospital," he explains to her.

"Mr. Edwards also wants to speak with you. This don't sound too good, Maddy. They were talking about removing the baby," Buford says concerned.

"Listen, my phone is about to die. I'll call you later." She hangs up.

"Now what?" Troy asks as he starts up the car.

"We follow him day and night until he gets the baby," Madeline replies.

Chapter 15 ANDREW

I arrive at Real Art Ways about an hour late. From outside I can see that the facility is already packed with Hartford's young professional and artsy crowd.

I never really liked big crowds. During a family outing when I was nine years old, I got separated from my brother Peter and one of his friends. We were at the Yonkers Raceway in New York for its yearly carnival. I spent the entire time searching for them and no time on the rides. Peter told me later that they spent the entire time eating cotton candy and chasing after girls. Peter said they thought I was fine so they didn't look for me.

Before I can make the decision to leave the line at Real Art Ways, a voice comes from my left.

"Are you a member or a guest?" a man asks.

I shake my head to regain my focus. "I'm a guest," I say, handing the guy my five-dollar cover and then walk inside.

The facility has a laid-back industrial vibe. There are some funky colorful chandeliers hanging high from the ceiling. The exposed bricks on the walls bring out the character of the building. On the stage to my left, a local artist is performing with his band. The crowd pushes me further inside. I spot Peter in the far corner conversing with a couple of women. I begin to weave my way toward him.

"What's up, bro! Good to see you," Peter says as he gives me a quick hug.

Peter is in his mid-thirties and is a couple of inches taller than my six feet one. He maintains his lean physique by playing basketball at the YMCA in downtown Hartford in the mornings. Peter is a very outgoing individual and enjoys socializing. I'm the complete opposite. I would prefer to stay home watching television. The girls always comment on Peter's hazel eyes and smooth unblemished brown skin. Peter received both his undergraduate and MBA from the University of Connecticut. He got his big break in real estate after flipping several houses. He now owns several fast-food chain stores in Hartford.

"Look at this tall one, man. She's mine tonight," Peter whispers in my ear as he holds me for a beat. "Ladies, this is my younger brother, Andrew, I was telling you about," Peter says as he introduces me to the two women he is standing with.

Myra, a tall, athletically built African American female, whom Peter was whispering about, is one of the artists in the exhibition. "Peter said you work for DCF. Don't you guys take children from their parents?" Myra sarcastically asks while taking a sip from her cocktail.

If it's not defending DCF with our clients; we have to attempt to educate the complete stranger about what we do as social workers. I decide to give her the short version. "That's not all we do," I reply with my hands in my pockets, forcing a fake smile.

"Well, there was this one year I was volunteering at an afterschool program in the South Bronx teaching sculpting. Jorge, this cute little Puerto Rican boy, was amazing. He picked up all the methods I was teaching. Needless to say, not all the kids in the program had perfect personal lives. One day in the middle of one of my classes, two social workers from Child Protective Services literally removed him from the class and brought him to a foster home. They didn't even wait until my class was over." Myra completes her story, looking at me.

A couple of years back, there was a story all over the news about Florida's Child Protective Services losing track of a foster child for an entire year. I guess people think all state-run Child Protective Services like Connecticut's DCF work the same.

Without giving any real reaction to Myra's story, I just look at her and say, "Interesting."

"Ladies, maybe we can go downtown for more drinks after the exhibition tonight," Peter says, holding me close and trying to break the tension.

Myra's friend Jane, a short, chubby Asian woman who was standing with us, begins to speak in her slow, monotone voice, "Real Art Ways was founded twenty-nine years ago by a group of artists. They wanted to create a place where they could exhibit their work. The original location was in downtown Hartford. They recently moved to this location on Arbor Street."

"This facility is really one of a kind! An artistic gem," Peter says as he sips his drink.

In my mind I'm laughing because Peter knows nothing about art. He knows a lot about women and how to fool them that he is some art connoisseur. I don't think Peter really got a good look at Myra under these lights, but I'm no judge. My thoughts begin to float over the jazz chords in the background. I find that I am suddenly drawn to a huge black-and-white photo over Jane's shoulder.

"I'll talk to you later, Peter. Nice meeting you guys," I say, shaking the hands of Jane and Myra before I walk away.

The photo hanging in front of me is so simple yet so powerful. A shirtless and shoeless boy cries as he tries to take a piece of meat from a dog. Below the picture is the information "Lost Meal" shot by Patricia Dos Santos in Rio de Janeiro, Brazil.

"The power in the photo for me is the people walking by and doing nothing," a voice with a foreign-sounding accent says from behind me.

With my eyebrows raised, I turn and am instantly blown away by the tall, lean, bronze-skinned muse in front of me.

"Patricia Dos Santos," she says, extending her hand to me.

Confused, I fumble my hand out of my pocket and take a second glance at the picture as I greet her. "Andrew Edwards," I say as our eyes lock. "Very powerful photo." I can't believe that is the best I can come up with.

Her hand feels so soft.

"Well, I try to capture emotions in my shots", Patricia says and then politely asks for her hand back. "I have several other photos in the exhibition. They will be here for the next couple of months," she says and points down the wall.

Stars seem to be spinning around me as she stands there talking. Now

65

I know why people say Brazil has some of the most beautiful women in the world.

"Excuse me, Patricia. Someone was interested in purchasing one of your photos. Do you have a minute?" one of the RAW employees asks.

"It was a pleasure meeting you. Be sure to look at some of the other photos. I'd love to know what you think about them," she says, smiling and walking to the opposite side of the gallery like she's working a runway.

Chapter 16 ANDREW

It's been only a couple of days, and I can't keep my mind off Patricia. I open my wallet and pull out the business card I managed to take from under one of her photos that was on display at the Real Art Ways event. Even the card has its own artistic flair. One of her photos is posted on it, and one side is in English and the other in Portuguese. She disappeared in the crowd after we spoke. That night I took her advice and checked out the rest of her work. Many of her photos are portraits of children and families in slums all over the world. She has a photojournalistic approach to her photography that makes the viewer feel like he or she is there.

I've been contemplating sending her an e-mail since meeting her. I know I don't have the courage to speak to her on the phone just yet. I open Microsoft Outlook on my work computer, skipping past my full inbox. I hit new message and begin typing.

> *Hello Patricia,*
>
> *I am not sure if you remember me. I had a conversation with you in front of your photo "Lost Meal" at the recent exhibition at Real Art Ways this past weekend. I just wanted to write to say that it was nice meeting you and to tell you that I took your advice and checked out the rest of your work that was on display. Your work is amazing! I wasn't sure where you would be displaying your work after you leave Hartford, but I was interested in maybe being put on your mailing list. Thanks for the pleasure in meeting you and your work.*
>
> *Andrew*

I press send before even reviewing the e-mail. *Man, wait, what did I just write?* I'm not sure if I sound like an obsessed fan or some guy that was afraid to say what he was really thinking. I should have said you are amazingly beautiful. I would love to see you again over a cup of coffee. Better yet, how about dinner and a movie? I have been out of the dating scene for ages. My eyes switch focus from the computer screen to Kay's picture in the little frame between the computer and wall. *Sweet Kay, how I wish it was you that I was sending the e-mail to.* A feeling of guilt blankets my heart. I turn my chair around away from the computer and see the time on my clock.

Shit! I'm late.

Chapter 17   ANDREW

I start the engine to the state car and head to the assistant attorney general's office on Sherman Street for the weekly Multi Disciplinary Team, or MDT, meeting. Stephanie would usually be there, but she is still out of the office, and it's my turn to cover. I'm quickly buzzed in and show my badge to the desk clerk who directs me to the second-floor conference room.

I slip into the room and see that the table is full. The meetings are held in one of the spare conference rooms in the building. There are about a dozen people around the large wooden table. I work my way to the empty seat on the opposite side of the table. The team consists of all familiar faces. The facilitator, Ted Gray, sits at the head of the table. To his right are the head physician and two forensic interviewers and family advocates from the Child Advocacy Center (CAC) at St. Francis Hospital. The Connecticut Sexual Assault Crisis Services (CONNSACS) has a counselor represented. Sergeant John White from the Hartford Police Department Juvenile Investigative Division and Assistant Attorney General Donald Webb are seated on the left side of the table.

"Nice that DCF could make it to the table," Prosecutor Brian Leroy says under his breath.

How could I forget Prosecutor Leroy? He's one of the biggest critics of DCF, even though we are all supposed to be working as a team. The concept of the MDT is to look at some of the critical reports like the serious physical abuse or sexual abuse cases that come from the Hartford region and pull from the expertise of all the specialties represented at the table. There are many occasions when the team has helped break cases with the police and the prosecution, getting a confession from the alleged perpetrator and getting convictions. There have been many complaints by my colleagues about the MDT process. They say some of the recommendations that are given by the team come months after the investigation is closed and a little bit too late to implement the recommendations offered by the team. The guns are aimed toward DCF when something goes wrong.

I place my jacket on the back of my chair and listen to the discussion that was already underway. The conversation is somewhat heated between Prosecutor Leroy and Sergeant White about a case the judge threw out of court.

"If your detectives would do their jobs right, maybe, just maybe, I can put some of these pedophiles away," Prosecutor Leroy says, looking down and writing on his legal pad.

With his face turning candy-apple red, Sergeant White restrains himself in his response. "It wasn't my detectives that missed the ball on this one. The thirteen-year-old female victim provided a clear disclosure of multiple incidents of fondling. There was also allegedly digital to vaginal penetration by her twenty-five-year-old male cousin when she was between the ages of eleven and thirteen. Plus penile to vaginal penetration by an uncle when she was ten years old," the sergeant explains.

"So, sergeant, how did this molester slip through your hands this time?" Prosecutor Leroy asks in his usual condescending tone.

Losing his patience, Sergeant White replies, "You know, the kid gave the initial disclosure to a peer and a teacher before DCF interviewed her a second time. It was only after DCF's interview that she recanted and refused to go forward with the interview at the Child Advocacy Center or provide a statement to us."

There are a couple of seconds of silence before the ball is passed to my court.

"Andrew, do you have the DCF protocol for this case? Maybe we can see the exact disclosure that was made instead of just making assumptions about what was actually disclosed. It's possible the investigator had a legal consult with the DCF principal attorney?" Assistant Attorney General Webb asks in order to break some of the tension.

In my rush to the meeting and my Hail Mary of an e-mail to Patricia,

I forgot to look in my inbox to retrieve the agenda items Stephanie usually sends to the covering worker. I feel an instant hot flash through my body. All of the eyes in the room are on me. I make a lousy attempt to search my bag for the files that I know aren't there. Looking up I say, "I must have forgotten the file on my desk."

From across the table, the CONNSACS counselor begins to provide statistics on children that recant their disclosures. "It's common for victims to be fearful to disclose. With the alleged perpetrator being a family member, there was possibly some extra hesitation regarding her providing a full disclosure to the police or DCF," the forensic interviewer from the CAC adds.

"Her reporting doesn't seem to be the problem. She gave the disclosure to the teacher and that should have been good enough for DCF to contact the center for an interview. It looks like DCF's ongoing issues with conducting multiple interviews with the victims have helped a couple of slim balls get away," Prosecutor Leroy says as he looks in my direction.

I want to jump across the table as I wrestle with the voice in my head. I sit for the rest of the meeting, pissed that I wasn't prepared, and it definitely showed. I take the names of the cases reviewed and add them to my growing list.

Chapter 18 ANDREW

Back at the office I pick up the new case on my chair assigned by the covering supervisor. It has a seventy-two-hour response time so there was no need to go out that day. I toss the case on my desk and go into my e-mail quickly. I scroll down the inbox and go to the one with "MDT agenda" written in the subject line. I review the case that had me ready to jump across the table and strangle Prosecutor Leroy. The narrative states that the case was closed over three months ago and had an unsubstantiation of sexual abuse. The uncle and cousin apparently lived out of the home, and their whereabouts were unknown during the investigation.

As I read further into the investigation protocol, the second interview that allegedly messed up the case was not the reason the girl recanted. The narrative documents that the girl didn't give a disclosure to the teacher; rather she told one of her girlfriends and that friend told the teacher. By the time DCF arrived at the school, the teacher to whom the alleged abuse was reported and the school social worker had attempted to speak with the girl, but she wasn't willing to talk. The investigator wrote that the alleged victim had her hands around her friend's neck after the teacher told her that it was the friend that reported her disclosure. The girl gave no information regarding the names of the relatives, and she denied disclosing to the friend.

Shit, so it wasn't DCF's fault as Prosecutor Leroy implied.

I decide to take a quick break. I buy a soda and then head to the bathroom. I turn on the faucet at the sink and splash some cold water on my face. I look up at my face in the mirror and see the bags under my eyes. I've had many busy nights in the recent days coming off the outing with Peter. I reach into my pocket and find that I'm running low on my wonder pills. I will have to give my dealer Chase a call for a refill.

Chapter 19 CASSANDRA

Inside her room Cassandra looks at herself as she stands in front of her full-body mirror behind her locked door. She wears a pair of her aunt Persephone's hip-hugger jeans that she had taken from the dirty clothes basket. Weeks from her twelfth birthday, her body is developing fast. She fills the jeans out from all angles as she turns from side to side admiring herself. She applies a stick of red lipstick that she found in the back pocket of the jeans. She presses her full moist lips together like she has seen her aunt Persephone do so many times before going out to the club.

There's been no talk about a birthday party or anything this year. She really doesn't expect one, just like she didn't expect one last year. Things have changed since she brought the big mess to the family. The last birthday party she can remember was when she turned nine. That year her grandmother gave her a big party at Chucky Cheese, and her aunts bought her a bunch of clothes. She also got her first kiss from a boy named Juan, who was twelve years old. He told her afterward that her breath stunk. Her first menstrual cycle came a couple of days after her party. Her aunt Debra told her that she got hers around the same age. The same night her menstrual cycle ended, Gordo, her mother's oldest brother, raped her in the basement of her grandmother's house.

"You're a waste of a good body. You're a woman now," Gordo said as he ripped through her.

After Gordo was done raping her, he made her throw her bloody panties in with the dirty clothes.

"Don't tell your grandmother. If she asks why they are bloody, just tell her that it was from your period," Gordo directs as he leaves Cassandra sitting on the cold basement floor.

From behind the door she can hear someone coming up the stairs. Cassandra fears that it's her aunt Persephone. She races to take the jeans off and throws them under her bed. The doorknob turns. Her head turns to the door in panic. She buttons the last button of her shorts and rushes to the door. Cassandra forgets that she has the lipstick on as she opens the door slowly. At the door is a little Hispanic girl from her aunt's daycare.

"Hello, my name is Ann Marie. Your aunt told me to ask you to take me to get my picture taken," Ann Marie says, holding a brown teddy bear.

With her heart rate slowing, Cassandra comes completely out of the door. The girl is about seven years old with her hair in a ponytail, wearing blue jeans and a pink T-shirt. Cassandra's aunt Persephone runs a daycare in the house for some of the mothers in the community. This is the second girl Cassandra has taken upstairs for a picture that day. She knows her job and will not mess up this time. Cassandra walks upstairs with Ann Marie and knocks on the door.

"Wait right here, okay?" Cassandra says, pulling the girl in front of her.

A couple of seconds later, Gordo opens the door, wearing a nice white button-down shirt tucked into his jeans. Inside the room Cassandra can see the purple backdrop and studio strobe lights. Her eyes widen.

"And what is your name, pretty girl?" Gordo asks with the worst display of friendliness.

"My name is Ann Marie," she says as Gordo rubs the back of his hand on Ann Marie's cheek.

"Now that's a pretty name. Come inside so I can take your picture. Can I call you Princess Ann Marie?" Gordo asks as Ann Marie enters the room.

"You think I'm a princess?" Ann Marie asks, looking up at Gordo.

"You look like one to me. Why don't you go play with some of the toys next to the bed," Gordo says as he turns back to Cassandra who is standing on the stairs.

Gordo puts his head out the half-closed door. "Now do your fucking job today. And take that lipstick off. It looks horrible on you," Gordo says as he begins to close the door.

Cassandra looks at him and then at the girl whom she can see through the closing door. Cassandra knows that there are at least two other girls she will bring upstairs that day. Gordo rarely takes pictures of her anymore. Cassandra has now moved to having video filmed of her performing sexual acts on adult men and women. Cassandra wonders what would have happened to her if she had told when she had a chance. It is too late now. She knows that she will be hurt if she tells anyone again.

Chapter 20 ANDREW

The climb to my second-floor condo seems so tiresome now. There used to be a time when I would just run up these stairs. It's not like my job requires much physical energy. I stand in front of my big red door and pause to catch my breath. I can remember when I surprised Kay with the keys to the unit.

* * *

"The real estate agent told me that we could see the unit one more time before the closing," I said and then handed the keys to Kay.

I watched Kay put her curly brown hair into a ponytail as she walked up the remaining stairs to the second floor. Her flawless cream-toned skin, high cheekbones, and light brown eyes complemented her biracial heritage. Her body fit perfectly in her white blouse and navy blue knee-length skirt that exposed her long slender legs.

"I love this big red door, Andrew. You know red is my favorite color," Kay said, smiling as she turned the doorknob.

The door swung open.

"Oh, Andrew! Oh, Andrew. When did you do this?" Kay turned and jumped into my arms, almost knocking us both down the stairs.

Inside the apartment were a couple of our storage boxes and her brown leather extra-cushioned chair from our room at our old place.

I had taken the day off and closed on the condo earlier in the day. Kay thought the closing would take place the following week.

"I was able to move some of our boxes in while you were at work," I said, holding her in my embrace.

I guess I still had a little bit of a romantic side to me. I picked her up in my arms and walked through the door, kicking it shut behind me.

*   *   *

A big pile of mail is on the floor in front of me. Taped to the door is a note from my neighbor Sinclair.

Andrew, I will be gone for a couple of weeks. Can you water my plants?

This guy is gone all the time. He has some type of Internet business and works a lot from home. Kay and I used to joke that he was probably a serial killer doing his murders while on vacation.

I open the door and rush to disarm the alarm system across the room. With the lights still off, I place my leather bag on the kitchen table and then walk around the unit closing the blinds. The phone rings, but it's not on the base. I grab my bag from the table and pick up the phone in my bedroom. The caller ID says "D&D Financing." I answer the phone and then quickly hang up. The telemarketers know exactly when to call.

I open my bag and take out a couple of my new cases and my assignment from Dr. Sol. Dr. Sol says things will get better in time. All I have to do is stay focused and work. I slide the plastic file holder from the back of my closet and place the assignment from Dr. Sol inside.

I walk toward the window, kicking through the clutter on the floor. My bed hasn't been made in days. I stand in front of Kay's favorite chair and fall backward on top of a pile of clothes. I sit motionless and aching. Aching to see her come around the corner to ask how my day was, aching to feel her touch and her kisses. I reach in my pocket and take yet another pill. I drink it down with a quarter glass of Jack Daniels left in the bottle from last night. I sink deeper into the cushions. Left with these memories of Kay, I drift to sleep and hope not to wake.

Chapter 21 RENEE

Renee meets Buford Donnelly at the nurses' station in the NICU.

"Hi, Mrs. Tisdale, I'm here to visit with Trevan," Buford says, holding a balloon from the gift shop in the hospital.

"I wasn't aware that you were supposed to visit today. Is Andrew meeting you here to supervise the visit?" Renee asks as she looks at Trevan's file, searching for any note that she missed about Andrew setting up the visit for that day.

"I met with Andrew at the DCF office a couple of days ago. He said he would speak with you about me visiting Trevan. Is there a problem?" Buford looks confused.

"Well, Mr. Donnelly, there is no note in Trevan's file showing that a visit was scheduled today. You didn't even call to say you were coming. Usually with DCF-related cases, the DCF worker has to supervise the visit. I'm surprised Andrew didn't tell you that before you came today," Renee explains.

"I wasn't informed that DCF had to be here to supervise the visit. I think I have the right to visit my son today, Mrs. Tisdale. I am his father, and I'm not the one that was using heroin," Buford says, looking down at Renee.

"Mr. Donnelly, do you mind waiting here for a couple of minutes?" Renee asks and then heads to her office to give Andrew a call.

Renee thinks, *Andrew knows that he should be here today. I wonder why he didn't call to tell me.* She picks up her office phone and dials Andrew's number. After several rings Andrew picks up.

"Hey, Andrew, it's Renee."

"Hey, Renee, what's up?"

"I have Mr. Donnelly at the hospital looking to have a visit with Trevan. Are you coming to supervise the visit?" Renee asks in a friendly tone.

After a couple of seconds Andrew answers with an attitude. "There is no reason for DCF to be at the visit, Renee. We don't have custody of Trevan, and DCF has no legal action pending on him. Just because DCF has an active investigation doesn't mean we have to be there. You know it's the hospital's responsibility to provide the visit for Mr. Donnelly. So why did you waste a call?"

"But, Andrew, Trevan's mother abandoned him at the hospital. This is a high-risk newborn case. You're telling me DCF is not taking any legal action on this case?" Renee asks, challenging Andrew.

"Renee, I'm the one that works at DCF now. I have it under control. Thanks for the call. Let me know how the visit goes."

Renee sits on the other end of the line listening to the dial tone. She has known Andrew for years and has never seen this side of him. Renee knows that working at DCF is stressful. She wonders if there is something else going on with Andrew. Renee agrees with Andrew that the hospital has to allow Mr. Donnelly to visit his son. She also knows in her time at DCF she would have attended at least the first visit to make sure everything went well. Especially since Madeline, Trevan's mother, abandoned him after the delivery. She hangs up the phone, pausing to regain her composure. She exits her office and returns to the nurses' station.

"Mr. Donnelly, follow me. I'll show you to the nursery," Renee says, picking up the file from the counter.

Chapter 22 ANDREW

I read the article in the *Hartford Courant* about the murder a couple of days ago on Love Lane. The police aren't releasing much information, only saying that this crime is very different from the others in the city.

It gets me so angry knowing that nothing has been done on Kay's case. There have been no leads, no witnesses, nothing.

My program supervisor, Tracey Hammer, walks toward me on her short skinny legs with an armful of cases.

"Andrew, can I see you in my office?" Tracey asks, not even slowing her pace as she continues to her office.

I didn't expect this. I place the newspaper in my bag and then follow her to her office.

"Close the door," she tells me with her raspy voice.

Tracey Hammer is a fifty-year-old white female with dirty blonde hair showing hints of gray. She walks behind her desk and drops the cases she had in her hand on top of a pile of cases she has to review for closing and transfer. She wears her red-framed reading glasses on the edge of her nose as she sits behind her desk. I sit for over two minutes watching her as she listens to several voicemails and checks her work e-mail.

Tracey is a twenty-five-year veteran with DCF. She was transferred from the Torrington regional office a year ago. The word around the office is she was involuntarily transferred to Hartford. Some rumors have gone as far as to say that she doesn't like working with Hartford's predominately Hispanic, Caribbean, and African American population. I've seen her rip through some of my colleagues for making what she felt were horrible assessments while in the field. Since she has been the program supervisor in investigations, three investigators decided to transfer to other units in the office. She personally moved two other investigators because of their inability to keep up with the pace and the workload.

So now I sit in front her. Why? I guess I'm about to find out as she hangs up her phone and turns her chair toward me. She wastes no time getting to the point.

"My stats show you have several cases due by the end of the week. Stephanie is going to be out a while longer. I want you to turn in your cases to me personally, not to the covering supervisor. I assume that won't be a problem. Am I right?" she asks, looking at me over the rim of her glasses.

"There should be no problems. I have to add just a couple of narratives to the protocol and make a couple of calls. I can have them to you tomorrow," I reply.

I just told her a lie. I guess I will be working late tonight. This can't be why she called me to her office.

She sits back in her chair and takes her glasses off. "I have an e-mail from Stephanie showing that you were supposed to be covering the last MDT meeting. I also received a call stating that you weren't prepared for any of the cases," Tracey says in her raspy voice, slowly leaning back in her chair.

How could I forget?

"Yes, I mistakenly left the file at my desk in my rush to the meeting," I reply with a little sweat building on my palms.

"Andrew, I understand the past year hasn't been the best for you, if you know what I mean. If there is any reason you can't keep up with the pace or think you need some time, I suggest you inform Stephanie and me. You know here in investigations we need the minds of our workers sharp at all times," she says and pulls her chair closer to the desk.

Was that a threat she just made? I think that was, Andrew.

I sit looking at her, emotionless. Usually I'm much quicker in my responses, but I'm still dealing with the hangover and the effects from the new pills from the previous night. I guess it's really starting to show in my work now.

"I'll make sure that cases are processed in time. I'll also make sure that I'll be prepared for the next MDT meeting," I say, not trying to come up with any excuses.

You should let me speak for you next time.

I walk back to my desk. I can feel that my blood is at its boiling point. With no wall near to punch a hole through, I sit at my desk and take out another pill. The red light from my phone blinks, showing that I have an incoming call. At first I think about letting it go to voicemail, but instead I pick it up.

"Hey, Andrew, it's Renee."

Renee tells me that she has Buford Donnelly at the hospital and that he is expecting a visit with his son. She asks if I am planning to be present in order to supervise the visit. As I react to her questions, I am still pissed from my conversation with Tracey. I wrap her up kind of quickly. So many people think DCF is expected to do everything.

On my right is a big pile of cases that I have to work on. In front of me on my computer screen is a bunch of unread e-mail. Scrolling through the messages, I see one from Patricia. I feel my blood pressure come down a level. I open her e-mail and read it.

> *Andrew,*
>
> *Thank you for the message. I guess I have a new fan of my work. It was a pleasure meeting you at the exhibition. I had a chance to visit the Wadsworth and Mark Twain museums this past week. I have been enjoying your city. You guys have just as many shootings as Rio de Janeiro lol. If you have time, maybe we could meet over a cup of coffee. I hear there is a nice café downtown named Xando's. Hopefully I will hear from you soon.*
>
> *Tchau,*
>
> *Patricia*

I sit back in my chair with both hands behind my head and take a deep breath. The day is looking much brighter now.

Chapter 23   DETECTIVE DUPRI

At her desk in the far back corner of the Major Crimes Division office, Detective Sandy Dupri reviews her notes from the Love Lane murder. Going into her fifth year in Major Crimes and her fifteenth overall in the department, she looks forward to knocking the next five years out and retiring somewhere hot.

Out of all her years in the department, this case sits differently with her. Most of the other cases are straightforward, drug-dealer killings over territory or gang related. This one didn't fit that MO. Sifting through the file, she pulls out the crime scene photos and spreads them across her desk.

As she looks once again at the photos, she thinks, *Who are you? What is your name? Maybe he was a crackhead on that side of town looking for a hit. What about a robbery gone bad? He didn't have identification on him. Why not use a gun? Why use a knife?*

She picks up one of the photos for a closer look.

Why cut off his penis?

A call over the police scanner breaks Detective Dupri's thoughts. There was another fatal stabbing near the Love Lane murder site.

Maybe my suspect resurfaced, she thought as she grabbed her portable radio off her desk. She then headed to her unmarked vehicle.

*   *   *

Detective Dupri takes a quick left onto Ridgewood Street, speeding toward the entrance to Kenny Park in Hartford's North End. A call had just come in of a fatal stabbing of a black female on the west side of the park. The suspect was last seen on foot heading through the woods. This is the second stabbing in a week in the same area. With no leads on the Love Lane John Doe, Detective Dupri hit this call with the hope that she is getting closer to her suspect.

Her cruiser is the first to enter the park. The suspect is in sight, cutting through the woods. Detective Dupri jumps out of the car, radio in hand, and follows the fleeing suspect.

"This is unit ninety-two. Code two, code two. I have my eyes on the suspect. I'm on foot cutting through the woods heading eastbound. I have a black male, six feet, mid-twenties, blue jeans and short dreads," Detective Dupri yells over the portable radio, gasping for air.

Five years ago she wouldn't have been sucking for air like she is now. Ten years ago she would have been on top of him with her knee in his back. As she breaks through the trees and runs into the open field, she discovers that he has about a thirty-yard lead on her.

"Send me some cars! Send me some cars! I got a Carl Lewis on my hands," Detective Dupri yells over the portable radio.

Out of the woods to her left, a black German shepherd darts toward the suspect.

"Unit ninety-two, this is unit fifty-one. Be advised that K-9 is in the area."

As the dog gains ground, it's like watching a greyhound chase the bunny at the racetrack. A jump and a quick bite to the arm, and the suspect is down on his face and screaming. Detective Dupri and the K-9 officer arrive at the scene. The dog is called off as Detective Dupri handcuffs the suspect and pats him down, uncovering no weapons, drugs, or ID.

"You little shit, you on the track team or something?" Detective Dupri yells.

"My arm is bleeding. That dog bit my fucking arm," the guy screams.

"No shit. When you run from the police, you get chased. When you run from a dog, you get bit," Detective Dupri says as she pulls the guy to his feet.

There is blood smeared all over the suspect's shirt and hands. With her hand under his armpit, she walks him to the cruiser and places him in the backseat.

"Why were you running?" Detective Dupri asks.

But he doesn't respond.

"At least tell me your name?"

He still gives no response.

Detective Dupri closes the door to the squad car. "Bring this guy to Major Crimes for further questioning," Detective Dupri directs the officer.

*   *   *

After many hours of interviewing the suspect, Detective Dupri concludes that he is not her suspect in the Love Lane murder. This suspect stabbed his girlfriend because he thought she was cheating on him.

Detective Dupri opens the folder that is on her desk. She sees that the Love Lane John Doe's prints were returned. She now has a name.

Chapter 24 ANDREW

After several e-mails, Patricia and I decide to meet at Xando's on Pratt Street in downtown Hartford. When I walk into the corner café, my senses are attacked by the variety of coffees they offer and the live music playing for the night. With a little mixture of Paris by day and New York SoHo by night, the area hardly resembles the Hartford I've known. The mayor has been pushing the idea of redeveloping downtown into "New England's Rising Star." The vision is to have a combination of luxury condos and affordable housing, with the hope of bringing a middle class and the empty nesters into the city. The city has been getting a lot of press from all the shootings lately. I'm surprised I'm still here instead of some suit trying to cut down on the commute and drink imported coffee.

I hear my name being called over the music playing.

"Andrew, Andrew!"

I look up to the second-floor mezzanine area. Patricia is waving and trying to catch my attention. I walk up the stairs and double-check the time.

She's early.

She stands in the narrow aisle, wearing black slacks and a black collared shirt tucked in at the waist. Her beauty seems to light up the café as she stands to greet me.

"The man behind all the e-mails," she says and then kisses me on both cheeks.

Kisses on the first date.

"Yes, finally we meet again," I reply with a smile.

A white, dreadlocked waitress comes and takes our orders as we sit under the low illuminating light. I order a cup of cinnamon tea and a turkey sandwich. She gets a refill on her coffee and orders a salad. We spend a little over an hour getting to know one another.

"I graduated from the Federal University in Rio de Janeiro, Brazil, with a degree in photojournalism," Patricia says as she sips her coffee. "I spent a couple of years working as a photographer for *O Globo*, Brazil's largest newspaper. My beat was the *favelas* or slums as you might call them. I had this one assignment where I went into some of Rio's most dangerous slums photographing the *traficant* leaders as a part of a special report one of my colleagues was working on regarding the effects of Rio's organized crime on the people of the slums," she explains as I watch her full brown lips move. "In Brazil, the *traficant* or drug lords have more power than the police. The politicians and police are so corrupt that the people rely more on the *traficants* for their protection and safety," Patricia explains.

Patricia does most of the talking for the first twenty minutes. I still can't believe this is the second time I have been out this month.

"For the past two months I have been traveling around the United States with my exhibition "Brazil's Lost Children." One of my friends invited me to exhibit at RAW in Hartford after I had a show at a small gallery in New York City. I will be staying with my friend in West Hartford until the exhibition is over," she says.

She tells me about her last relationship. "About a year ago I ended a long-term relationship with Luciano," who she says is an Italian businessman. "I caught him with a much younger woman in our condo on Ipanema Beach," Patricia says with a sad tone in her voice.

I guess we all have some heartbreak in our lives.

I can hear from the crack in her voice that it is hard for her to tell this story. Why anyone would cheat on her surprises me.

"So, Andrew, I feel like I've been talking the entire time. Tell me a little about yourself. Are you married?" she asks, looking down at the wedding band on my finger.

I'm suddenly jolted back into reality. "I figured you would ask," I say and then pause. "I'm a widower." I take a sip from my tea.

"Oh, Andrew, I am sorry. I saw the ring and had to ask," she says with a tone of embarrassment in her voice.

"For the past year I have tried to avoid this conversation. I only go into this corridor and many others in my mind with Dr. Sol. Yes, I'm in therapy," I say as my eyes begin to focus on the dancing flame from the candle on the table. "Her name was Kay Edwards. She was a good woman, real sweet, and kind with her words. I met her at a birthday party of a mutual friend we had from college. I remember the night of the party. I couldn't take my eyes off her," I say with a smile on my face.

"She must have been a pretty woman," Patricia says smiling.

"Yes, she was very beautiful."

"So did you speak with her that night?" Patricia asks, sipping her coffee.

"When I finally got the courage to speak with her, we talked all night. During our conversation I learned that Kay graduated from Eastern Connecticut State University the same year as me. We never saw each other on campus because she took many of her classes at night and I lived off campus."

"Hey, it sounds like you guys were meant to find each other. You had a chance while you attended college and then finally met at a party of a friend from college. There are no coincidences in life, Andrew. The universe aligned for you," Patricia says, sharing some of her wisdom.

"Did you get her number that night? Tell me more. Tell me more," Patricia asks, engaged by my story.

"That same night we exchanged numbers. I spoke with her on the phone several times before we met again. It was truly love at first sight." I pause for a couple of seconds.

"It seems like you really love her, Andrew," Patricia says as she looks across the table with a smile.

"Yes, I love her very much. I miss her too," I say, staring into Patricia's eyes. "Kay was such a happy person. She loved to be around people, especially children."

"It always feels good when you're helping someone," Patricia adds.

"I remember when she was offered the job at one of the elementary schools in Hartford. I had already been working and living in Hartford at the time so I knew the city. Kay never lived or worked in an urban setting. She was raised in West Hartford, which is one of the suburbs outside of Hartford. I tried to tell her that the kids were going to be very challenging and the environment wasn't the safest. The school she was going to be working at was next to the dangerous Dutch Point housing project."

"When you truly want to help, Andrew, you sometimes look past the danger that may be around you. Some people live in dangerous environments, and nothing ever happens to them. Then there are others who live in so-called safe environments where dangerous things happen all the time. You can only try to stay alert, that's all."

"Yeah, that's true, Patricia. Kay always loved a challenge and insisted on taking the job. She had an extra bonus with her best friend, Betsey, already working at the school," I say, recounting my memories of Kay.

"See, you had an extra set of eyes on her. A best friend would always look out for her sidekick," Patricia smiles, holding her coffee with both hands as she brings it to her mouth.

"They were like sisters, Kay and Betsey."

"If you don't mind, Andrew, how did she pass away?"

I sit with my eyes fixed on the dimly lit room behind Patricia's head. The music and the voices in the room seem to fade to the background.

"I'm sorry, Andrew. I should have never asked you that. You don't have to answer the question," Patricia says embarrassed, reaching her hand across the table.

"It's okay. Many people already know the story," I say as I tilt my head back and close my eyes. "Kay and I both hoped to make a change in the lives of the people around us. We both had jobs that involved teaching and helping people in need. The years went by so fast. One day we meet at a party, and two years later we are getting married in a rose garden in Hartford. Our life wasn't perfect."

"No one's life is perfect, Andrew. Trust me," Patricia says, holding my hand tighter.

"We had our moments. I guess a part of me was just waiting for something bad to happen. It was a time that the gang violence in Hartford was just so crazy. There were random people being killed and retaliation murders. I never would have thought that the violence would hit so close to home. My life changed with one call from Betsey. I remember Betsey was crying and just telling me to quickly get to the Dutch Point housing project and that something terrible had happened to Kay." I can feel the tears running down my cheeks.

Patricia stands and moves her chair to my side. She moves close and puts her right arm around my shoulder. I lay my head on her shoulder and continue with the story.

"When I got to the crime scene, it was taped off. There were some residents from the housing project outside, crowded around one building. All I thought was, I had to see her, I had to touch her. I ran past the officer, screaming out her name. As I got closer, I could see a white sheet over a body that was lying in the doorway of one of the vacant units. That was when my heart dropped. I was completely empty, lost. Why my Kay? Why not me?" I say crying harder.

I pause and take a deep breath. The joy and happiness that filled my heart minutes ago has now turned to sadness and anger. I have entered the gate of darkness and fight to control myself, squeezing my leg under the table.

What do you think that squeezing is doing, Andrew? Nothing. You know where it goes from here if you keep talking. The rage will come. It will build and build and then what? Let me out, Andrew.

"Andrew, Andrew, we can talk about this another day," Patricia says and pulls me closer to her.

I open my eyes and try to regain my focus through the tears. I look at Patricia seated at my side. The tears on our cheeks glisten in the candle's soft light.

"Please excuse me, Patricia," I say. I get up from my chair, and her arm falls to the side.

I walk to the stairs toward the bathroom on the first floor. I lock the bathroom door behind me. I barely catch myself as my knees give out. I place both hands on the marble vanity, and my breathing intensifies. My head hangs as the sink catches my past dreams of my love. This pain I feel never leaves me. It has a grip around my heart that only gets tighter over time. I search my pockets almost frantically, forgetting that I left the pills in the car.

You don't need any pills, Andrew. You know how to release this pain, how to loosen the grip. You can't stop now.

90

My fingers rub my temples, trying to massage away the thoughts. *No, no, I'll call Dr. Sol. He'll know what do.* I turn on the faucet, splash a handful of water on my face, and take in a deep breath. *Why Kay? My sweet Kay. Maybe Dr. Sol is right. The work that we are doing may be the only way to heal.*

The knock at the door interrupts my thoughts. I wipe my face with some paper towels and then open the door. Patricia stands in front of me. She takes my hand and leads me to the exit. Outside, Patricia pulls me close as we walk down Pratt Street. The night's refreshing air cools my body down. We stop in front of a black Toyota Camry.

"Do you mind sitting in the car with me, Andrew?"

"I'm not sure, Patricia. I already made this night into a sad fest," I say pitifully.

"I'm enjoying my time tonight. Just have a seat in the car if you don't mind," she says as she walks to the driver side door.

I guess being with Patricia is better than being home alone. I open the passenger door and get inside the car. As hard as it was to speak about Kay, there is something about Patricia that makes me feel safe. There are no expectations with her. She just listened and seemed to caress my heart with her eyes. Part of me wanted to pull away out of my love for Kay. The other half wanted to jump into Patricia's arms. Inside the car Patricia turns on the engine to warm us up a little.

"My therapist has been trying to get me to attend a bereavement group for a while now. I wasn't sure if I was ready to speak about Kay around a large group of people," I say as I feel Patricia reach out and grab my hand.

"Well, the group sounds like a good idea, Andrew. Maybe you should try going to one meeting to see how it is," Patricia suggests as her warm eyes look into mine.

I can't believe the support Patricia is giving me. How can she do this? She doesn't know me. I look at my watch. It's almost midnight.

"Thanks for coming out tonight to meet with me, Andrew. I really enjoyed my night and would love to see you again," Patricia says, caressing the top of my hand.

"I enjoyed my time also. I would love to see you again," I say almost hypnotized by her eyes and her touch.

I can't hold back my urge any longer. I pull her toward me and our lips meet. She smells like a spring garden, and her lips are soft, oh so soft and sweet. Our lips pull away after what seems like minutes but is only a couple of seconds.

"I was waiting for that gift all night," Patricia says with a smile.

"You make me so relaxed. You put my mind off somewhere very far away. Being with you tonight, you took me away from this life. I was feeling no pain. No loss of love, rather a new boost of energy of joy and hope," I say and then pull her close for a tight embrace.

"Thank you," Patricia says.

"No, thank you," I say as I open the passenger side door.

Chapter 25 MADELINE

Madeline rocks back and forth with her hand across her stomach looking out of Troy's bedroom window. She waits for the arrival of her special delivery. A cramp builds in her legs so she stands and paces the room. Almost twenty minutes have passed since Troy left. Madeline begins to lose her patience. She bites her nails and walks back toward the window. The bedroom doorknob begins to move. Someone is trying to enter. Startled, her eyes widen. She suddenly hears Troy's voice on the other side.

"Maddy, it's me. Open the door," Troy says.

Madeline unlocks the door, and Troy rushes in, shutting it behind him. Madeline shuffles through his pants pockets, looking for the bag, before he can lock the door.

"Slow your ass down, girl," Troy says, nudging her back with his elbow.

Troy then puts his hands down his pants and takes the dime bag of heroin out from under his crotch.

"Shit, the boys are all over the street. I had to walk like all the way to Main Street for this shit," Troy says.

Troy is a small-time marijuana dealer. When he was ten years old, he started as a lookout for some of the older guys on the block.

Speechless, Madeline snatches the bag out of his hand and then goes to her purse on the floor next to his bed. She takes out a little mirror and cuts a couple of lines, electing to snort it instead of smoking it. Madeline feels the effects immediately. As she lies on the bed, she begins to feel a warm rush flow through her body.

Madeline rubs her hands on her face and sucks her fingers, trying to get a bit of the residue of the heroin in her system. She watches Troy walk to the window and pull the blinds. A stream of sunlight hits the walls. The bed bounces as Troy lies next to her. Madeline looks up at Troy who is watching her enjoy her high. She begins to feel him kissing her neck and rubbing her breast under her shirt.

"What you doing?" Madeline says, barely opening her mouth.

Madeline opens her eyes and sees Troy take a little of the heroin from the mirror. He puts it on his finger and then brings it to her nose.

"Snort," Troy says.

Madeline takes a strong snort of the heroin, and then Troy pulls her shirt off, exposing her bare breasts. Seconds later Madeline is in the middle of the bed naked. She feels Troy enter her as she lies paralyzed.

Chapter 26 ANDREW

It was the kiss I couldn't get out of my mind. I felt so comfortable around her. I was able to pull down my wall and allow her to experience my world even though there are sides she has not seen. I've tried so hard to control everything in my life. Now I feel that it's time to let go and to let someone new in. I will be cautious, but I have to see her again.

I have been in the office all morning, going to back-to-back meetings on several of my active investigations. With my thoughts on Patricia, I've been able to take some of the strain out of the daily grind. Patricia is something new to look forward to. I sit in a meeting with the principal attorney.

"I don't understand why you didn't remove these girls. You're telling me that the mother's boyfriend was a perpetrator of sexual abuse on one of the mother's older daughters. On your current investigation the same boyfriend was living in the mother's home where there are two teenage girls?" Principal Attorney Cory Hines asks, reviewing his notes from our legal consult.

"I understand that it is of concern that the boyfriend returned to the home. During my interviews with the two teenage girls, neither made disclosures of sexual abuse. I don't see the imminence to remove the girls like you do," I say, defending our decision in investigations.

"Good that you understand how this is of concern, Andrew. I completely disagree with investigations' decision to just draft a safety plan for the boyfriend to leave the home. At the minimum at this time, neglect petitions should be filed on the mother for allowing a known perpetrator of abuse to return to the home where there are minors. At this time you don't have a guarantee that she will keep him out of the home," Attorney Hines says in a condescending tone and then turns to his computer and begins typing.

Now that was rude. I manage to keep my cool, thinking of the possibilities of seeing Patricia again or, at the least, hearing her voice.

After several minutes of typing, he turns back toward me.

"For the record, Andrew, the process in place is for all supervisors to accompany their workers to all legal consults. Also, I just sent an e-mail to your supervisor and the program supervisor informing them that I felt that the girls should have been removed. As a result of your two-week delay in having a legal consult, the imminence has passed, and at this time neglect petitions should be filed immediately." Attorney Hines slides the legal consult notes across the desk and turns back to his computer.

I take the legal consult notes and leave the office. Something must be wrong because I'm not blowing steam out of my ears. Back on the investigations floor, I walk to my desk with a smile. Next to me a couple of my colleagues are gossiping about some of the recent murders in Hartford, in particular the Love Lane murder.

"My cousin is an officer in the Hartford Police Department. He told me that the detectives think the Love Lane murder was not gang or drug related. He said there was some crazy shit they discovered that he really couldn't tell me," the male worker says to the three workers sitting around him.

"Well, I think you have to be a coward to kill someone," the female worker says.

I hear that they don't know anything different than what the news is reporting. I find my cell in my bag. I check my voicemail. Patricia wants to meet again.

Chapter 27 GORDO

The Starbucks in West Hartford at Bishops Corner is a little slow with only a handful of customers. Gordo sits next to the window and a couple of tables away from the closest customer. He sips his latte grande while surfing the Web on his MacBook. He has been a very busy man the past week, adding three more girls to his collection of pictures and videos. Gordo is so amazed how easy it is to sell pictures of naked girls compared to selling drugs. In his underground world of trading images, only those referred from a friend in the network can join. Gordo now has a network of about fifty clients. He also controls who's in or out.

A couple of weeks ago, he received an e-mail from one of his clients named Chester. He offered to pay a pretty penny for a large amount of Gordo's pictures. In the past, Gordo and Chester have gone back and forth trading small files. In one of the last e-mails, Chester mentioned that it was getting too risky to keep the files on his computer. He asked Gordo to copy the files to a CD and to arrange a time to pick them up. Gordo knows that many of his clients have a legitimate concern about getting caught with the files on their computers. Saving the files in an alternate format makes it easier to hide or destroy the files and images.

Gordo goes into one of the open forums on his site. The thread is giving a step-by-step tutorial on how to download encryption software to a computer and how to erase a hard drive in less than a minute. This was a good tool in his line of work. In the networks, there are forums about the newest antipedophile sites. Others run the gamut from new technology about the best computers and cameras to buy to the latest news articles about the recent arrests of those caught trading. The forums allow people in Gordo's trade to always stay ahead of the police and to learn from the ones that were caught.

Gordo looks at his watch. Chester is running late. Then he hears the password.

"We'll close on the house this week." A tall, middle-aged Caucasian male with a nicely fitted gray suit and matching tie speaks the words into his cell phone as he enters the coffee shop.

Gordo looks up from his computer, and they make eye contact. Gordo nods for Chester to come over to the table.

"Hey, next time let's meet at the playground," Chester says sarcastically as he sits down and places his cell on the table.

"No, next time we'll meet at City Hall," Gordo says with a smile.

Gordo did his homework on Chester Malroni. He is one of the aides to the mayor of Hartford.

"So let's get down to business. Did you bring the money with you?" Gordo asks, locking his computer screen.

"I want to see all the images in high resolution before I pay you anything," Chester demands as he reaches into his coat pocket and then places an envelope on his knee under the table.

Gordo smirks and then unlocks his computer screen. He minimizes his Firefox Web browser and then opens his iPhoto application on his MacBook. A tall, cute brunette waitress takes an order from the lady sitting a couple of tables away from them. The waitress then comes to their table to take an order.

"Hi, sir, would you like a refill on your latte?" the waitress asks Gordo with a smile.

"I'm all set, sweetie," Gordo says.

"Sweetie, my father calls me sweetie," the waitress says and turns her attention to Chester. "And how about you, sir? Would you like to order something?" she asks Chester.

"Yeah, I'll take a blueberry muffin and coffee," Chester says and then turns back to Gordo. "She was looking at you hard man."

"She's a little too old for my taste, if you know what I mean," Gordo replies as he attempts to locate Chester's pictures.

Gordo scrolls down past twenty different princess albums. He double clicks on the album labeled "Princess Iris." In an instant, hundreds of images pop up on the screen. Gordo angles the laptop screen toward Chester, keeping an eye on the lady sitting next to them.

"Now that's what I'm talking about," Chester says, moving the screen closer.

Gordo quickly turns the laptop back toward himself. "You want to get us caught?" he hisses.

Gordo watches as Chester takes a quick look over his shoulder. They both see that the woman is on her cell phone and paying them no mind.

"Move your chair closer," Gordo directs.

Gordo scrolls slowly through the images on the screen, giving Chester a taste of the product.

"I took these with my new camera. You see the details in the close-ups of her pussy?" Gordo whispers to Chester as he admires his own work.

Gordo can see that Chester likes what he sees. He watches as Chester grabs his penis under the table.

"Man, these are better than the ones you sent me," Chester says excitedly.

Gordo minimizes the images and then reaches into his bag. "This is what you were looking at and more," Gordo says, placing a CD on the table. "Now where is the money?" Gordo asks as he leans back in his chair and looks out the window to his car.

Chester hands Gordo the envelope under the table.

"I will give you the other half when I see the girl in person," Chester says, reaching for the CD.

Gordo puts the envelope in his bag and reaches the CD before Chester.

"What the fuck you think you doing, buddy?" Chester says under his breath, leaning closer to Gordo.

The waitress returns to the table with the muffin and coffee.

"Nice tattoos. I love that one," the waitress says, pointing to the words surrounded in flames on Gordo's forearm: Amor de Rey.

These are words used by the Almighty Latin King Nation. In the 1940s, young Puerto Rican males in Chicago organized the Almighty Latin King

Nation into a club. The club's goals and intentions were to fight prejudice and racism. As time passed, the club transformed into one of the largest and most violent gangs in the nation.

"Like doesn't that mean King's Love? Well, I know it means King's Love. I'm in honors Spanish at Hall High School, and my mother is half Spanish," the waitress says, speaking very fast and in a valley girl tone.

"You mind getting me some sugar?" Chester asks, annoyed by the interruption.

Without trying to make a scene, Chester turns back Gordo. "What the hell are you doing? Either you give me the CD or the money," Chester demands.

Gordo leans forward, unfazed by Chester's frustration. "Look outside to the red Honda Civic in front of the store," Gordo directs Chester.

Gordo watches Chester's eyes light up.

"Is that who I think it is?" Chester asks with a big smile.

Iris sits in the front seat of the car. Next to her is an older girl wearing her iPod headphones and sketching in a book.

Gordo puts his cup on the table and offers Chester the new deal. "I want fifteen hundred dollars for the CD and an hour with the girl," Gordo says calmly.

"How you gonna jump up one thousand dollars, man?" Chester says angrily, looking around to make sure no one is listening.

Gordo calmly shuts down his computer and puts it into his bag. He stands up and takes a bite out of Chester's muffin. "You have ten minutes. The bank is across the street," Gordo says. He then exits the coffee shop.

From outside, Gordo can see Chester eating the rest of the muffin. Gordo watches as Chester quickly exits the store and heads across the street to the bank.

The woman who was sitting at the table next to Gordo and Chester notices that Chester left his cell phone on the table. She takes her bag, picks up the cell phone, and rushes after Chester.

Chapter 28 ANDREW

I park my state-issued vehicle next to a red Honda Civic in front of Starbucks. I turn my work cell phone on vibrate, hoping for no calls from the office. I have some time before my next home visit. I spot Patricia walking toward the store from Albany Avenue.

"Hey, Andrew, I see you got my voicemail," Patricia says and greets me with a warm embrace.

"Yeah, sorry I wasn't able to call you sooner. I was in meetings all morning. You mind if I grab a cup a tea from the Starbucks?" I ask.

"Sure, I actually want a refill on my coffee," Patricia says and follows me inside.

"Were you able to catch up with him?" the young waitress asks Patricia as we wait in line to place our order.

"Yes, I caught him as he was crossing the street," Patricia says, smiling to the waitress.

"What's that all about?" I ask.

"Some guy sitting next to me earlier left his cell on the table. I caught up with him and gave his phone back to him. Oh, there he goes," Patricia says, pointing outside to a Caucasian male speaking with a short Hispanic male next to my state car.

"You did your good deed for the day," I say, moving forward to place our orders.

"Have you seen the rose gardens at Elizabeth Park yet?" I ask Patricia as we exit the store.

"Not yet," Patricia says and sips her coffee.

"You want to take a quick ride over there? I have some time before my next case," I say.

"My friend dropped me off today so I don't have my car," she says as we stand in front of the store.

"You know what? Jump in the backseat of the state car. If I run into any of my colleagues, I'll say you're a client," I say as I open the back door to the car.

The park has very little traffic since there are no flowers in bloom. As we walk toward the rose gardens, our fingers touch. She then takes my hand in hers.

"This *jardim*, or garden as you say, is *muito bonito*," Patricia says as we walk down one of the many arched aisles.

"A big-time insurance giant named Charles M. Pond willed his estate to the city of Hartford. As a part of his will, he wanted the garden to be named after his late wife Elizabeth who had passed away several years earlier. This garden is one of the oldest municipally operated rose gardens in the country," I say as we walk hand-in-hand toward the gazebo in the center of the garden.

The long flowerless vines weave themselves around the gazebo like Kay's hand wove itself to my heart. My mind takes me back to the day I said I do. It was only a couple of years earlier that I stood here with Kay in front of our friends and family and the garden filled with the most beautiful assortment of roses. The guitarist played our favorite song as she walked down the aisle of arches filled with roses. As I turned to see her, my eyes filled with tears and my lips quivered uncontrollably. Kay was an angel. That day we spoke our own vows and promised to carry each other's hearts for eternity.

I begin to feel a gentle squeeze of my hand.

"Andrew, are you okay?" Patricia asks.

"I'm fine. Sorry about that," I say as I regain my focus, wiping the tears from my eyes.

There is no music, no roses, and no Kay.

"This is the rose garden I was telling you about the other day. Kay and I got married in this very spot," I say, looking out over the lifeless garden.

"I'm sure she would have loved that you returned. I'm sorry that she couldn't be here with you," Patricia says and pulls me closer to her.

I don't have too many expectations of this new friendship with Patricia. My work cell phone vibrates in my pocket.

"You know what, Patricia? I don't know what it is about you. You're not like other women I've met. The feeling I have when I'm around you tranquilizes my mind and soul. You don't get jealous when I speak about Kay. The pain of Kay's loss is not as intense when I'm with you," I say, looking into Patricia's eyes.

"Well, thank you for your kind words, Andrew. There is no reason for me to get jealous about Kay or anyone else. You love her, and I'm happy that you love her. I can't take away that love that you feel for her. Nor will I try to take it away," Patricia says, holding me tightly in her arms.

I take Patricia's hand, and we begin to walk out of the garden. "Thanks for listening to me the other night," I say softly and squeeze her hand.

"Thanks for sharing. To be honest I haven't been able to keep you off my mind since the other night," she says, pulling me closer to her side.

"Really? I thought you would be changing your phone number after that." I smile as we reach the state car.

"Not a chance," she says, leaning toward me.

I close my eyes, melt into her arms, and enjoy our passionate kiss.

"I owed you that from the other night." She smiles and pulls away from me.

"I've been really thinking about going to the support group. Thanks for the encouragement the other night," I say, holding her in my arms.

"Like I said, if you want, I can go with you to the first meeting." Patricia gives me a quick peck on the lips.

"You know what? I think I'll try to go to the first one on my own. I'll definitely let you know how it goes," I say. "My work phone has been vibrating since we left the coffee shop." I pull the cell phone from my hip.

"You must be an important man," Patricia says as she takes her camera out of her bag.

"Jump inside. I'll give you a ride to your friend's house."

"I'll call my friend to pick me up later. I want to take some pictures in the garden," she says and then gives me a hug and kiss.

"Well, I do have to get back to work. I'll call you later. Maybe we can go out for drinks."

"That would be great. Call me."

I start the engine to the car and blow her kiss. As I'm driving away, I can see her taking several shots of me. I pick up my cell phone to check the voicemail.

*   *   *

My supervisor was trying to reach me to assist one of my colleagues with an emergency. I hang up the phone and speed out of the park on my way to the Stowe Village housing project. This location has a significant and gruesome history in the north end of Hartford. It's the site of the 1944 Ringling Brothers and Barnum & Bailey Circus fire where 167 people died. Many decades later the housing project was built near the lot. The flames burned down the big canvas tent, leaving behind the ashes of many lives, mostly children. Fires still burn in this area of the city. Now the fire comes from the ends of blunts and crack pipes. It burns the hopes of many who live in the housing project and many others throughout the city.

When driving through the different neighborhoods in Hartford, everyone can see that they are no different from any other inner city. Hartford is the poorest city in one of the richest states in the nation. It is a city that once had so much innovation and national and international importance. The insurance capital of the world still has its high skyscrapers that leave a stark shadow on the haves and have-nots.

As I turn onto the street I observe several patrol cars, an ambulance, and many people in the distance. As I drive slowly through the crowd, I spot a couple of state vehicles. There are dozens of residents and spectators in front of the door that is being guarded by several officers. I exit the car and make my way through the crowd toward the front door of the apartment. All of a sudden I hear a voice scream out.

"Here's another one!"

Before I know it, I'm pushed through the crowd like a ping-pong ball, and hands, feet, cans, and spit hit all areas of my body. One of the officers steps forward and pulls me into the apartment while another attempts to calm the crowd.

"Back up, people, back up. Let him through," the Hispanic officer yells out to the crowd, waving them back.

"You're lucky you didn't end up like the other worker," the officer who saved me says as he walks back outside to help his partner calm the crowd.

I navigate through the cluttered apartment. I step over the jumble of garbage, toys, miscellaneous fluids, and clothes. The sink is piled high with dirty dishes, and water cascades onto the floor. The common nocturnal roaches race across the countertops with no fear of the light coming through the windows. Water pours in through a large hole in the ceiling. Another officer who is talking on his cell phone stands in an open back door in the living room, letting air flow through the unit.

"I'm from DCF," I say and hold up my ID.

He takes a quick look at me and continues his cell phone conversation.

At the bottom of the stairs in the middle of the apartment, I can hear voices at the top. The railing hangs off the wall. The walls are smeared with what appears to be feces. I walk with my hand over my nose. The stench in the apartment is a combination of foul, rotten matter combined with shit and piss. At the top of the stairs I turn toward the bathroom and the source of the reeking odor. It looks like a Port-a-Potty was turned upside down. The toilet is topped off with a dark soupy mix of feces, toilet paper, and a couple of Legos. Clothes and garbage are lying soggy across the floor. The worst is the bathtub, which resembles a second toilet. It is half full with feces, water, and what looks from a distance like a dead cat floating facedown.

I walk to the bedroom where all the voices are coming from. Another officer stands at the door. He takes a quick look at my ID and moves into the hallway to allow me to pass. I'm shocked at what I see when I enter. Piles and piles of clothes, food, and feces are spread across the floor. In the far corner of the room, a paramedic is wrapping a bandage on the head of an adult female. In the other corner, a Hartford police detective and Isaiah, a DCF investigator from my office, are standing over a second paramedic. I look closer and see that the paramedic is treating an eight- or nine-year-old African American girl. I move toward the adult female on the floor. When I get closer, I see that it's Claudia, one of the newest investigators who transferred from treatment services.

"Andrew, you're here," Claudia says breathless, looking up at me.

"What happened to you, Claudia?" I ask nervously and reach my hand out to hers.

"I got hit in the head or something. Where were you? You were supposed to come out with me on this mother-unknown case today," she says as she rubs her head with her hand.

Fuck! What did I just get myself into?

"Shit, Claudia, I got caught up with another case and lost track of time," I lie to her, coming up with a bullshit excuse.

You can't live in this fantasy that is Patricia for too long. You're going to have to come back to me.

Isaiah catches my eye and walks over.

"What's up, Andrew?" Isaiah says as we greet each other and walk to the hallway.

"Guy, what happened to her?" I ask Isaiah concerned.

"I just got here myself. My supervisor, Paul, received a call from Claudia, who said she was just hit over the head. I was standing next to him when she called, so I was asked to come out to see what was going. Claudia left a note on her computer saying you were going to accompany her to this address. Shit, after seeing her, I thought we were going to find you in one of these rooms knocked out on the floor too," he says as he pats me on my shoulder and smiles.

Oh shit, that's not good.

"So what's up with the little girl?" I ask.

"When I arrived, the officer and the paramedics were already present. I guess the girl was hiding in the back of the closet under some clothes. It appears that she was in the closet for a while because they found some food and her clothes were soiled," Isaiah says.

"What about Claudia? How did she get knocked out?" I ask, looking over to Claudia who was being helped to her feet by the paramedic.

"Well, I haven't spoken to her myself. The detective spoke with her before I arrived. Claudia told the detective that when she arrived at the unit the front door was broken open. She told him that she was responding to a mother-unknown case. I guess from outside she could hear the girl yelling for help, so she entered the unit," Isaiah explains, reading from his notes.

"She came into this place before calling the police?" I ask, shaking my head side to side.

"Yeah, that's crazy. This is a shithole. Rookie mistake," Isaiah says.

"Anyhow, the girl's voice led Claudia to the closet. When she got to the closet door, there were clothes packed up against it. Claudia reported that it was impossible for the girl to push her way out. As Claudia was pulling the door open, she was struck from behind on her head and knocked unconscious. Now that's some crazy shit," Isaiah says and closes his field book.

"Have the police spoken with any of the neighbors outside? Do they even know who this little girl is?" I ask while peeking back into the room.

"I don't think the girl has said a word to anyone. The officers have been asking around to the neighbors, but they're not saying anything," Isaiah says. "This is a removal, for sure. I'll be right back. I have to call the office to give Paul an update," Isaiah says, picking up his work cell and stepping a couple of feet away from me.

And you were so busy, Andrew, but doing what? Nothing! Get focused because they will blame you for this in the end.

After a minute or so on the phone, Isaiah walks back toward me.

"That was an easy call. We got a ninety-six-hour hold on the girl. I'm going to follow the ambulance to Connecticut Children's Medical Center. Paul will meet Claudia at the emergency department at Hartford Hospital," Isaiah says and then walks past me back into the room.

Isaiah and I walk behind the detective and the paramedics as they take Claudia and the girl out of the unit. More spit and hands fly in our direction as the officer escorts Isaiah and me to our state vehicles.

"You fuckers are always too late for shit," a voice says over the yelling and swearing.

"Baby snatchers!" another voice shouts.

It amazes me how the majority of people in the community react to DCF. We didn't put the girl in the condition she was found. Yet we get the foot in the ass and the label of baby snatchers. Did no one know this girl or her parents? Did they not see the unit themselves? Maybe it was one of them that called the report into DCF. People are so afraid to be called snitches that they are willing to allow people to die before selling out. I put my car in drive and barrel out of Stowe Village, knowing that I could be back the next day on a new case.

*   *   *

I arrive at the office a little before five. My supervisor has left a note on my desk requesting to see me before I leave for the day. Stephanie is on the phone when I enter her office, but she hangs up quickly.

"Hey, Andrew, have a seat," Stephanie says as I close the door behind me and prepare for the worst.

"Andrew, I don't think I need to tell you that something very scary happened today to Claudia. She said you were supposed to be out in the field with her. Where were you?" Stephanie asks firmly.

Part of me wants to tell the truth, but I can't.

Yes, you can, Andrew. Tell her where you were or where you weren't supposed to be. It will give us more time together.

"I was so sorry to hear about Claudia. I was out on some other cases and lost track of time," I say, knowing that if anyone ever tried to verify my lie, I would be caught.

No, you were with Patricia in the park on state time. That's the truth, Andrew.

"Well, it's good to hear that because everyone thought you were knocked out somewhere in the apartment with Claudia," Stephanie says, leaning back in her chair.

She believes me?

Yeah, this time but maybe not next time.

"I called you in to see how you were doing. I also wanted to see if you wanted to go to the hospital with a couple of the guys on the floor to see Claudia tonight. You should come with us. We may go out for drinks later," Stephanie says. She gets up from her chair and picks up her purse from the coat rack.

"You know what? I have another engagement tonight. Here's a couple of dollars for a card and some flowers," I say, digging in my pocket for some spare cash.

"Okay. I'll let Claudia know you asked about her," Stephanie says.

"Thanks," I say and leave her office. I pick up my phone to make a pill order from an old friend.

*   *   *

I park my car on Gillett Street across from the Mark Twain House and Museum. The beautiful Victorian mansion designed by Edward Tuckerman Potter was built in 1870 and was the primary residence of Samuel and Livy Clemens from 1871 to 1891. Clemens loved his Hartford home but had to leave the United States for Europe because of his financial problems. Over the past 120 years, the home went through many owners, and at one point was going to be demolished in order to build apartments. If Clemens were alive today, what would he write about the residents of his beloved city? Hartford is a city whose citizens can't escape from the grips of poverty, drugs, and crime. Hartford is a city where some have never experienced the world outside its borders. Many are trapped in the generational and psychological dependency on the government with their hands out and waiting. Who will write about them?

I walk into the apartment building and take the elevator to the third floor. Inside the elevator I rub my temples thinking how stupid I was to leave Claudia hanging like that. In the hallway a young Hispanic woman and her two children, around five and seven years old, walk toward me.

"Hey, he's from DCF. Look," the boy says to his older brother as he points to my work ID.

I look down and see that I forgot to take off my ID. I slip it in my pocket and then knock on the door of apartment thirty-five. About a minute later Chase answers.

"What's up, Andrew? You got here fast," he says as he holds the door open for me.

It's interesting how life has its connections. Chase was in DCF custody for many years before he signed himself out of our care as an adolescent. His mother was an addict and died of AIDS. Fatherless and mentored by the streets, kids like him are a dime a dozen out here. Now Chase is my supplier—how ironic. Inside the two-bedroom unit, the galley kitchen is stacked with empty forty-ounce bottles of liquor. We walk through the living room where a couple of his friends are playing video games and smoking blunts.

"Yeah, nigga, I'm passing on you all day," one of Chase's friends yells out in joy as he plays the latest edition of John Madden Football.

Chase opens his bedroom door with a key.

"So what you need today?" Chase asks as he opens the top dresser drawer.

It seems like every time I see him, I'm looking for more pills and a higher dosage. He pulls the bottles out like he works at CVS Pharmacy. He has pills for all the major moods. Tonight I'm picking up more oxycontin and adderall.

"This should last you about a week. I'll even throw in a couple more days' worth since you're a good customer," Chase says and passes two plastic bags full of pills.

"Thanks, I'll see you next week," I say. I toss the money on the bed and then walk out of the bedroom to the front door.

Chapter 29 CASSANDRA

Cassandra and Iris sit in the backseat of the car as Gordo drives down the eleven-mile stretch of highway that is the Berlin Turnpike. In the past couple of years, Cassandra and many other victims of Gordo have been taken to the cheap motels on the turnpike. The turnpike allows easy access for Gordo's clients from Hartford to New Haven. Many of these clients live on the fringes of the cities that line the highway. The motel Cassandra and Iris are being brought to that day is very familiar to Cassandra. The manager is a client of Gordo and raped Cassandra three times in the past.

Cassandra and Iris exit the Honda Civic while Gordo goes to speak with the manager of the motel.

"Take Iris to the room. The door is unlocked," Gordo directs Cassandra as he walks to the main office.

"Come on. Let's go," Cassandra says, putting her bag on her shoulder and then grabbing Iris's hand.

The room is in the far corner of the motel. Cassandra gets to room eighteen and turns the knob.

"Just as I remembered," Cassandra says as they walk into the room, frozen in '70s decor.

"You've been here before?" Iris asks with a smile as Cassandra closes the door.

"Go play on the bed," Cassandra directs Iris, ignoring her question.

Cassandra watches as Iris walks across the shag carpet toward the bed with a muted green bed set. The stylish circle and square patterned wallpaper is peeling, showing a water stain. The room is a time capsule filled with smoke permeating the furniture and hanging in the air. Cassandra waits by the window as Iris plays on the bed. Cassandra cracks the window to get some air into the musty smelling room.

"Cassandra, look. Look how high I'm getting," Iris says as she jumps on the bed.

Cassandra turns her attention out the window. She sees Chester pull up in a dark green Land Rover Discovery. From where she stands, Cassandra can see two car seats in his backseat.

"This guy has kids," Cassandra says under her breath, peeking through the curtains.

Cassandra cautiously watches and listens from the window as Chester walks to the front of the Land Rover, carrying a bag with balloon prints.

"This is the rest of the money," Chester says as he hands Gordo a bank envelope.

"And here is your CD," Gordo says. He gives Chester the CD and then places the envelope in his computer bag.

Cassandra turns to Iris who is still jumping on the bed.

She has no idea what's about to happen, Cassandra thinks.

Cassandra pulls the curtain back. She catches a final glimpse of Chester walking toward the room, loosening his tie, and taking off his cufflinks.

Cassandra moves to sit on the edge of the bed where Iris is still jumping. Gordo and Chester are close enough for Cassandra to hear them speaking outside the door.

"No biting and don't leave any marks," Gordo whispers to Chester as he opens the door a crack. "Don't make her bleed or tear," Gordo says, holding Chester back by his arm and giving him one last directive before he enters the room.

Cassandra watches through the cracked door as Chester pulls his arm from Gordo's grasp.

"You do your job and make sure the police don't come," Chester hisses. He pulls his arm from Gordo's grip and opens the door completely.

Iris stops jumping on the bed as Chester closes the door behind him.

"Hello, you must be Princess Iris," Chester says, walking toward the bed and looking at Iris.

Cassandra slides off the side of the bed, leaving Iris sitting in the middle. She knows her job and won't mess up this time.

"Cassandra, where are you going?" Iris calls out, but Cassandra ignores her.

Cassandra walks to the table next to the front door and picks up one of Gordo's digital cameras. Cassandra watches as Chester sits on the edge of the bed facing Iris.

"Hi, Iris, how are you?" Chester asks in a very soft fatherly tone.

Is that how you speak to your own kid, you freak?

Chester places the bag he came with between him and Iris. Iris's eyes light up with excitement as she looks up to Cassandra.

He brought gifts? Great.

"Is that for me?" Iris says, looking at the colorful bag Chester brought into the room.

"Well, have you been a good girl?" Chester asks with a smile.

"I've been a good girl. Yes, I'm a good girl," Iris says, bouncing on her knees.

Don't get so excited. Things will get worse.

"And what will you do for your gift?" Chester asks as he waves the bag in front of Iris's face.

"Let me see. Let me see," Iris says as she tries to grab the bag from his hand.

Cassandra turns on the digital camera and holds the four-inch screen in front of her face. She watches through the camera's screen as Chester peeks inside the bag and pulls out a huge lollipop.

"Can I have it? Can I have it?" Iris asks with joy, reaching for the lollipop and almost falling on top of Chester.

"Will you give me a kiss for the lollipop?" Chester asks timidly.

"Yes, yes, I will," Iris says, cupping her hands in front of her face like she is praying.

Cassandra takes several shots with the camera as Iris gives Chester a big kiss on his cheek. Cassandra sits thinking how she was tricked in this same motel and offered a gift of her own. The first couple of times Cassandra felt just like Iris and so many of the little girls she's come to the motels with. The men make you feel so special. They bring you beautiful things, candy, clothes, and movies. It's only when you get a little older and you're worn out that they don't even look at you. You receive no more presents or requests, Cassandra remembers.

Cassandra focuses the camera very tightly on Chester's hand.

Are you serious? A tiara and a gown?

Cassandra takes several more shots as Iris bounces on her knees when Chester hands her the gown and tiara.

"Look, Cassandra. He brought me a tiara and a gown. I'm a princess for sure now," Iris says with joy, looking over to Cassandra.

If you are a princess, who is he in this tale?

Cassandra turns the camera to Chester. He squints at Cassandra with an evil look. Cassandra feels the message he is sending with his eyes: *You know your job. Don't interfere.*

Cassandra takes a close-up shot of his face.

She takes multiple shots as Iris takes off her clothes to try on the gown. Cassandra received the orders very clearly from Gordo not to miss a shot.

"Slow down. You don't have to do it so quick," Chester says as he begins to help Iris take off her shirt, exposing her flat bare chest.

Cassandra's lens follows Chester's fingertips as they rub across the two pink dots that are Iris's nipples. His fingers then travel down Iris's side and then unbutton her pants.

"That tickles," Iris says and pulls her arms down quickly.

Iris reaches for the gown, but Chester pulls it away from her grasp.

"I helped you get undressed, now you can help me," Chester says while holding the gown behind his back.

Iris pauses for a couple of seconds.

"Okay, I'll help you," Iris says innocently with a smile.

Cassandra snaps multiple shots as Iris unbuttons his shirt. Cassandra's unwanted act of voyeurism leaves her in disgust as she watches Chester's fingertips travel around Iris's body. The camera focuses on Chester squeezing his penis as the blood stiffens him.

"You have hair on your chest. You look like a monkey." Iris laughs with her hands over her mouth.

"Now that's not very nice, is it?" Chester asks as he pulls off his shirt.

Chester lies back on the bed and begins to tug at his pants, faking that he can't unbutton them. He sits up and places the tiara on Iris's head.

"Can you help me with my button? I think my button is stuck," he says, tugging at the waistline of his pants.

Is this guy for real?

Cassandra looks at her watch. *This is progressing fast.*

Chester looks back to Cassandra as Iris is unbuttoning his pants.

Yeah, I know. I won't miss this.

Chester pulls Iris up to his face and begins kissing her on her neck as if she were a wife or girlfriend. But behind his broad shoulders lies a little girl, someone's daughter.

"That tickles," Iris says and pushes away.

Cassandra watches as Chester squeezes and turns Iris. Iris looks toward Cassandra, but Chester turns her head back toward him.

"Close your eyes," Chester directs Iris in a less than fatherly tone.

This is the part you are not going to like.

Chester slowly guides Iris to her back. He holds Iris's hands over her head with his left hand. Chester's right hand begins to rub Iris's vagina over her underwear. His fingers quickly move under her underwear, digitally penetrating her.

"Ow, that hurts!" Iris gasps and screams out with her eyes wide open.

Iris attempts to free her hands, but Chester anchors them down with just one of his strong hands.

"I want to go home," Iris yells out, twisting her body from side to side.

Cassandra grips the camera tightly in her hands and grinds her teeth.

"Gordo said you're a player. You're not going anywhere. I paid for you, and my time is not up." Chester smiles, amused by her attempt to break loose.

Cassandra sits as the only spectator of this assault. She continues to follow Gordo's orders and takes pictures.

Relax. It will get worse if you move.

Chester penetrates Iris deeper with his fingers and holds her hands tighter.

"No! Stop! It hurts! It hurts!" Iris screams at the top of her lungs, frantically trying to break from his grip.

"Like I said, you are mine for at least another twenty minutes," Chester says, entertained by her pleas.

Cassandra watches as Chester takes his bloody fingers out of Iris and flips her on her stomach, ripping her panties off.

Iris's screams are now muffled by the mattress, and her body is restrained by Chester's weight as he straddles her.

Cassandra stops taking pictures, pulling the camera from in front of her face.

She is telling him to stop. This has gone too far.

Cassandra watches as Chester pulls Iris by her hips, forcing her to her knees. He holds one hand over her mouth and then attempts to enter her from behind, but his penis doesn't go in.

"You're a feisty one." Chester laughs while grabbing the back of Iris's neck and forcing her face-first into the mattress. He looks into the camera as he spits on his right hand. "Lubrication." Chester smiles into the camera, rubbing his penis with his saliva and trying again to enter Iris.

"Help, Cassandra, help!" Iris yells with tears flowing from her eyes as he enters her from behind. Iris pushes the pillows and sheets from the bed as she screams into the mattress in pain.

Cassandra is supposed to take pictures, nothing more. She can't hold back any longer. She has been where Iris is right now many times. Cassandra had no one to help her, so why should she help Iris?

Chester continues with his assault with no worries or concerns that he will be stopped. But then a voice is heard.

"Stop, she said stop!" Cassandra yells in anger and is shocked by her voice as it bounces off the walls and rings in her ears.

Iris looks to Cassandra as the left side of her face is planted in the mattress. Chester gives no reaction to Cassandra's command. Cassandra turns to her bag that is on the table, places the camera down, and then shuffles her hand inside the bag.

"Where is it? Where is it?" Cassandra nervously says as she frantically searches her bag. Cassandra's hand finally wraps around it.

Rushing back to the side of the bed, Cassandra yells again, "She said stop!"

Chester turns with his face grimaced.

"Shut the fuck up, you little bitch, and pick up the camera," Chester commands and then takes one swipe at Cassandra's face, knocking her several feet backward onto the floor.

Cassandra slowly sits up and touches her cheek. She can feel her face is tender to the touch. Cassandra's blood boils as she sits on the floor. Still holding it tightly in her hands, Cassandra opens it up and pushes herself from the floor with a burst of adrenalin. She runs full speed toward the bed. With one slash, Cassandra suspends Chester's moment of bliss and transposes it into agony.

"Shit! You little bitch! Fuck!" Chester yells as he falls backward onto the floor, holding what is left of his penis.

Cassandra moves quickly and grabs Iris's naked bloody body from the blood-soaked bed. Halfway out the door she turns back to get her bag from the table. They then exit the room in full sprint.

*   *   *

Cassandra sits with Iris in her arms in the back eat of the Civic as Gordo speeds down the Berlin Turnpike back into Hartford.

"You stupid little bitch! What the fuck did you do?" Gordo yells at Cassandra as he crosses into Hartford.

Cassandra saw Gordo's shocked face as she ran with Iris's bloody body to his car. Cassandra knows that Chester is not stupid enough to report the incident to the police. She wonders how he will explain to his wife and doctor how his penis was cut off.

"You know how much money you just lost me, you dummy? You're gonna pay for this shit, trust me," Gordo says, banging his fist on the steering wheel.

Cassandra cradles Iris in her arms and lets Gordo's threats float out the window. She wishes someone would do the same for her. She knows that can never happen, especially since the only person that cared for her is now gone. Cassandra can never reveal to anyone again what happens in her home or what happened today. Now somewhat calmer, Iris lays her head on Cassandra's chest with her eyes closed.

"Everything will be okay," Cassandra whispers to Iris as she caresses Iris's head with her hand.

The next couple of days will be very painful for Iris. Cassandra will have to help clean Iris up, just like she's done for the others. Cassandra's job moved from lying spread eagle on the bed with someone's father ravishing her to being the mother bird to the girls that come through her aunt Persephone's daycare. Cassandra has to warn the girls about the consequences of telling the truth. She teaches them how to construct lies about scratches, marks, and tears.

Cassandra softly rubs her fingers across her bruised cheek.

"Yeah, keep rubbing your cheek. You got more where that came from," Gordo says with a smile as he looks through the rearview mirror at Cassandra.

Cassandra can see her aunt Persephone waiting at the back door of the apartment building as Gordo parks the car. Persephone walks to the back door with eyes piercing through Cassandra.

"It's time to get up," Cassandra says softly, shaking Iris, who fell asleep.

Persephone opens the back door slowly, taking Iris from the backseat into her arms. "Come with me, baby," Persephone says with the sweetest voice as she walks inside the unit with Iris in her arms.

"And your stupid ass is coming with me," Gordo says angrily as he grabs Cassandra by her hair from the backseat and drags her to the apartment building.

Cassandra is thrown by the hair down a short flight of stairs into the basement. Her body crashes hard onto the damp concrete floor. She watches as Gordo locks the door. She leans up on her knees attempting to stand.

"Lay your ass back down," Gordo says. He punches Cassandra in the face, snapping her head to the side.

Cassandra is laid out again with her face on the cold floor. She lies there for a couple of seconds before she feels her hair being pulled again from the back. Gordo slams her face to the floor, but she is able to shield most of the impact with her hands. She sees through the hair that covers her face that he is taking off his belt.

"You stupid little bitch. You always seem to mess the simplest shit up!" Gordo yells with the belt dangling from his hand.

The first lashing with the belt is to her back. It stings so bad and makes her spring up to her butt. Gordo begins flogging uncontrollably like a wild animal. Cassandra deflects many of the lashes with her hands but can't protect herself from all of them. Her mind transports her to a different dimension to escape the throbbing pain.

*   *   *

Many of her friends were talking about all the fun they were having at the afterschool program at Kinsella Elementary. The school is right next to the Dutch Point housing project where she lives. Sometimes Cassandra would stay a couple of minutes after school and stare from a distance. Cassandra wished that she could be at the program like so many of her friends. Instead she had to return home and help her aunt Persephone with her daycare and her uncle Gordo with his pictures.

One day she took a permission slip and saw that a parent or guardian had to sign for their child to attend the program. Cassandra knew she couldn't have her mother sign it because she didn't know where her mother was.

"Your mother is a crack whore. Go out on the street. You will probably see her selling her ass out there for sure," she remembered that Persephone and Gordo would say.

Over the past year, Cassandra has seen her mother only a couple of times. Her aunt Persephone never allows her mother in the apartment and threatens to call the police if her mother visits.

Cassandra has one aunt named Persephone and an uncle named Broga, but everyone calls him Gordo. A couple of years ago her mother signed temporary custody over to Persephone. Cassandra always felt that Persephone took custody only for the welfare check. People don't talk about her father. Persephone and Gordo have said in the past that her father was a top-ranking Latin King who was murdered over drugs and that he was the reason her mother was an addict.

Cassandra looked at the permission slip in her hand and knew Persephone would never sign for her to attend. She decided to have one of her friends with good cursive penmanship sign it for her. After she was permitted to enter the program, Cassandra came up with a plan to attend the program a couple of days out of the week.

The first day at the program was better than school. All of Cassandra's friends were there. They received help with their homework, got snacks, and were able to watch a movie. After a couple of weeks, Cassandra began helping her peers in the program with their homework. The teachers took notice, especially the best one, their Miss Kay. Miss Kay always paid Cassandra so much attention and told her how beautiful and smart she was.

"Thanks for helping the other kids, Cassandra," Miss Kay said as Cassandra left the program for the day.

After the program was over, Miss Kay would walk many of the students back to Dutch Point.

"Miss Kay is crazy for bringing us home. The police don't even come into this place," one of Cassandra's friends from Dutch Point said one time.

"Why aren't you coming to the program every day," Miss Kay asked Cassandra while Cassandra was helping her hand out snacks.

Cassandra attempted to avoid the questions the first couple of times, but Miss Kay was persistent.

"Hey, Cassandra, you should be here tomorrow. We're going to watch *Ice Age*."

Cassandra began to feel the pressure of the constant questions from Miss Kay so she stopped attending the program for a while.

"Hey, stranger, I haven't seen you at the program for a while," Miss Kay said when she ran into Cassandra in the hallway at school.

"Hi, Miss Kay, I can't come to the program every day. I have to help my aunt around the house with chores," Cassandra lied.

"Chores? You can't do them after the program? I've wanted to tell you that I want to speak with your aunt to tell her what a great helper you've been in the program," Miss Kay said with a smile.

"I'll try to make it this week," Cassandra said, cutting her short and walking toward the main office to drop off the attendance sheet.

It was the day after one of Cassandra's arranged encounters by Gordo that Miss Kay noticed that she was down.

"Why so gloomy?" Miss Kay asked Cassandra who sat at a corner table alone.

Cassandra looked up from the sketchpad and didn't say a word.

"Wow, that's a nice sketch, Cassandra," Miss Kay said as she looked down to her sketchpad.

"Thanks," Cassandra said, closing the sketchpad.

"Was the face you drew of someone you know?" Miss Kay asked, sitting down next to Cassandra.

"Sort of," Cassandra said as she sat up in her chair.

"I'm going to go outside for a little," Cassandra told Miss Kay as she stood from the chair.

"I'll come with you if you don't mind," Miss Kay said as she followed her to the door.

This lady doesn't give up, does she?

"You look a little down today. Everything okay?" Miss Kay asked as they walked toward the front of the school.

"Yeah, everything is okay," Cassandra said as she looked toward the Colt factory's blue onion dome across the street from the school.

In her heart Cassandra wanted to tell Miss Kay everything that was going on. Cassandra wanted to tell Miss Kay how her uncle Gordo raped her. How he took pictures of her and other little girls. Cassandra knew she couldn't say anything. She knew what her uncle Gordo would do to her if she ever told.

"You see that onion-shaped dome over there? An inventor named Samuel Colt built that factory under the dome," Miss Kay said, pointing across the street to the factory.

Cassandra really knew very little about the city where she was born.

"Well, Mr. Colt invented something called the revolving cylinder. This allowed five to six bullets to be shot one after another without reloading," Miss Kay explained.

"Why is that so special? My uncle's friend has a gun that can shoot fifteen shots," Cassandra said innocently.

"Well, that's after one hundred years of innovation, silly," Miss Kay said with a smile.

"How are things going at school, Cassandra?" Miss Kay asked as they walked back to the school's main entrance.

Cassandra paused. "It's not school; it's home," Cassandra said as they continued walking.

Cassandra wished she could take back what she had just said.

"Are there issues with food?" Miss Kay asked as they stopped in front of the door to the afterschool program.

"No," Cassandra said as she wished it were issues with food. Cassandra remembered that her uncle Gordo and aunt Persephone had told her many times what would happen if she ever told someone what was going on in the home. Already feeling like she had said too much, Cassandra made up a fictitious story.

"I just hate that I have to miss so many days of the program to do my chores. My aunt yells at me all the time for nothing. I wish I could do them after the program, but my aunt won't let me," Cassandra said as her eyes began to tear.

"I know it can be difficult when someone yells at you. Like I told you before, if you want me to speak with your aunt, I would love to do so. You know what? If you ever want to talk after school or on the weekends, give me a call," Miss Kay said as she wrote her cell phone number on a piece of scrap paper from her pocket.

Cassandra then walked inside the school in front of Miss Kay.

*   *   *

Cassandra squints her eyes. Her body aches and her skin is welted from the beating. The only light comes from a small window at the far end of the room over the washer and dryer. Her face rests on metal and her body smells of urine. She turns on her back and notices that she is inside a metal dog cage. Cassandra is not sure how long she was unconscious. She hears someone coming. The door to the basement opens.

Chapter 30 ANDREW

The cocoon is broken. I feel air on my back. I lie still with my eyes closed. The snake-like creature's tentacle wraps around my hip and slowly pulls at my clothes. A noise comes from the hallway. My eyes open wide.

She will save me this time.

The creature swiftly moves through the door, knocking my baseball cap off the dresser with its long waving tentacle.

*　　　*　　　*

I lie on my back and stare at the ceiling. It's easy for me to blame the dreams on the pills and alcohol. I know that the dreams were here long before my dependencies. No, they're just dreams. That's all, nothing more.

*　　　*　　　*

I'm a couple of minutes early for my session with Dr. Sol. I sit in the corner of the waiting room and lean over in the chair with my hands between my shaking legs.

"Mr. Edwards, Dr. Sol will see you now," the secretary calls out.

Dr. Sol is putting away a file in his desk when I enter the office.

"I can't take it anymore—the dreams, the pain," I say frustrated as I walk into the office, gesturing with my hands in front of me.

Dr. Sol calmly locks the desk drawer and walks to the middle of the room where I pace the floor. With his hand on my shoulder, we walk to the wall-length window overlooking downtown Hartford and the Connecticut River.

"Andrew, this is a normal reaction to what you've been going through. Not everyone can pass through the pain and loss you have endured. Yet you are able to continue to do what I suggest in order to help you get better," he says.

"It's the voices, my job, Kay—this has to stop." I ramble on and then shake my head.

Dr. Sol leaves me at the window and walks to the table in the middle of the room. He pours me a glass of water.

"Hey, Andrew, come have a seat so we can talk." He motions toward the chair with his hand.

I turn and walk to the chair and sit next to him.

"You've been working hard for a long time, Andrew. Let's talk about it before you throw all your hard work away. Let's take your concerns one by one. Tell me about the voices," Dr. Sol says as he places his writing pad in front of him.

"We've had this conversation over and over. I feel like I'm going crazy. The voices come and go whenever they please," I say frustrated.

"Okay, go on," Dr. Sol says, guiding me through my frustration.

"I fight myself not to allow the voices to consume me and control my behavior and thoughts," I say, leaning forward with my head in my hands.

"Andrew, you're not crazy. People go through difficult situations like you all the time. Some people have out of the ordinary or bizarre experiences," he explains.

I think it's the pills.

"To be insane is to have an unsound state of mind, to be seriously mentally ill. That doesn't describe you, Andrew," he continues, leaning forward close enough to put his hand on my shoulder for comfort.

I sit with my face in my hands thinking differently, fading him to the background.

He continues speaking. "Some studies attribute the majority of the audible hallucinations to psychic experiences."

I sit, shaking my head in my hand.

If I'm psychic, why didn't I know that Kay was going to be killed?

I move up in the chair and wipe my face with my hands. I pick up the water next to me and take a sip. I feel that I have to change the subject before I really go crazy. Over the years I put a lot of trust in Dr. Sol. He's been able to help me sort out some of the confusion in my head. In ways he is like a father to me.

"You know the only thing that is making me feel better is Patricia," I say calmly.

"Patricia? Who is she?" he asks, sitting up in his chair.

"I met Patricia recently at an art exhibition. She is such an amazing woman. It's like she hears me out. She has patience with me," I say, feeling at ease again.

"I didn't know you were seeing someone. This will be the first woman you have dated since Kay's passing," Dr. Sol says as he jots down a couple of notes.

"She's no replacement for Kay. I don't know if I can call it a relationship exactly either. We've seen each other only a couple of times. I feel she is just someone I am growing to trust," I say and look toward the window.

"Again it was good that you decided to move forward, Andrew. You've been very cautious over the past year since Kay's passing. Just take it day by day, and keep me posted if you don't mind," Dr. Sol says and puts the pen down.

"Well, I knew I could see you and have you make me feel a little better. Thanks for the time," I say as I stand from my chair.

"You know what? We'll slow down on the assignments for now," Dr. Sol says, standing next to me.

"That would be good," I say. I shake his hand and then head to the door.

Chapter 31 CASSANDRA

Cassandra watches from the dog cage as Persephone walks down the stairs with a basket full of clothes. Cassandra sits up on her knees and hands like a dog as Persephone drops the basket of clothes on the floor and opens the cage.

"Get the hell out of there, you stupid bitch," Persephone says, pulling Cassandra out of the cage by her hair. "Wash the clothes, and after you're done, get back in the cage," Persephone says and dumps the basket of dirty clothes on top of Cassandra.

Cassandra begins to pick up the blood-soaked clothes from the floor. She wonders how Iris slept last night. Cassandra remembers the stinging sensation she had when she went to pee after Gordo raped her. It felt like her insides were ripped up. Her aunt Persephone kept her from school for almost a week and a half to allow her to heal.

Cassandra stands after placing all the clothes back in the basket. As she walks to the washer, she overhears Persephone on the phone.

"Hey, Carmen! Yeah, Iris is fine over here. She is having so much fun with Cassandra. No, no rush to get her. Better yet, she can stay for a couple more days if you want. Yeah, girl, go do your thing. I'll have her call you when she wakes up later," Persephone says, lying to Iris's mother.

Cassandra knows as mean as Persephone is, she isn't stupid. Many of the children she has in her daycare have parents that are involved with DCF and drugs. Cassandra knows Persephone takes full advantage of this. None of the parents will say shit to her because she always will have something to use against them. Cassandra hears from the conversation Persephone had with Carmen that she was just awarded a couple of more days for Iris to heal.

Chapter 32 ANDREW

I parked my car in front of the multiuse brick building in the South End of Hartford. I exit my car and double-check the address and time from the note Dr. Sol gave me a couple of weeks ago.

This is the right place.

It was only after I met Patricia that I built up the courage to join the group. I take a deep breath, place the paper in my back pocket, and head inside the building. I stop at the main bulletin board near the front desk. I look down the list of meetings being held and see that the Bereavement Support Group is located in room 116. As I walk down the hallway, I can see several other groups in session and at least two adult education night classes being held. I stop in front of the glass door of room 116. Inside I see several adults sitting in the middle of the room in a circle and others by the refreshments in the corner.

Maybe I can leave before someone sees me. What will I do at home? Sit there and stare at her pictures?

I take a deep breath and begin to turn around to return to my car. I suddenly bump into a young African American woman in her mid-twenties as she tries to enter the room.

"I'm sorry about that. Are you going inside?" she says with a smile as she reaches for the doorknob.

"Uh, yeah, I'm going in," I say and hold the top of the opening door to let her pass under my arm.

I guess there's no turning back now.

I slowly walk inside toward the refreshment table with my hands in my pants pockets. Several people look up briefly but go back to their conversations.

On the pastry table there are sticker nametags and several Sharpies. I scribble my name on the tag and place it on my brown blazer.

Next to the pastry table, I read the nametag of an older Hispanic woman named Estrella who is having a conversation with a red-headed Caucasian woman in her mid-thirties named Stacey.

"I think it's ridiculous with all these shootings in Hartford. Two murders in the past two weeks," Stacey says as she shakes her head.

"I live right in the middle of it," Estrella says in a very strong Spanish accent.

Evander, a tall, athletically built African American male, gets up from his chair in the middle of the room. He must be the group facilitator.

"We will be starting in about a minute. You can also grab a cup of coffee or tea during the meeting," he says in a soft voice.

I pour a quick cup of tea and walk to one of the empty chairs in the middle of the room. I look around the circle and see it is a very diverse group of about eight people including myself.

"I see we have a couple of new people in tonight's group. If you all don't mind, I would like to go around the circle for everyone to say their name," Evander says, making eye contact with everyone around the circle as he speaks.

Estrella speaks first. "My name is Estrella Mendoza. I live in Hartford for over thirty years. After my amor, my Ricky, died of lung cancer last year, it was hard to be without him. I felt lost and alone. He was my first love, my first partner. We were together for fifty years before God took him," Estrella says in her accented English and wipes her eyes with a tissue.

I see there is no particular format to the discussion. Estrella goes on for several minutes speaking about the emptiness she feels without her husband, Ricky. I look around the room and see tears in many of the participants' eyes. Stacey rubs Estrella on her back to give her support.

Next is the young African American woman who ran into me in the hallway. "My name is Althea. I live on Albany Avenue in Hartford's North End. I'm the oldest of four children. I'm here because a couple of weeks ago I lost my three-year-old son during a fire in my apartment." Althea pauses for several seconds as she begins to cry.

"It's okay, Althea. We are here for you," an African American woman in her forties named Pam says as she pats Althea gently on the back.

Althea sits up in her chair and takes a deep breath, continuing with her story. "I was living with my aunt at the time in an attic apartment. I couldn't afford to live on my own, and my mother's three-bedroom unit was too small for all of my siblings and my son to live in. I remember that night I lit a candle before my son, Jabar, went to sleep. I guess I was stubborn because my aunt would always tell me not to light candles around the baby and that something terrible could happen if it fell." Althea began to cry a little harder but continued. "I actually put the candles away in a chest for a while and didn't light them. It was after an argument with Jabar's father that I returned home and lit several candles to help me relax. I went downstairs quickly, very quickly, to get something to eat while Jabar was sleeping. My aunt came from the living room and asked if I had burned something because she smelled smoke. I told her no but instantly knew what it was. I ran up the stairs and saw smoke coming from under the door." She cries uncontrollably along with most of the group, including Evander.

"I trapped him in there. I killed him. I tried opening the door but the knob was too hot, and my aunt said it would only make things worse to let oxygen into the room. The smoke forced everyone in the building to run to the street. I was crying on my knees and looking up to the attic window as the fire ripped through the building." Althea ends her story with everyone, including me, kneeling next to her and giving her words of support and comfort.

The entire night goes on like this, each person telling a story of loss. I've never seen so many tears in my life as each person encourages the next and patiently listens to every word. After about an hour into the group, most of the participants have spoken except for me.

"Andrew, we would love to hear from you if you would like to speak," Evander says as he looks over to me.

All the tear-filled eyes look my way. I feel that the pressure is definitely off after hearing all the stories that evening.

I take a deep breath and then speak. "My name is Andrew Edwards, and I live in Hartford. This is my first time at the meeting tonight," I say, gazing ahead and falling into a trance as I tell them about Kay.

"Her name was Kay, and she was the love of my life. She's been gone for about a year, but it feels like forever. My heart is so filled with love for her, but I can never share it with her again. Sometimes I think I didn't show her how much I appreciated her. I guess we never know how much we will miss a person until she's gone." I pause for a second and hear words of encouragement in the background urging me to take my time.

"Her body was found not too far from where we are sitting. I received the call from her best friend, telling me that something horrible had happened to Kay and for me to rush to Dutch Point housing project. When I arrived the police had the area taped off. I ignored the tape and ran under it toward the body that was on the ground in the doorway of an empty unit. Before I could get to the body, several officers grabbed me and held me back. I yelled out asking who was under the sheet. I was in complete panic. They finally let me through, and a detective showed me her school identification. I didn't understand why she was there." I pause for several seconds, bowing my head toward the ground. The tears cascade down my face and fall on the floor at my feet.

"I'm so sorry, Andrew," one voice is heard from across the circle.

"We're here for you, Andrew," another voice says as someone rubs the center of my back.

"You can stop if you like, Andrew," Evander says in a supportive tone.

I lean back in the chair and wipe my face with my hands. I take a deep breath and continue. "They wouldn't let me get close to her at the scene because they were still gathering evidence. Hours later I headed to the coroner's office. I'm was led into a room adjacent to the autopsy room where Kay's body was being held. A television monitor was on top of a metal table. I was told prior to arriving that Kay's body had to be preserved for evidence. I wasn't able to hold her that night. I stood in front of the moinitor still in shock about what happened. The medical examiner turns to me and begins to speak. His words were muffled. The room was spinning.

"Are you ready Mr. Edwards?"

I nod my head yes and watch him turn on the monitor. In front of me was a close up video feed of Kay's face. I felt like vomiting. My legs gave out. The tears flowed uncontrollably. My Kay was lying lifeless on a stainless steel table. I reached out and touch the cold monitor with my fingertips. Kay's eyes were closed and her skin color drained. I asked to see the entire body, and he obliged. He picks up a joystck and pans the camera to show a full body view. It was then that I saw the extent of her injuries. Her throat was cut from ear to ear. There were stab wounds around her torso and defense wounds on her hands. That was the hardest day of my life." I finish the story feeling drained.

The group's participants all come next to me. I feel hands on my back and shoulders.

"You are a strong man, Andrew," Estrella says with tears in her eyes.

"I'm so sorry, Andrew," Stacey says as she rubs my shoulder with her hand.

As hard as it was to tell the story to a group of strangers, I feel so relieved afterward. This is the second time in the past week that I have told the story about Kay. It was a different sensation to sit and listen to everyone's story and then add mine. I've had loss in my life before Kay. My father passed away when I was a very young boy. I sit up in the chair, feeling much more relaxed. I don't even feel like I have to pop a pill or have a drink.

"Andrew, thank you for coming tonight," Evander says. He places a hand on my shoulder and shakes my hand as I stand next to Estrella.

"Andrew, I remember hearing about your wife's murder. I lived in Dutch Point at the time but recently moved out," Estrella says. "For a long time I didn't want to move out of my apartment because I didn't want to leave Ricky behind. We lived in the same apartment for over thirty years. We had so many memories there. It took a long time to leave, but after encouragement from my children, I left Dutch Point. I have a little duplex in the South End of Hartford not too far from my old apartment."

"I'm sure you loved him," I say with encouragement.

"You know, Andrew, the most powerful part about leaving my old apartment was cleaning the house. When I was cleaning, I was able to find love letters and pictures I hadn't seen in years. The story of our life is now in boxes in the basement of my new place."

"I know that had to be hard to put all your memories in the basement," I say.

"It was hard, but I knew I had to start over. I have memories of Ricky all around my new apartment, but they aren't overwhelming," Estrella explains.

My life feels like hers because I haven't touched anything since Kay's death. "Thank you for listening and for the extra time and suggestions. I know I can't move, but maybe I could start with packing some of Kay's belongings," I say with a smile.

I walk her to her car.

"I hope to see you at the next group," Estrella says as she closes the door to her car.

"Yes, I hope to see you also," I say and then walk toward my car.

Chapter 33 ANDREW

I open the kitchen curtains and stand in my black jogging pants and Champion sweatshirt. The morning sun beams through the clouds into my face. Garbage and branches litter the lawn from last night's storm. I watch from my window as the old Hispanic woman from down the street lets her dog crap in my front yard yet again.

"I don't want the dog shitting in my yard. Use the park across the street," I say as she smiles and then walks away.

I wipe the sleep from my eyes and walk into the living room. I live in a twelve hundred square foot two-bedroom apartment in the South Green section of Hartford. Kay loved the unit's floor plan with the kitchen, living room, and dining room all open. The unit is its usual mess since Kay has been gone. Kay was very organized and neat. Her side of the closet was always perfect. Everything had its little place. She would always say I kept the place like a dorm room.

The doorbell rings as I'm walking back to my bedroom. I look at the clock.

I wasn't expecting anyone right now.

I open my front door.

"Hey, guy, you should keep the front door locked. You got some crazy people out here," Peter says as he walks up my stairs with two coffees and a box of doughnuts in hand.

"I wasn't expecting you so early on a Saturday morning," I say as he walks into the unit handing me a coffee.

"I didn't know I had to be invited. Plus I've been trying to call you for days, but you don't pick up your phone," Peter says. He takes off his brown leather jacket and then sits on the cluttered sofa in the living room.

"So what's up with you?" I say, sipping the sugarless coffee.

"I met a girl last night at the Bar with No Name in downtown Hartford. She lives right down the street from you so I figured I pass by."

"Are you ever going to settle down, man? It has to get tiresome never to be in a committed relationship at your age," I say as I sit on the arm of one of the sofas in the living room.

"Me? Never in a committed relationship? I guess you were too young to remember Linda. When I was in high school, I was with her for an entire six months," Peter says smiling.

"Only to break up with her after prom because you had sex with her. That doesn't count, man," I say, grabbing one of the doughnuts from the table.

Peter has been like this for as long as I can remember. He is seven years older than I am, and I remember him bringing different girls home all the time. Peter was rarely around, so that left me with my mother or alone with my stepfather when she was out.

"Anyways, player hater, you missed out last night. They had mad women there," Peter says. He waves his hand and hits a couple of empty boxes near the sofa that fall to the fall.

"What, you moving or something?" he asks as he restacks the boxes.

"No. I'm just finally getting around to packing up some of Kay's things," I say, leaving out the details that I attended the group.

"Yeah, that's good. Sitting around here with all her things would have gotten me depressed," he says. "You ever speak with that chick you met at Real Art Ways?" Peter continues with a mouth half full of a jelly doughnut.

As much as I love Peter, I don't share everything with him. I'm a very private guy some would say.

"We've traded a couple of e-mails and spoke on the phone several times," I say, giving him the short version. "Hey, since you're here, maybe you can help me pack some things." I walk over and hand him one of the boxes on the side of the sofa.

"Guy, when was the last time you made the bed?" Peter asks in a joking tone as he enters the master bedroom behind me.

"Are you here to help or what? How about you start packing up all Kay's clothes in the closet," I say and walk to the opposite side of the room to the dresser.

I pull up a little stool from my corner of the room and sit in front of her side of the dresser. I don't think I've ever opened this drawer before. I knew Kay was very private and never really liked me going through her things. It was no problem for me because I never liked anyone picking through my stuff. The drawer has shirts and socks. One by one, I stack the shirts in one of the empty cardboard boxes. The scent of her Victoria Secrets peach body spray travels through my nostrils, and I close my eyes. I remember buying it for her the last birthday we celebrated together.

"What's up with these files and newspaper articles?" Peter calls out from the closet.

I open my eyes and rush over to the closet.

"Give me that, man. I said Kay's clothes, nothing else," I say annoyed, snatching the files and papers out of his hands.

"Hey, man, I didn't know it was top secret stuff," Peter says laughing. "I gotta go to the bathroom. I hope it's not as dirty as your room." He smiles as I place the files and papers back in the plastic file box on the floor of the closet.

I pick up the file box and store it on the top shelf in the hallway closet. As I'm turning around, Peter walks out of the bathroom.

"What, you steal one of Mom's old family albums?" Peter says as he opens one of the albums from the bookshelf in the hallway.

"Mom knows I have it. You're the one that likes to take things from Mom without asking. You remember her car you snuck out with and crashed when you were seventeen?" I remind him as we walk back into the bedroom.

"Okay, you got me," he says. "Oh, man, you got some old pictures." Peter points to a photo of him holding me after I was born.

I hear a big sigh from behind as I'm taping up my first full box of clothes. I knew the pictures would bring back memories.

"You have a lot of Dad in here, man," Peter says in a sad tone.

"I know I was young when he died, but I miss him too," I say, sitting next to Peter on the bed.

"He died of a freaking heart attack," Peter says shaking his head.

"Well, that's why I asked Mom for the album. Most of my memories are through old pictures and stories from you and others," I say as I flip the page of the album.

"He was a very good man. Everyone loved him. Last month I dropped by White Plains High School back in New York and saw teachers who worked there when he did," Peter says and wipes a tear from his eye.

"I'm surprised Mom didn't move from White Plains. I've been trying to get her to come to Connecticut ever since Robert's death," Peter says flipping the page to a picture of our first family vacation with our stepfather, Robert.

Our mother, Annie Edwards, remarried three years after our father's death.

"Weren't you mad that Robert bought you the wrong flavor ice cream or something like that?" Peter asks as he points to the picture with me frowning.

I try not to remember that far back sometimes. I've trained my mind to block it all out.

"Yeah, something like that," I say.

"What's up with these cut-up photos?" Peter asks turning the page.

"I started making a collage but couldn't finish it," I say, walking to pick up the packed box in front of the dresser.

"Isn't she lovely, isn't she wonderful." My ringtone plays Stevie Wonder in the kitchen.

"I'll be right back," I excuse myself to answer the phone. I know exactly who it is.

"Hey, Andrew, I'm downstairs," Patricia says on the other end.

"I'll be right down," I say and then hang up the phone.

Last night after the group, I called Patricia to let her know how amazing it was. I was so excited by Estrella's suggestion of cleaning the house. I went to Walmart and bought a couple of boxes after speaking with Patricia. Patricia thought it was such a good idea that she offered to come help me this morning. I can see her taking a picture as I walk down the stairs to open the door. This is her first time visiting.

"*Bom dia* or good morning," I say, mangling the Portuguese language.

"*Bom dia*. You learn fast," Patricia says and gives me a kiss on the cheek.

"So what were you taking a picture of?" I ask her as we walk up the stairs.

"You have a classic Volvo 1800 in front of your house," Patricia says as she unbuttons her jacket.

"Oh, my neighbor's piece of junk out there?" I say as I watch her waiting for me in front of my red door.

"That's not junk, that's a classic. Roger Moore drove it in the 1960s television show *The Saint*. My father also restored a beautiful red one when I was a child living in Brazil," Patricia says smiling.

"I never heard of the show. The car is a little too small for my taste," I say as I walk up the final couple of stairs.

I stand frozen on the stairs for a second as I see Patricia standing next to the big red door. No woman has been in the apartment since Kay's death.

"Should I open it?" Patricia asks with a smile, snapping me out of my daydream.

"Sorry about that. I just had a quick flashback of the day I surprised Kay with the keys to the apartment. Excuse the mess, but sure, open it up," I say and stand behind her as she turns the doorknob.

"Wow, this is a very nice place. Those windows let in a lot of light. Those brick walls give a nice touch also," Patricia says, looking past the clutter throughout the apartment.

"I guess you and Kay have the same taste. She loved the windows, high ceilings, and brick walls too." I close the door behind me.

Peter walks into the living room from the back. I forgot for a minute that he is here.

"And hello, hello, you sly dog," Peter says with a smile as he walks toward Patricia and me. "You look familiar. What club have I seen you at?" Peter asks.

What a dumbass. He picks up woman with that?

"Peter, this is Patricia. I met her at the Real Art Ways exhibition a couple of weeks ago," I say formally introducing them.

137

"Oh, yeah, how is your friend? Her name is at the tip of my tongue," Peter says as he seemingly strains every brain cell to shuffle through the list of girls he has been with.

"Myra," Patricia replies as she stands next to me.

"Yeah, that's her. How is she?" Peter asks excitedly.

"I'm not sure. I really don't know her very well. She was just a fellow artist in the same exhibition," Patricia says, taking her bag and placing it on the sofa.

"So, Peter, Patricia is here to help me with the packing I was telling you about," I say as I gesture with a nod to the door.

"Hey, look at the time. The mall should be open by now. Patricia, it was nice seeing you again. Andrew, give me call later, okay? I'll see my way out." Peter winks at me as he walks to the door.

"Yeah, I'll call you," I say and close the door behind him.

"Would you like some coffee and a doughnut," I ask Patricia as I take her jacket and put it next to her bag on the sofa.

"American coffee tastes like hot chocolate compared to Brazilian coffee. I'll pass on it right now," Patricia says with a smile as she walks with her hands in the back pockets of her jeans toward some of the pictures on the bookshelf.

I stand next to the closet and watch Patricia as she moves from picture to picture. My heart doesn't feel as heavy as it used to. I don't feel guilty with her being here. I wonder if Kay would approve of her.

"Oh, I love this one with you guys posing next to Niagara Falls," Patricia says as she picks up the frame from the shelf.

Kay and I went to Niagara Falls for one of our anniversaries. I remember she was so scared to take the boat into the falls.

"So where do we start?" Patricia asks, rubbing her hands together.

I lead her to the master bedroom.

"You already have one box packed. Good job. I love this leather chair," Patricia says, falling into its soft cushions. "I can fall asleep right here." She smiles and reaches her hands out for me to help her to her feet.

"I have fallen asleep in that very spot so many times." I pull her up and pause just to look at her standing in front of me. "I feel so tranquil around you," I say as I hold her in my arms.

The feeling I have around Patricia is so much better than any pill I have ever popped or bottle of liquor I ever drank.

"This is the beginning of your new life. You will still have Kay in it with you. I'll make sure of that, Andrew," Patricia says and kisses me on the lips.

"I'll complete the dresser drawers. Peter was working on the clothes in the closet. Maybe you can finish what he started. There should be a box in the closet," I say.

"Yes, sir." Patricia smiles as she marches to the closet.

We spend over ten minutes of straight working and no talking.

"Hey, Andrew, I think I found some old love letters. The envelope reads 'To my love Kay, from Andrew with love.' How romantic," Patricia says from the closet.

"Those are from the beginning of our relationship. You can put them in the box. I don't think I'm ready to read through them right now," I say.

Every piece of clothing, accessories, or jewelry has its story.

"Have you thought about sending some of Kay's things to her family?" Patricia walks out of the closet with her first complete box.

"Kay's mother actually came and picked up a lot of Kay's belongings a couple of months ago. She told me that I could keep the rest or do whatever I wished with the remaining items." I take the box out of Patricia's arms.

"You know what you can do, Andrew? You can donate some clothes and other items to local women's shelters or to families in need. Keep the items that hold the most sentimental value in your possession."

"I can't believe I didn't think about that before. That's an excellent idea, Patricia."

I switch spots with Patricia for a while and take the closet. On the back shelf I open Kay's beautiful antique jewelry box with an angel carved on the top. Inside are birthday, holiday, and anniversary jewelry I bought for her over the years. Before meeting Kay, I wasn't much of a jewelry shopper. Kay, on the other hand, loved antique jewelry and inherited many pieces from her grandmother. I returned them to her mother after her death.

In one of the compartments inside the jewelry box I find a Polaroid picture. As I look at it closely, I can see it is a photo of Kay and a student at her school. The student in the Polaroid looks too old to be in Kay's third-grade class. On the bottom there is a date. It was taken a couple of weeks before Kay was killed.

Who is this girl? And who took the picture?

I know just the person to ask but will have to wait until next week.

After a couple of hours, we were able to pack pretty much everything in the bedroom and some stuff from the hallway closet. There was one last drawer to clean out on Kay's side of the bed.

"Thank you for helping me, Patricia. We got a lot done today," I say as I hand her a cup of orange juice.

"No problem, Andrew. Let me know when you're going to complete the rest of the place. I would love to come back," she says, leaning back in Kay's leather chair.

"Estrella from my support group was so right. I really do feel much better right now after packing some of Kay's things." I take a sip from my glass of juice and continue. "If you don't mind, can you clean the last drawer next to Kay's side of the bed? I think she stored some of her papers from school there. I'm going to take a quick shower." I grab my clothes from the drawer.

"Sure, just hand me another box," Patricia says and hands me the empty glass.

As I walk back from the kitchen, I peek into the bedroom. Patricia is sitting on Kay's side of the bed opening the box. A chill shoots up my spine.

I'm going to be happy again.

PART II
Kay's Journal

Chapter 34 PATRICIA

P atricia places the box on the floor and then sits on the edge of the bed. She pulls on Kay's drawer, but it only opens partially.

Something must be stuck.

Patricia squeezes her hand inside the drawer and takes some of the papers from the front. She places the papers in the box and tries to open the drawer again.

Still not working.

Patricia reaches her hand to the back of the drawer. She can feel a book stuck in the back that prevents the drawer from opening. Patricia tugs hard at the book while manipulating the drawer at the same time. The book is released, and Patricia is able to pull open the drawer. She sits with both hands wrapped around the book.

This is not a book. It's Kay's journal.

Without too much thought, she tosses the journal into the open box on the floor. Patricia quickly walks to the hallway and puts her ear to the bathroom door.

He's still taking a shower.

Patricia returns to the bedroom and stands over the open box staring at the journal. She picks up the journal and walks to the living room. She heads to the bookshelf and looks at some of the pictures of Andrew and Kay.

They still look happy in the photo.

As a photographer, Patricia knows that pictures can hide emotions and deceive the viewer. Patricia's struggle is whether or not to read the journal. She wouldn't want someone to read hers.

Kay can't get mad. She's not here anymore.

Patricia tries to find justification for reading the journal.

Maybe there is something in here that can help Andrew. He did say they don't know who killed her.

The bathroom door begins to open.

Shit, he's coming.

Patricia looks at the journal and then to the hallway. Her bag is on the sofa in front of her. Her decision is made. It will be like it never existed.

*　　*　　*

After a long day of packing, Andrew drops off Patricia after a late lunch. At the kitchen counter, Patricia begins to open her bag but closes it quickly. She decides to take a quick shower to relax her body and mind. Patricia's friend will be in Boston for a couple of days so she has the apartment to herself. After her shower, Patricia returns to the kitchen wearing her white robe and carrying a towel to dry her hair. She finally takes the leather-bound journal out of her bag and places it on the counter. Her fingers trace the embedded angel on the cover. A button secures the journal.

"I can't believe I just stole something from a dead woman," Patricia says to herself, holding the journal in front of her face. The guilt begins to build in her chest.

"Maybe this was the wrong thing to do." She picks up the phone to dial Andrew's number but quickly hangs up the receiver.

"I need a drink, that's what I need." She walks to the refrigerator to grab a bottle of wine.

Patricia takes a wine glass from the cabinet. She places the wine bottle under her arm and then picks up the journal with her free hand. She slowly walks to the love seat in the corner of the living room and pours a glass of wine.

"Kay Edwards, what was on your mind?" she muses as she fans the pages with her fingers and takes a sip from the glass. "I'll just skim through and then return it like it was never taken. It's only to help him, right? That's it, only to help him."

Patricia opens the front cover.

December 31

I told myself that I was going to write in a journal this year, so why not start now hours away from a new one? I would sometimes sit and think why people would wait all year in order to make resolutions about what they will change or do differently in the New Year. Couldn't they make a change in any month or day of the year?

In college in one of my ancient history classes, we actually learned the origin of the New Year. In modern times we only know it as the ball dropping in Times Square and watching the news on New Year's Eve to see all the different countries around the world enjoying their New Year's celebrations. But what I learned is that it was originally celebrated on March 1. Why can't we go back to that? It made sense back then, I guess, because it was near the time of the spring equinox. The ancient Greeks celebrated theirs during the winter solstice. It was only during the time of the Roman king Pompilius and the creation of twelve lunar months from the previously established ten that we began celebrating it on January 1, the month named after the Roman god Janus.

So why do I write this in my journal? I write it because I will follow the path of tradition and pray for the gods to help me be a better person, teacher, friend, and wife in the next year.

January 1

I am still so tired from last night's party. Andrew, Betsey, her husband, and I all went to see the ball drop in Times Square. They said they planned it all year because they knew I had never experienced it. Andrew actually kept a secret from me. *Wow.* What an awesome time, but need I say *cold*?

January 8

First week back to school after the holiday recess. I really didn't get much time with Andrew because he usually takes his vacation during the summer. I did have a chance to READ. My mother said I've always loved reading and would sit in my room with a book in my lap making up stories for the pictures. Andrew bought me leather-bound copies of the classics *The Odyssey* and *The Iliad*.

January 30

Andrew is stressed again about some of his cases. I hate it when he is like this because it's like he is a different person. I try to get close, but he pushes me away with his words. When I ask to speak about why he's so upset, he says he doesn't remember being upset. I know his job is very difficult and I could never do it. Working with the children at the school has its own challenges. We actually saw one of his cases on the ten o'clock news tonight.

*   *   *

"Hey, Andrew, I'm going to go to bed," Kay said as Andrew sat on the couch and stared blankly into the television.

Kay's initial reaction was to walk into the bedroom and accept that Andrew had ignored her again. Instead, she stood across the room from him, took a deep breath, and then walked toward him. Kay had made a promise to herself that she would be a better wife. She fought the urge to allow Andrew to continue to live in his own isolated world. Kay sat beside Andrew and smiled as she admired his beautiful caramel-colored skin. She reached out to caress his hair with her hand.

"Andrew, I said I'm going to bed," Kay repeated in a soft tone.

As her hand touched his head, Andrew flinched and then he quickly turned toward her.

"I'm sorry. You startled me. I didn't hear you the first time," Andrew said and then turned his head back to the television.

Andrew sat on the couch and felt buzzed from the four drinks he had that evening. With his glass nearly empty, he took the last swallow of liquor left in the glass. As the reporter on the television spoke about his shaken baby case, Andrew picked up the half empty bottle of liquor that was on the floor. He filled his glass to the rim, with the goal to have at least one more drink after finishing the one in his hand. Andrew watched the news segment intently. Earlier that day, he noticed that the media had taken an interest in his shaken baby investigation. With all the media attention his case received, he wanted to stay up to see how the news reported on it.

Kay sat close to Andrew. She felt that he didn't even notice her. She laid her head on his shoulder and grabbed his left hand. Kay saw that Andrew had poured another glass of liquor.

"There I go," Andrew said as he pointed to the television.

Kay watched as Andrew walked out of a house in Hartford to his state car. She knew Andrew's job brought him into many clients' homes. She always feared that one day an upset client would attack Andrew.

"They actually taped you walking out of the family's home?" Kay asked.

"Yeah, that's crazy," Andrew said and then took a sip from the glass in his hand. "The mother is only nineteen with two sons, a five-month-old and a two-year-old. The boyfriend isn't the father of either child. The mother left the five-month-old, who was sleeping at the time, with her boyfriend and was only gone for twenty minutes. When she returned, the boyfriend was in a rush to leave the house. She went to check on her son, and when she saw him, he was gasping for air, blood was coming out of his nose, and his eyes were red. She called the ambulance, and they brought him to CCMC," Andrew told Kay.

Andrew explained the case to Kay as if he were giving an update to his supervisor. He spoke very mechanically and in a serious tone.

"When I spoke with the physician from the Suspected Child Abuse and Neglect Program at the hospital, he told me that this case was a prime example of shaken baby syndrome."

"This world is crazy. What would make a person do something like that?" Kay asked.

"More than likely the baby was crying and the boyfriend wanted him to stop so he shook him. When a baby is forcefully shaken, the brain moves from side to side, hitting the skull. Because babies don't have fully developed neck muscles, they can't control their heads. The doctors said that the baby likely would have brain damage from the shaking because blood vessels and nerves were damaged in the brain," Andrew explained. "At least the baby will survive. He will remain in the NICU for further monitoring."

*   *   *

After the news segment, I went to bed, but Andrew was up a while longer and had another drink.

February 3

Tonight I made a beautiful dinner for Andrew, but he got home too late for us to eat together. Every day it's a new emergency with him. Andrew removed a couple of children on a new case and had to place them in a foster home. I can't imagine taking a child from his or her parent. What must that feel like to tell a parent that you are taking his or her child? Andrew said in the beginning he would get nervous, but now it was second nature.

I was thinking about picking up a second job since I have so much time after school. Plus I'm usually home alone. One of my colleagues told me about an opening in the afterschool program and it was a couple of extra bucks that I could earn. Maybe I will check it out. Andrew will never know I was gone since he is never home before me.

February 8

Today was my first day at the afterschool program. It was so much fun. We helped the children with their homework and then did some fun activities and played outside. I'm so excited about starting.

February 14

Andrew brought me to Hot Tomatoes in downtown Hartford for Valentine's Day. I remember we ate there our wedding night.

*   *   *

Kay held Andrew's hand tightly as they walked down Church Street in downtown Hartford. The streets were busy as spectators left an event at the Civic Center. Kay didn't care who watched them as Andrew periodically stopped to give her a kiss. During their reception earlier in the day, Kay was so excited that she forgot to eat, so they decided to walk from the Hilton to Hot Tomatoes for a late dinner.

While they waited to be seated, several couples in line with them watched as they beamed with their newlywed glow and flirted with one another. Kay's name was called by the maître d', and they were seated in the far corner of the room.

Andrew ordered two glasses of red wine for the two of them. This was the happiest he had felt in his life. He sat next to his soul mate and expressed his love by softly kissing her neck. The electricity from the day still flowed strongly through him. Andrew felt connected and in tune with Kay.

The waitress who came to their table to take their order broke Andrew's focus on Kay.

Andrew said with pride, "This is my lovely wife, and we'll take the largest steak."

Andrew kissed Kay and touched her leg under the table throughout dinner. He was so excited that he forgot to eat. After dinner he left the waitress a substantial tip.

Back at the hotel, they had several drinks in the bar and then made their way to their room. There was a couple in the elevator who got off before them. When the door closed, Andrew pulled Kay into his arms and kissed and caressed her. The excitement from the day slowly intensified to its peak and searched for an outlet to release.

When they reached their floor, they both composed themselves and exited the elevator. Kay observed that there was no one in the hallway. She looked at Andrew whose eyes were squinting at her. He growled like a tiger and then began to chase her toward their door. Kay giggled as she tried to escape Andrew's pursuit. She slowly stalled her pace as she got closer to their door. Andrew grabbed her arm and pushed her back against the door. Kay tilted her head up as Andrew kissed her and pulled at her dress.

An older woman exited the elevator and walked unnoticed in their direction. The woman paused initially, shocked by the scene in front of her. She watched as a younger woman was kissed and groped by what appeared to be her boyfriend or possibly her husband. The woman watched as the young man dropped something, and her gaze then changed to one of envy, admiring the young woman and the love and passion between the couple.

With Kay still in his arms and his back to the door, Andrew searched his pants pockets for the card to open the door. He found it in his back pocket. He dropped the card as he rushed to open the door. He picked it up from the floor and noticed a woman staring at them down the hallway. He slipped the card in the slot, and the door opened on the first try. They both fell to the floor. Andrew kicked the door closed behind him.

Kay lay on the floor in the dark as Andrew removed her dress and panties. That night they made love on the floor, then on the bed, back to the floor, and finally ended in the shower. At the end of the night Kay lay naked in the bed with her head on Andrew's bare sweaty chest.

"I love you," Andrew whispered as he kissed Kay on the top of her head.

*   *   *

Tonight Hot Tomatoes was packed. After thirty minutes we were seated. Our old table was occupied, but we were seated fairly close to it. It was supposed to be a special night, but Andrew looked and sounded withdrawn. It was like he was in another world and didn't want to be there. I asked him what was wrong, but he said nothing. After several drinks and some small talk, we returned home. No wild lovemaking tonight. Only another bottle of wine and the television in the living room for him.

I sit here writing as the love of my life is out of tune with me. Is it me? What can I do? He's been in therapy for a while but doesn't talk to me about it. Shouldn't it be working? In my time of knowing him, he has his periods like this. In the past he has said it was because of the job or things that are "too complicated to explain." Sometimes I don't know what to do or say so I write.

SOLITUDE
Solitude why do you come in this time of need?
I resent you for taking his mind, his soul.
He is mine not yours, but I see your power is stronger.
Loneliness, find your space in another life away from me.
Leave us at peace. Stop draining the emotions that I have so grown to love.
Did you create an illusion for me to swarm to
Only to transform and sting me when my heart has unfastened?
Depression, don't alienate him from my advances.
You leave me deserted, quenched with love, eyes burning and fleeced of tears.

February 16

The afterschool program has been so fun. It looks like the children enjoy the activities, and it seems that they like me. It feels good to be appreciated.

February 18

Andrew actually surprised me with flowers, chocolates, and a long kiss tonight. After the program, I went to buy some groceries and spent some time at the bookstore. I know it's not Valentine's Day, but I will take whatever love he is giving.

*   *   *

"And these are for what?" Kay asked as Andrew held her tightly in his arms.

"They are for the love that you give me past, present, and future," Andrew said.

"The poet," Kay said accepting his embrace.

Kay walked to the bedroom with a big smile while Andrew unpacked the groceries. She hoped that the Andrew who was in the kitchen would be like that every day. The shower relaxed her body. The thought of having the old Andrew back even for one night excited her heart.

Andrew prepared two grilled chicken breasts and vegetables for dinner while Kay took a shower. A little before Kay arrived home, he had taken a pill to help him relax. Over the past couple of months he had taken his focus off Kay. The stress of his job consumed him. He knew that Kay didn't deserve the lack of attention and love.

The iPod was playing some bossa nova, and the table was already set. Kay walked up behind Andrew, wrapped her arms around his torso, and kissed him on his neck.

"And what can I help you with, my love?" Kay whispered.

Andrew turned and gave Kay a strong and love-filled hug. She was one of the only people that knew the sensitive and loving Andrew. His heart felt cold and hard at times. Kay's love and energy shot through him, warming his soul.

"All I want is for you to relax and enjoy the night," Andrew said as he gave Kay another kiss.

Kay stood in the kitchen with a smile while Andrew brought the wine to the table. She felt that the universe had answered her call.

*   *   *

This is the Andrew I miss, the guy that I married. I want him to feel this way all the time but don't know how to do it. I will work hard for him to stay this way. I will keep my New Year's resolution and be a good wife.

February 25

Last week we had a couple of new members join the afterschool program. I guess the word is out ☺.

March 5

I noticed today that many of the children in the program walk home alone. Most of them live in the Dutch Point housing project. I decided that I was going to walk some of them home after the program. A couple of the other teachers didn't think it was a good idea. They felt that the neighborhood was too dangerous for me to go alone. Needless to say, none of them volunteered to accompany me. I knew if I told Betsey she would try to talk me out of it.

You know, it's funny that we can teach the children in the same neighborhood that they live, but we're afraid to venture outside the walls of the school and interact with them in their own environment. How can we ever relate to our students if we can't see what they experience? We all knew when we came to teach at the school that it was in an urban setting. *Get over it.*

I actually did my research on Dutch Point and wanted to know how it got its name. I was surprised to find out that back in the 1600s Henry Hudson, the same guy that has a river named after him in New York state, was hired by the Dutch to find a shorter route for the Northwest Passage to Asia. Years after Hudson, Dutch explorer Adriaen Block erected a fort called House of Hope and controlled nearly thirty acres of land, trading exotic skins and furs.

In the 1940s the barricade-style apartments were built in the Dutch Point housing project. Generations of families grew up and lived there. When you walk around, you see that it's no different than any other housing project. Just the style of the building is different. Unfortunately, it has the same drug activity and crime that infest many of the city's neighborhoods. It's the history of the area and the innocent children and families that you want to save from this cycle of fear, addiction, devastation, and dependency. What I can do is teach them and help them find a way out.

*   *   *

There were several children with Kay on the walk home. The first drop off was on Stonington Street adjacent to Colt Park. Neighborhood children played with a football in the middle of the street as Kay and the group she was with sang and skipped down the sidewalk. Cassandra trailed behind the group and broke off completely before they entered Dutch Point.

Inside the grounds of the housing project there were many people outside their units conversing, kids running around the buildings, and loud music playing. Several of the Hispanic and African American males whistled at Kay and asked her name as she passed. Some of the females gave Kay weird looks, but they didn't bother to speak.

In Dutch Point there were many hardworking families. The drug dealers and gang members that terrorized the community created a false picture that did not represent the honest and hardworking families living there. Kay observed that the life that her students lived was completely different from the safe and comfortable suburban life she was raised in. She now understood the fears of her colleagues. They came from the same world of privilege that she had, but they preferred to do their goodwill behind the secure walls of the school.

Kay returned to the school without incident and eager to tell the other teachers.

March 11

Things seemed to have picked up with Andrew at work. I rarely see him anymore. Some nights he arrives home and I'm heading to bed. He says it's all for the cause, helping the children, his job. I mean donate to our cause I want to say but know he works hard. I get a quick kiss good night, and he's either reviewing paperwork or watching the news to see if one of his cases will be shown.

Andrew is drinking much more now, but he's somehow able to wake up the next morning with no problems. I told him in the past to stop working on-call, but he says we need the extra cash. I think it's DCF that has him like this. I know he went to college for psychology and his father was a great social worker, but I feel that it's draining him. He works some of the most horrific cases in the state, and I think it's taking a toll on him.

Andrew has been seeing Dr. Sol for a while now. I knew he was going initially to work on some of his issues about his father's death and some other issues that he never wants to talk about. I give him space, but we've been together for a while now, and I feel like there are so many things I just don't know about him. Andrew says the work he is doing with Dr. Sol is helping him filter through his issues at the same time he's helping others. Whatever

155

that means, because it's not helping me. It's not giving me more time, rather it's taking it away. I think he sees Dr. Sol more than me. This may sound like I'm jealous because I am. I want my husband back. I miss him. Sometimes I want to speak with Dr. Sol myself but stop every time. It's my poetry that keeps me sane sometimes.

ABOUT A SECOND
Sometimes I'm so confused.
Sometimes I feel like
I'm lost. I don't know why.
It could be because the weather is cool.
Could be the distance, could be my job, the routine.
But I know I have sunshine.
I know I have a bridge.
I have every reason to be here, to be alive.
But when I lose you for about a second,
That is when nothing makes sense anymore.
Sometimes I make you confused.
Sometimes I make you feel like you are lost.
I don't know why. Please don't ask.
This boat was lost at sea.
But your light tower, it guided me. Guide me, boy.
You anchored me. You anchored this love, so take this love.
But when I lose you for about a second,
That is when nothing makes sense anymore.

March 20

I haven't seen Cassandra in the program lately. She usually comes a couple of days out of the week. She's such a sweet girl and a great helper. The interesting thing is she always seems to disappear during the walks home. I'm not too sure I want to tell Andrew about the program. He would probably be upset that I was walking the kids home into Dutch Point.

March 24

Andrew had another nightmare last night. Ever since I met him, he's been having these nightmares but never wants to speak about them. Andrew wakes up screaming and swinging his arms sometimes. One time he got me right in the head with one of his arms. I knew he didn't do it on purpose, but it hurt. I tried to comfort him, telling him that everyone has nightmares, but he got defensive. I wonder if I should try to meet with Dr. Sol. I need to find out how I can help Andrew. Maybe I'll call Peter, but I really don't like Peter. He's such a womanizer and can be a pain in the ass sometimes.

March 25

Andrew and I met with my mother today for lunch.

March 27

Andrew called after his session with Dr. Sol to tell me he had to return to work late tonight. I'm going to try to find a nice frame for the beautiful sketch Cassandra drew of me today.

March 31

Today while I was washing our clothes, I found a folded piece of paper in the back pocket of Andrew's pants and some pills in the front. The pills didn't look like Tylenol, and I knew he wasn't on any prescribed medication. Initially I was going to throw the paper away, but I took a look first. On the top of the page were the words "assignment three" and an address. Maybe it's something from work. I put the paper and the pills on the table next to the bed and waited for him to say something, but he didn't.

April 3

It wasn't right how he spoke with me tonight. Sometimes it's like I don't know who he is.

*   *   *

Kay paced back and forth for hours in the living room as she waited for Andrew to return home. She tried calling his cell phone, but it went straight to the voicemail. Kay contemplated calling Peter but chose not to get anyone else worried. It wasn't unusual for Andrew to work late. But he usually called to tell her when he was going to work after hours. Kay's ultimate fear was that Andrew was injured somewhere in Hartford. It was close to midnight when he walked in the door, still under stress.

"Why didn't you call me, Andrew?" Kay asked worried.

"What do you mean, Kay? I work late sometimes. I have emergencies. I can't call you all the time like that. I get out of cases late. You know this," Andrew said angrily as he walked past her.

"It's like I don't know you anymore, Andrew," Kay said as she walked away from him.

"As if my job isn't stressful enough, I have to come home to this shit," Andrew said, throwing his jacket on the sofa.

"If you call someone worrying about you stress, then fuck you," Kay said and then walked into the bedroom and slammed the door behind her.

Andrew yelled out as he kicked over the table next to the sofa. He knew his anger and stress weren't Kay's fault. His frustration was more a reaction to Kay than to any issue at work. He got caught up in the moment, and he knew he couldn't take his words back at that point. Andrew picked up his jacket from the sofa and then slammed the door as he left the condo.

Kay sat on the bed in their room crying into her pillow. She didn't know how she could help Andrew. She felt that the closer she got to Andrew, the further he pushed her away. Time had changed Andrew. He was no longer the person she had married. It was as if he wore a mask.

MASK

I'm suppressed and depressed,
Laying dressed in my flesh,
Staying stressed and confused,
No direction no clue,
Ideas in my queue,
Nothing more, nothing new.
I reflect and discuss:
What is trust? What is just?
It was death of a soul,
Growing mold, no control.
Let it roll, and it will fall.
Heard him call, standing tall,
Not for long was not strong.
Love is here, love is gone,
Broken dreams, written songs.
Memory, remember me.
Climbed a tree I tried to flee,
Broken branches, broken me.
Painted face sprayed with mace.
Tears are streaming, broken dreaming.
Clean the closet as you have it.
You're my prey, but I'm your target.
Camouflage it, can't disguise it.
Masqueraded dancing puppet,
Hidden face behind a veil
Covering my imperfections.
What's the lesson? Give a clue.
Reveal yourself and just be you.

April 7

Cassandra was back at the program this week. She looked a little down, so I took her for a walk. She cheered up for a second when she saw my antique angel necklace that Andrew bought me last year. Cassandra said my necklace was so pretty. She said her mother bought her an angel necklace years ago and told her that the angel was going to protect her. Cassandra said her aunt took the necklace from her and she hasn't seen it since. While we were walking around the school, I gave her a little history lesson on the Colt factory. Cassandra is such a smart girl. Cassandra is having some problems at home with her aunt and put it down to having to do chores. I suspect something different. I gave her my cell phone number and told her to call me if she wanted to talk. Maybe I should leave the social work to Andrew?

April 9

Tonight was girl's night out. Betsey and I went to have a couple of cocktails at Vito's by the Park in downtown Hartford. At least once a month we get together like this. We've been friends since freshman year at Eastern Connecticut State University. During our senior year in college, the Hartford public school system was recruiting on campus. We both put in applications and were lucky enough to be offered to teach at Kinsella School the following year. We've had some really good times in and out of college and some very tough times. I was happy she was there on one of my worst days.

*   *   *

It was close to nine at night and the campus library was closing. Kay sat alone in a study area at the far end of the library. Her best friend Betsey and several of her roommates had invited her to an off-campus party, but she elected to study for the weekend. Kay packed her bag, and put on her jacket and hat. Kay, along with several dozen students shuffled out of the library into the brisk eastern Connecticut night. Kay walked alone but stayed close to a group of students headed toward her dorm. The campus was quiet, not much activity. On the weekends many of the students left campus since the majority of them were residents of the state.

Inside High-Rise, one of the campus apartments, Kay checked her mailbox and picked up some promotional flyers for Domino's. High-Rise was like a ghost town on the weekends. Kay ran into one of her classmates in the campus laundry room. She headed to the elevator but forgot that it was out of service, so she walked up the four flights to her floor. Her apartment was next to the stairway. She noticed that the light on her side of the hallway was off, which was odd. She made a mental note to notify the resident assistant in the morning.

Inside the apartment the lights were off. Kay flipped the kitchen light and saw the mess Betsey and the others left behind. There were several empty beer bottles on the table. A bag of potato chips was ripped opened with half of the bag's content on the floor. Kay had never lived with a messier set of girls. She took her hat off and placed her bag on the living room sofa. She grabbed the empty cans and tossed them into the garbage and placed the bag of chips on top of the refrigerator. She turned around with her back to the sink. On the counter there was a can of beer. Kay opened the can and took a sip. The last thing on her mind was to clean up someone else's mess.

In the unit, there were six separate bedrooms. Kay picked up her bag and then walked around the corner to her room. She tried turning on the light in the hallway, but the bulb was broken with some of the glass still on the floor. She wondered whom Betsy and the other girls had in the apartment before they went to the party. At her door, she took her keys from her back pocket and struggled to get the key in the hole. She finally slipped the key in after a couple of tries. Kay's roommate's door behind her began to open. She thought she was alone.

"Pam, I didn't—"

Without warning from out of the shadows a large figure pounced on Kay from behind. The unidentified male swept her off her feet by the waist and covered her mouth with a gloved hand, as he forced her into her bedroom. The man was startled, by Kay's arrival at the apartment. He was able to kick Kay's roommate's door open as Kay entered the apartment earlier. The intruder held Kay tightly as she tried to turn. In the struggle they both fell on the bed. The grip around Kay's waist and mouth got tighter.

"What the fuck?" Kay screamed through the gloved hand on her mouth.

The intruder breathed heavily, trying to keep Kay under control. A terrible pain shot through his hand as Kay bit his fingers. He struck Kay in the back of the head with a powerful blow. A searing pain tore through Kay's head and everyting went black. The intruder felt her body go limp.

161

Kay struggled to regain consciousness as she lay dazed on the bed. She squinted her eyes, trying to focus on the large hooded figure standing over her. Then, out of nowhere, an excruciating strike connected to the side of her head. More searing pain. She felt her pants being pulled down as she went unconscious.

Betsey and her roommates returned home a little after two in the morning. Betsey entered the apartment first and instantly knew something wasn't right. The television in the living room was gone, and the doors to several of her roommates' rooms were wide open. Betsey thought about Kay and panicked as she ran to Kay's room in the back while her roommates ran to their rooms. Betsey saw that Kay's door was closed. She turned the doorknob but it was locked. She banged on Kay's door as she simultaneously turned the doorknob.

Kay lay on her back in the center of the bed. She found it difficult to open her eyes. She touched her eye with her hand and felt that her face was swollen. Someone banging on her door had awakened her. Kay looked down and saw that her pants and panties were down to her ankles. Blood ran down her legs and soaked the bed. Kay screamed out and then tried to stand but fell to the ground. She heard the banging on the door get louder and someone calling her name. Kay managed to crawl to the door and opened it with the last ounce of strength that she had. Betsey knelt next to her, holding her in her arms and screaming for someone to call the police.

That night sealed Kay and Betsey's bond forever. Betsey stayed by Kay's side, from the interview with the police to the time at the hospital. Medical personnel did a rape kit and took Kay's clothes for evidence. Kay felt empty, damaged, and ripped apart.

The police told them of another rape several blocks off campus a couple of hours before the attack on Kay. The police were not sure if the rapes were related but said it was possible. They were not sure how the person got into the apartment because there was no indication of a break-in. Betsey was upset because she thought that maybe she had left the door unlocked. There were several items taken from some of the other rooms, and there were many complaints of robberies on the same day in other apartments in the building. They never found the person who raped Kay.

After that day, Betsey promised to never share what happened with anyone. I felt too embarrassed to tell my parents. I also never had the courage to tell Andrew or any other partner before him. I think it's better this way. Since that day I've always been so honest with Betsey. We spend hours talking about life. Betsey and her husband are out every weekend trying to find a party. Usually Andrew and I accompany them, but he's working so much we haven't been out for a while.

I told her about Andrew being so withdrawn and the things I found in his pocket last week. It was odd and really didn't make sense. Betsey asked me if I thought he was cheating, but I definitely didn't feel that. My theory was his job is at the root of some of his issues. Andrew seems to be fine after his sessions with Dr. Sol but then falls back into his depression. Sometimes I catch Andrew having entire conversations with himself. I mean, I know we all talk to ourselves, but what I saw was different. Betsey said Andrew's behavior is a phase and for me not to worry. I wish he would come back to me. It was such a good time to be out with her and not home alone.

April 10

Tonight I walked into the bathroom and saw Andrew cleaning a cut on his arm. He said it happened during work while he was helping a client move some things. I told him to get it checked, but he said it was minor. I worry about Andrew and feel that he is in danger sometimes at his job. When I try to have a conversation about it, Andrew avoids the subject only saying that his job can be dangerous at times. Andrew actually apologized for the other night with a card and a poem he wrote.

IT WAS ME
It was a squeeze without an embrace.
It was tears that couldn't release.
It was silence by me not you.
It was anger for reasons too many to name.
It was not for anything you did, but what I continue to do.

It was me that was not pushing to change.
It was you who tried and who cried.
It was me who wanted but couldn't.
It was you who could and did.
It was this feeling that happens with sadness.
It was the pressure in my head that fades me out.
It is a voice that directs and commands.
It was my excuses, my abuse, my secrets.
It was me not you.
Love, Andrew

April 15

Today while cleaning the closet I mistakenly turned over one of Andrew's folders. I picked up the same paper I had found in his pants pocket a couple of weeks back, but this time things were crossed out. In the back of the closet he has a plastic file box that he usually keeps his work-related stuff in. I put the papers, including one of Dr. Sol's business cards, back in the file and then placed them in the box.

April 17

I dreaded calling Peter but had to see if he noticed any changes in Andrew. Peter told me not to worry about Andrew, saying that Andrew has always been quiet and kept to himself. It got me really upset when Peter asked me, " Don't you know that already? You're married to him." I mean, it's not a joke. Yes, I know Andrew can be quiet. I live with him. I wondered if there was more to this than I thought. Next time I will keep Peter out of it.

April 19

Today after work I took a ride to Bloomfield. I was just too curious about this paper that I found in Andrew's things. When I got to the address, it was in what appeared to be a working class neighborhood next to the Copaco Center. There was no car in the driveway, and it didn't seem like anyone was home. What do I think I'm doing? This is crazy.

April 21

Over the past couple of days, I've received three hang up calls on my cell from a private caller. I hope the telemarketers didn't get my number.

April 23

Today I took some Polaroid pictures with some of the children and gave them copies. They were so happy. During the drop off in Dutch Point, I saw the police arrest a group of guys who were selling drugs. The closest I've ever come to something like this was watching the television show *COPS*. I think I was more scared than the children I was dropping off. Yet again Cassandra seemed to disappear. I need to find out where she lives so I can speak with her aunt about how well she is doing in the program.

April 25

I took the address for Dr. Sol's office from the business card that was in the closet the other day. I need to see if Dr. Sol can help me understand what is going on with Andrew.

*   *   *

Kay exited the elevator and made her way to Dr. Sol's office. She was a little nervous and unsure how Dr. Sol would receive her. The waiting room was empty when she entered. The secretary was on her cell phone as Kay patiently waited in front of the counter for her to end her call.

The secretary hung up her cell and acknowledged Kay. "Hello, how can I help you?"

"Hi, my name is Kay Edwards. I'm not sure if you can help me. My husband, Andrew Edwards, is a client of Dr. Sol. I was wondering if I could speak with Dr. Sol today if he has time," Kay asked.

"Well, Mrs. Edwards, I really can't say if your husband is seen here or not. Confidentiality laws," the secretary said as she looked up at Kay.

"I understand the laws, but it's really important that I speak with Dr. Sol," Kay insisted.

"The only thing I can do is leave Dr. Sol a message to let him know that you are here to see him. You can have a seat," the secretary said and picked up her phone.

Kay walked over to one of the tables and picked up a magazine. She looked over to see that the secretary was back on her cell phone. Several minutes after Kay's arrival the door to the back offices opened.

"Mrs. Edwards?" a male voice called out.

Kay turned and saw a tall, well-dressed Caucasian male standing in the doorway.

"Dr. Sol?" Kay asked as she walked toward the man.

"Yes, please come inside," Dr. Sol said as Kay shook his hand.

As they walked down a short hallway to his office, Dr. Sol wondered why Kay had come to see him. He thought briefly that maybe Andrew spoke with her about their sessions. He allowed that thought to quickly pass through his consciousness because he knew Andrew wasn't ready to speak with Kay about some of the issues he was going through. That brought him back to his first thought. *Why was she here?*

"You can have a seat over there," Dr. Sol said, pointing to the leather chairs in the middle of the office.

Behind his desk were his academic credentials from Stanford University and a beautiful framed photograph.

"That's a beautiful picture of the Golden Gate Bridge. I love how the fog seems to engulf the entire bridge," Kay said as she sat down in the chair.

"Thank you. I took that many years ago. I think that was my best one out of the dozen shots that day," Dr. Sol said as he closed the door and walked toward Kay. "So, Mrs. Edwards, how can I help you today?" he asked as he sat in the chair next to Kay.

Kay paused for a second in order to frame her thoughts. "I really don't know how to say it. I guess I will say it directly. I came here today because I really didn't know to whom I should turn. It's Andrew. He's been very withdrawn lately. He works so much that we don't even speak. He doesn't communicate his feelings to me anymore. He seems to always be drinking. I don't know, it's like he's a different person." Kay rambled on to Dr. Sol.

Dr. Sol picked up the pitcher of water from the table next to him. He was not sure what answers Kay expected to get from him regarding Andrew. He knew exactly why Andrew was withdrawn. He knew why Andrew worked late. Just because he knew these things didn't mean he was going to tell Kay or anyone else. He knew he had to control this and many other situations. *Let's see how this plays out*, he thought.

"Would you like a glass of water?" Dr. Sol asked in a therapeutic tone as he poured a glass for himself.

"No, thank you."

"Is there anything else?" Dr. Sol asked and then took a sip from his glass.

"Since you asked, yes. The other day I found a piece of paper and some pills in our room. I mean, it was really nothing. I really don't know where the pills came from. They weren't Tylenol or anything. This paper, it was some sort of assignment or something. I put the pills and the paper next to Andrew's side of the bed and left it alone."

Dr. Sol didn't allow Kay to see his uneasiness about the information that she shared. He wasn't aware that Andrew was taking pills but graciously nodded as if he knew the information. The paper with the assignment was another matter that he would have to address at a later time.

"Why let a piece of paper and a random pill you found get to you so hard?" Dr. Sol asked.

"I guess it was because Andrew continued to act withdrawn. I don't feel I am able to speak with him directly because he just doesn't seem open to talk. I can't say I thought he was cheating on me or anything, but I wondered why he had an address on the paper I found in the room," Kay said.

"Well, you said you put it on his table and left it alone, correct?" Dr. Sol asked.

"Yes, that is what I did after I found the paper. But I was just so curious that I took the address from the paper and checked out the house to see what this assignment was all about. I mean, he never speaks about having assignments or anything for work. Needless to say, it was nothing, just some empty house. I don't know if I'm going crazy trying to figure out what's going on in Andrew's head." Kay finally stopped because she ran out of breath.

Kay watched as Dr. Sol stood from the chair next to her and walked to his desk. She sensed that he was trying to avoid her questions and concerns.

"Those are some interesting observations, Mrs. Edwards," Dr. Sol said.

"I'm just so concerned about Andrew and want to know how I can help him. Andrew just looks depressed to me," Kay said.

"I didn't know depression had a look," Dr. Sol said nonchalantly as sat in his chair and looked at Kay with a smile.

Kay thought, *Is this guy serious? This isn't a joke.*

"So, this paper you found. You mentioned that it was some sort of assignment? And had an address written on it?" Dr. Sol asked as he was writing on a pad at his desk.

"Yeah, like I said, I went to the house, and it was just some little house with no one home. The house is the least of my worries. It's Andrew that I'm concerned about. How is he doing in therapy with you? Do you feel like there is any progress? Do you think he needs to be on medication?" Kay rapidly asked, rising from the chair.

Dr. Sol's next words to Kay made her want to throw a chair at him, deepening her frustration.

"Well, Mrs. Edwards, I understand you have some concerns about your husband, and I appreciate you coming down to speak with me. But per confidentiality laws, I can't speak about Andrew and what goes on during our sessions. To be honest, I can't even say if he is my patient," Dr. Sol said as he placed his pen down.

Dr. Sol knew he had her in a position of frustration and vulnerability. She exposed her hand showing all of her cards. He felt that he gained more from the visit than she did.

"Dr. Sol, I understand the laws just as I told your secretary, but I don't think you understand what I'm here asking you for. I am very worried about Andrew. I am here for your guidance, for your help," Kay said, gesturing with her hand as she stood in front of his desk.

Kay was seething with anger. In desperation she had just opened her heart to this complete stranger and he barely acknowledged her. She was no better off than when she walked through the door. *This is all bullshit*, she thought.

"Mrs. Edwards, I understood you very clearly. I'm not sure if you understood me, but I can't speak with you about your husband's treatment. What I suggest is that you speak with Andrew about his progress. In order for me to discuss any patient, they need to first sign this release," Dr. Sol said and handed Kay a form authorizing release of information.

Kay's heart sank. She felt lost and alone. The only person she thought could help her understand what was going on with Andrew had just thrown cold water in her face.

"Andrew has spoken with me in the past about how you are helping him. He talks about this cause for the better good. Helping the children. I don't know what it all means, but to be honest with you, I don't see Andrew getting any better. He's good for a couple of hours after sessions with you, and then he seems to fade off." Kay was growing more frustrated with every second that passed.

"Mrs. Edwards, as a psychotherapist my job is to help my clients push through issues in their lives and try to balance things out among many other things. I understand your frustration with the current situation, but all I can say is speak with Andrew. Unfortunately, I can no longer entertain anymore questions about Andrew," Dr. Sol said as he got up from his chair and walked in front of the desk to stand next to Kay.

Kay felt like crying but held back her tears. Dr. Sol didn't deserve the satisfaction of seeing her cry.

"Well, thank you for your time." Kay took a deep breath through her nose and walked toward the door. As Kay's hand reached for the doorknob, Dr. Sol called her name and she turned around.

"My colleague has some openings for individual therapy. She does some good work," Dr. Sol said.

Kay forced a smile and walked out the door. She couldn't believe his boldness.

When Kay reached the hallway, her cell phone rang. It was another call from a private number. The person hung up again after she picked up.

April 26

I still can't believe Dr. Sol won't help me. I wonder if he knows how it feels to have someone you love in so much pain and you have no control over it. I hope he doesn't tell Andrew that I came to see him.

I went to the store to have my cell phone checked. I asked if there

169

was anything they could do about these calls coded private. The sales guy suggested that I don't pick them up. Oh really? Can you believe he also tried to sell me a new cell phone?

May 1

Andrew was working on-call late last night. I really don't know why he does this to himself. What's interesting about Andrew is he looks energized on some days and down on others.

May 3

I dropped the last kid off at Dutch Point, and before he walked away, I asked him if he knew where Cassandra lived. He pointed me in the direction of her aunt's unit.

*   *   *

Kay made her way to the other side of Dutch Point where the boy said Cassandra lived. She received more stares and catcalls as she walked across the housing project. She found Cassandra's apartment. There were a couple of cars parked in front of the unit with several guys smoking and blasting rap music. One of the Hispanic males pointed in her direction while another yelled something in Spanish and then began to laugh. *Maybe this wasn't a smart idea,* Kay thought. She knocked for about a minute and then saw someone look through the blinds. Several seconds later Cassandra cracked open the door.

"What are you doing here, Miss Kay?" she whispered nervously.

"You split from the group again so I just wanted to make sure you got home safely," Kay said as she looked at her through the cracked door.

"Well, I'm safe. Now you have to leave, miss," Cassandra said in a whisper and then closed the door.

Cassandra looked toward the stairs. She can hear that her aunt Persephone was still on the phone and unaware that someone was at the door. Persephone was the last person she was worried about. One of the guys next to the cars outside of the unit was her uncle Gordo. Cassandra cautiously looked through the blinds as Kay walked away. Her heart jumped when she saw her uncle Gordo and his friend begin to follow Kay. She knew she couldn't leave the house. Her aunt was on the phone so she had no way to warn Kay that she was being followed. Kay and her uncle Gordo were suddenly out of view from the window. Cassandra's heart sank.

As she walked back to the school, Kay remembered Cassandra saying her aunt wasn't very nice. Maybe she was out of bounds coming to Cassandra's home in the first place. Kay noticed some of the men who were in front of the house are now following her. She picks up the pace and closes in on a group of young girls walking ahead. She takes a quick look over her shoulder just in time to see the men disappear into one of the apartments.

Yeah, I'm paranoid, Kay said to herself.

*   *   *

May 6
Today, before the afterschool program, Cassandra came to speak with me.

*   *   *

Cassandra walked into Kay's classroom and closed the door behind her. She saw Kay behind her desk preparing some activities for the program. Cassandra worried about Kay after the day she visited her home. She was happy to see that her uncle Gordo didn't hurt Kay.

Kay noticed that Cassandra entered the room. She called her over to her desk.

"Miss Kay, I'm sorry about closing the door on you the other day," Cassandra apologized.

"That's no problem, Cassandra. I should be the one apologizing," Kay said as she stacked several papers and placed a box of color markers on top.

"Good thing my aunt Persephone was on the phone. She didn't know so I wasn't punished. My uncle Gordo was one of the guys that followed you," Cassandra said as she sat in the chair next to Kay's desk.

"Well, maybe you can help me carry this material to the program," Kay said and then slid the papers and markers in her direction.

Kay was still kicking herself for going to Cassandra's home unannounced. She hoped in her heart that she truly didn't get Cassandra into trouble that day. Today she didn't want to pry for information. Then suddenly out of nowhere Cassandra spoke.

"If someone told you something really bad happened to her, would you keep it a secret?" Cassandra asked as she looked down to the floor.

Kay paused for a second. She knew in her time she had kept secrets from others and had asked the same question as Cassandra. This was different. This was a student. She couldn't possibly do what she asked.

"It is not my job to keep secrets, Cassandra. I would listen to that person and try to help her as much as possible," Kay replied and sat down next to her.

Cassandra was silent for several seconds.

Kay didn't want to play this game. "Are you the person that something really bad happened to, Cassandra?"

Kay then noticed Cassandra's tears. She moved closer to comfort her.

Cassandra lifted her head and looked Kay in the eyes. "Yes, it was me." Cassandra cried harder in Kay's arms.

Several minutes passed, and Cassandra began to tell Kay what happened.

"I was forced to do things I didn't want to do. I was touched in my private parts and forced to touch other people," Cassandra said, crying uncontrollably.

Kay was completely surprised by her words. This was the first time that anyone had ever told Kay something so serious. She really didn't know how to respond. Just as Betsey did for her in college, she knew she needed to support Cassandra.

"Have you told anyone else about this, Cassandra?" Kay asked with her arms around Cassandra's shoulders.

"No, you are the first person I told," Cassandra said still in tears.

Kay knew from her own experience that the police would have to be notified and that Cassandra should go to the hospital.

"Cassandra, you are so courageous," Kay told her with her arms still around Cassandra.

Several weeks ago Cassandra had commented on Kay's angel necklace. Kay took her necklace off and placed it around Cassandra's neck. Cassandra's eyes instantly lit up, and she calmed down a little.

"I remember you said you had a necklace like this before," Kay said as

Cassandra sat with her hands around the necklace. "Cassandra, you did the right thing telling someone about what happened to you. No one should have something like that happen. You have to understand that as a teacher I am what they call a mandated reporter. By law I have to call DCF," Kay explained to her calmly with Cassandra's hands in hers.

Cassandra pulled her hands from Kay's. Her entire demeanor suddenly changed.

"No one can find out. You can't call DCF. I will surely get in trouble if they come to my home," Cassandra said frantically.

"Cassandra, it's okay. Calm down, okay? This is something that I can't keep from the authorities. I know you put your trust in me, and I hope you continue to do so. DCF will just come out to make sure that you are okay," Kay tried to explain.

"No, they won't. They will try to take me from my home. They will put me in a foster home, and I won't be able to see any of my friends. I know how it works. I've seen DCF do it before. My cousin was removed, and we haven't seen her for years. Now that I think about it, what I told you happened so long ago maybe I told the story wrong," Cassandra said with her head on Kay's desk, having this conversation with herself. She stopped crying and lifted her head from the desk. "You know, when I think about it more, nothing happened. I was never touched. I only wanted to see how you were going to react," Cassandra said and wiped her tears from her face.

Kay knew this was not true. She was not trained to speak with children that were abused. She was cautious about how she responded to Cassandra at this point.

Cassandra stood up from the chair and said in a very clear and calm voice, "If DCF or the police come to my aunt's home, I will tell them that it didn't happen." She then turned and walked out of the room.

*   *   *

After my conversation with Cassandra, I spoke with Andrew later that night. Andrew said I should report it to the DCF hotline right away. By state law I have twelve hours to make the report.

May 7

Today I made the report to the DCF hotline. I asked to remain anonymous. They said per state law as a mandated reporter I could not remain anonymous to DCF but I could with the family. After making the report, I asked the worker if I could call back to see if the case was accepted. I was told that they would not tell me anything about the case as it is confidential. Cassandra wasn't in the program this afternoon.

May 10

Several of Cassandra's teachers said she hasn't been in school for a couple of days. I knew going to her home wasn't a good idea. I asked Andrew what the process was with a case after it is called into DCF. He said depending on the severity of a case, it could be a nonaccepted case or coded same day, twenty-four-hour, or seventy-two-hour response time. It's been past seventy-two hours, so DCF must have responded by now.

During my drop off today, I asked some of the children if they have seen Cassandra. I hope she's okay. While in Dutch Point today, I felt like the stares were getting harder, definitely ever since my phone call to DCF. I wonder if they know I was the one that called in the report. These private incoming calls continue on my cell phone. I feel like I'm being followed. No, maybe it's just my mind playing tricks on me.

May 12

Tonight Andrew came home with another cut, this time on his hand. He said one of his clients pushed him in the back after he told her that it was a possibility that her child would be removed. Andrew's hand went through some glass causing the cut. When I suggested that he get it checked and to call the police next time, he got upset and asked me what I expected from him and that it was the nature of his job.

I DON'T EXPECT
No,
I don't expect you to smile.
How can one smile while the whole world is collapsing and

175

The chaos seems inevitable?
When there is no sign of near salvation.
No,
I don't expect you to be calm.
How can someone remain calm in the middle of a storm?
While dreams and hopes are being covered by sand
And there are no signs of an easy rescue.
No,
I don't expect you to speak.
How can a person find good words if there is confusion,
If there is a loud noise?
There is nothing but a wish.
No,
I don't expect anything.
I just wish.

May 17

Cassandra hasn't been in school all week. I wonder if I should ask Andrew to look her up in the DCF system. No, I don't want to bring him into this. He has other things to worry about. Lately I've been the stressed one around the house. During the program today, I saw Cassandra's uncle Gordo drive by the playground real slow, staring at me with a cold look. Maybe I should tell Andrew. No, I can't because he will know that I'm going into Dutch Point. I'll speak with Betsey about it. These damn calls are still coming to my phone. I think I may change my number.

May 18

This morning Andrew's tires were slashed. He said it was probably some kids in the neighborhood. I know we live in Hartford, but the way my mind has been going, I thought it was related to my call to DCF. I think I am definitely going crazy now. Today I spoke with Betsey about all the things happening.

*　　　*　　　*

Betsey noticed that Kay was withdrawn all week. She finally caught up with Kay in her classroom after school to speak with her. Ever since Kay was raped in college, Betsey had been protective of her. They were not just best friends. They were sisters.

Kay knew if there was one person she had to be honest with, it was Betsey. Kay sensed that Betsey knew something was wrong so Kay had to be careful about what she said in order not to alarm her.

"Is everything all right with Andrew?" Betsey asked as they sat in Kay's classroom.

"Surprisingly, it's not Andrew this time," Kay said taking a deep breath. "I've been walking the children home into Dutch Point after the program," Kay said and then took a sip from her bottled water.

"Why are you doing that, Kay?" Betsey asked concerned.

Kay rolled her eyes. She thought that maybe she should have kept it to herself. She knew deep inside she couldn't keep any secrets from Betsey. She also knew Betsey was right to be concerned considering the close call with the guys following her from Cassandra's home the other day.

"I'm doing it because the kids need it, Betsey. We can't limit ourselves to just the classroom. If not me, then who? No one," Kay said in a defensive tone.

Betsey sensed Kay's frustration with her question, so she backed off a little. She knew Kay wanted to help the children. But she felt that Kay was putting herself at risk by going into Dutch Point.

"Are you at least being accompanied by one of the other teachers?" Betsey asked as she opened her own bottle of water.

"No, I'm going in alone," Kay said and then heard Betsey sigh.

"Kay, you have to be careful out there. Just last week I saw on the news that there were some shootings over there," Betsey said shaking her head. "Does Andrew know at least?"

"No. Andrew can't know. I know he will be upset, just like you. I'm telling you so at least someone knows that I'm going there. You have to promise me that you won't tell Andrew," Kay said as she looked into Betsey's eyes.

"Kay, that's a big promise. I don't think I would be able to live with myself if something happened to you," Betsey said.

"I'll be fine, Betsey. Just promise me that you won't tell Andrew until I'm able to, okay?" Kay asked and took Betsey's hand.

"You have to tell him soon, all right?" Betsey said squeezing Kay's hand.

"I will, sister," Kay said with a smile squeezing Betsey's hand tighter.

"My gosh, you're going to break my hand, Kay." Betsey laughed and pulled her hand out of Kay's.

"I'll call you later," Kay said and then stood from the chair and left her classroom.

Kay knew she couldn't tell Betsey about Cassandra or even about Cassandra's uncle staring at her as he drove by the school the other day. She also didn't know when or if she would tell Andrew about her walks into Dutch Point.

May 20

Tonight I uncovered something very interesting about Dr. Sol. I wonder if Andrew knew about this. I was planning on speaking with him tonight about it but had to push it to the back burner. Now I have a better understanding of what's been on Andrew's mind.

*   *   *

Andrew sat on the sofa staring aimlessly at the blank television screen. He felt that he was falling deeper into his depression. He suffered from the stress of his job, the sessions with Dr. Sol, and his complete disconnection to Kay. He felt that the more he did for others the less he received in return. The sadness wrapped around his head and numbed him to the very thought of life. He recognized the change in his personality that Kay spoke of. He didn't know how to change back to the person he once was. Dr. Sol explained that Andrew's transformation was necessary in order to release him from his stress and pain.

Kay arrived home to see Andrew staring at the television. She placed the grocery bags on the countertop, then sat next to him, and kissed him on his cheek. Andrew leaned his head on her shoulder and closed his eyes. Kay wanted to ask him what was on his mind but felt that she'd get the same response—"Nothing." Kay reminded herself of her New Year's resolution to be a good wife and friend. She remained silent and caressed his hair with her fingers.

Andrew sat, relaxed by Kay's touch. His mood changed in her presence. That was the power he slowly took from Kay. The power to calm him and keep himself relaxed. He hoped to change and transform back to the person she had met years earlier.

Several minutes passed before he broke the silence. "Do you feel like you're not appreciated sometimes? It's like no matter what I do or how hard I try, it doesn't change anything," Andrew said with his head on Kay's shoulder.

Kay continued to listen, not sure if he was speaking of his appreciation for her or by her or something else.

"When I was growing up, I would always hear these stories about my father, about how people admired him as a great social worker and person. The stories made me want to be a social worker like my father. In college I learned about DCF. All I wanted was to make a difference in someone's life and to help those children that were abused and neglected," Andrew said.

"You are helping them, Andrew. Every day you're helping them," Kay said, trying to reassure him.

"I don't know. It's like when you help one family, hundreds more are right behind it." Andrew stopped speaking.

Kay heard him sigh deeply, and he began to cry.

"You are a good social worker, Andrew. You are a better person than you give yourself credit for. I know there are days you struggle, but we all do," Kay said as she rubbed his back with her hand.

"It's not the physical work with DCF, rather it's the emotional baggage. When I close my eyes, I sometimes see images that play over in my mind of children I've removed from their homes. The worst for me are the sexual abuse cases," Andrew said, crying in her arms.

Andrew's comments about the sexual abuse cases struck a chord with Kay. Not only because of her own sexual assault, but it also got her thinking about Cassandra and her sexual abuse.

"You wouldn't believe how many sex offenders live in the Greater Hartford area. Never mind the victims. Hundreds maybe thousands." Andrew sat up in the chair and wiped the tears from his eyes. "Many victims never disclose their abuse. Some hold their secrets from the world. Sometimes DCF is able to find the source of the abuse during our investigations, but then there are other cases that are multigenerational and have multiple perpetrators. The hardest time for me is when I'm sitting with a victim and I know something happened because they have physical proof, but the victim denies it or later recants. Without a victim, the police can't arrest anyone, and all DCF can do is possibly confirm the allegations of abuse," Andrew said, moving from point to point.

"I understand how all of this can get to you, Andrew," Kay said and pulled him closer to her.

"It's the victims, Kay. The victims have fears. They feel guilty and are embarrassed. They have a feeling that they won't be believed or fear that the perpetrator will only return to do it again. And it's my job—yes, my job—to help them move past their worries about the monsters hiding in the shadows. The more of these motherfuckers I eliminate or get off the streets, hundreds more take their place," Andrew said and took a deep breath through his mouth.

Kay knew Andrew was inspired to help the families that he served every day. What she didn't know was many social workers had experienced firsthand what their clients have gone through. Some had been through the state system as children and were victims of abuse and neglect themselves.

With tears in his eyes, Andrew held Kay close. "I'm sorry for everything, Kay. I'm sorry for not listening, for not being myself. I don't want to blame it on one thing, but there's just so much going on in my mind sometimes. The voices that scream in my head or the nightmares I have at night. That's why I'm going to Dr. Sol. Believe me, everything will get better with us. You don't deserve to be treated the way I have been treating you. I love you so much, Kay." Andrew gave her a strong embrace.

Kay cried in Andrew's arms. She squeezed him tightly and hoped to see the real Andrew again. She missed him so much. She didn't want to feel alone anymore. Kay wondered if Dr. Sol told Andrew that she visited him. In her heart she wanted to tell Andrew that she spoke with Dr. Sol, but she didn't think it was the right time for that. She now had a better understanding of why Andrew worked for DCF. He wanted to protect the victims while at the same time making sure that the perpetrators didn't get away. Andrew had the ability to change the world, one person at a time. The ability that he had through his job was an opportunity everyone has but takes for granted.

*   *   *

I held Andrew close and fell in love with him all over for the person that he is. After our conversation, I left with a new respect for Andrew and the work that the does. I told him I was going to give him all the support that he needed in order to help as many victims as he could. I will sleep better knowing that when Andrew is out late, he is working to protect children and people like me. I knew it wasn't the time to tell my secret, but I will, in time.

SO SPECIAL
Every day you make this love so real.
When you smile at me, it means so much to me.
When I saw you there, I knew that we could live
A life together in ecstasy.
So you took my hand and you walked with me.
I hand you my heart and ask for you to marry me.
You make me feel so special.

May 25
I worry less about Andrew since our conversation the other night. Now my sleepless nights are not because of Andrew, rather they are because of Cassandra. Even though I know I was supposed to call DCF, I feel that I betrayed Cassandra's trust. I will go visit Cassandra after the program tomorrow to see how she's doing and try to get this paranoia out of my mind. Today I have a new resolution to add to my list this year. I'm going to tell Andrew everything and will never lie to him again. Tomorrow will be my last day of taking the children into Dutch Point.

IT VS. YOU: THE BATTLE FOR THE SOUL

It grapples you to the ground leaving you defenseless.

Suffocating and overwhelming, its power is numbing, coming unannounced.

Triggered by the senses, the thought to surface only allows its grip to pull you further and deeper.

The body and mind remain weak, aching, and silent, confused by its presence.

The influence is evident on behavior and lack of emotion.

The weight increases. Seconds, minutes, hours, days, and weeks pass.

The face in the mirror ages. The skin sags and hair falls out by the touch.

The body is on opposite poles of gaining or losing.

The stomach is fed by your unwillingness to fight, conquering mind, body, and soul.

You give power and control unknowingly.

Your eyes are open and your heart is closed to the hands that surround you.

Your head hangs. The room is cold. Your heart is beating.

The bridge is high. The knife is sharp. The gun is loaded.

The rain is falling. The clouds are thick. You put hope in a prayer.

Your sword is drawn for an endless battle to take *You* back from *It*.

*   *   *

Patricia closes the journal and sits next to an empty bottle of wine. She now has questions, many of them. What did Kay learn about Dr. Sol? Why was Gordo following her? What about the phone calls? Who killed her?

Patricia's immediate thought was the police should have had this journal. These pages could hold the key to Kay's killer. Patricia knows that if she gives it to the police now, they will wonder where she got it, and then she will have a lot of explaining to do.

How can I tell Andrew without him thinking that I betrayed him? Remember, no one knows it exists. Not even Andrew.

PART III
The Revelation

Chapter 35 ANDREW

As I enter Kinsella Elementary School, the hall is empty except for a group of kids running toward me.

"Give me back my bag," a little curly-haired Hispanic girl yells out to the boy that zips by me and out the door.

Betsey is waiting for me at the front desk.

"Hey, Andrew! That little one almost ran you over," Betsey says as she walks around the desk to greet me.

"Yeah, he nearly stepped on my feet. How are you?" I ask and give her an embrace.

"The school days are always busy with the constant running around. Love it though," Betsey says. "How about you? How are things going?"

"I'm doing much better. Things are finally kind of leveling out."

"That's good, Andrew. How about we meet in my classroom?" Betsey says as we walk down the hallway.

"Thanks for taking the time to meet with me Betsey," I say as we head to her room.

"I was happy to hear your voice. It's been a long time."

I know Kay's loss is just as hard for Betsey as it is for me. They had been friends for a very long time.

Her classroom is typical for third grade, with students' drawings on the walls and glue sticks and markers on some of the desks.

"I tell the same group of kids every day to put their markers away. In one ear, out the other," Betsey says, smiling as she cleans off the desk.

"Hey, I was no different. I was always the first one out of the class when the final bell rang," I say smiling.

I pull a chair next to Betsey's desk and notice a picture of her and Kay.

"This was a fun night," I say as I pick up the frame from her desk.

"Yeah, that was the night we went to New York City to see *Rent* on Broadway. I remember somebody had a little too much to drink," Betsey says smiling as she sits behind her desk.

"Good thing we took the train into the city that night. Time seems to really pass by fast," I say, returning the frame to her desk.

"I miss her so much, Andrew," Betsey says as she begins to cry. "It's like I'm waiting for her to walk into my classroom right now. It's been so hard, Andrew." Betsey cries with her hand over her mouth.

"I know, Betsey. It's been hard for me too." I lean in and give her a hug.

"For a long time I thought about leaving the school, maybe transferring across town. Maybe even leaving the city altogether. But that's not what Kay would have done. She would have stuck around for the children," Betsey says, regaining her composure.

"It's good that you stuck around. I'm sure that's what Kay would have done."

"I can't believe the police have no leads on her case. It was right down the street, Andrew. There were people outside. Why won't anyone talk? Why won't they say who did this?" Betsey asks frustrated.

"I get where you're coming from. I don't understand it either. I call the detective every once in a while to see if they have leads, but nothing. As far as the community goes, if there are people who know what happened, they will never snitch and tell the police. That's just how it works on the street"

"I know we really never sat down to talk about everything since Kay's death. It's just so hard to think about, never mind talk about."

"I have to say that my therapy is helping a bit," I say, handing her a crayon that was on the floor next to her desk.

"Thanks. Constant cleaning in here." Betsey cracks a little smile from the corner of her mouth. "You know, Andrew, Kay just wasn't her usual cheerful self before her death. She looked almost depressed. I could never catch up with her during the school day or after school to see what was up. With the search for and purchase of our new house, things were just so crazy. I was such a horrible friend," Betsey says beggining to cry again.

"No, Betsey, you're the best friend anyone could have," I say in a comforting tone.

"Kay was just so busy with the afterschool program. I was usually gone before she would return from dropping the students off at Dutch Point after the program," Betsey says wiping her nose with a tissue.

"Afterschool program? Dutch Point? What are you talking about?" I ask, surprised by Betsey's comments.

"Kay was working in the afterschool program, Andrew. She was also walking some of the students home after the program into Dutch Point. Kay told me to promise not to tell you because she was going to tell you herself. I guess she never got around to telling you," Betsey says still crying.

"Kay told you not to tell me? How long was she doing this Betsey?" I snap, still shocked to hear about the afterschool program and the walks into Dutch Point.

"It was for a while, Andrew. Kay said you were working a lot back then. Kay was always home before you even with working at the program." Betsey wipes the tears from her eyes as she says, "I'm sorry, Andrew. I should have told you. Maybe she wouldn't have been killed."

"I'm sorry about snapping at you. I wish I had known. I know Kay thought I would have never approved of her walking into Dutch Point. It's not your fault."

"You know Kay. Even if you knew, she probably would have still done it. That's just who she was. Kay loved the kids and was always trying to help them."

Before Kay's murder, there was a huge void in our communication and relationship. I'm sure she must have wondered what was going on in my head.

"So, Andrew, what was it you said you wanted to talk to me about?" Betsey asks, trying to move from the subject.

"I was cleaning out some of Kay's things this past weekend and came across this picture. It looks like it was taken somewhere in the school. I wanted to see if you knew the girl standing with her in the picture," I say handing her the Polaroid.

"They're standing in front of a wall next to the gym. The girl's name is Cassandra," Betsey says looking at the picture.

"Cassandra? This girl looks too old for Kay's class."

"Cassandra wasn't in her class. She was from the afterschool program. I recall Kay talking about Cassandra and telling me how much she helped with the younger kids in the program. I think Cassandra was one of the kids that lived in Dutch Point also," Betsey says, returning the Polaroid.

"I don't know, Betsey. I feel like I need to speak with this girl. Maybe she knows something. Kay had this Polaroid in a little compartment in her jewelry box. Obviously, she didn't want me to find it. Is there any way you can get any contact information on Cassandra?" I ask, placing the Polaroid in my coat pocket.

"I don't have access to the school's main computer right now. I can try to follow up and see what I can do, Andrew. To be honest, I haven't even seen Cassandra this year in school. May be possible that she moved," Betsey says. "Do you really think there is some connection between Kay's murder and Cassandra?"

"I really don't know. I'm only trying to piece together a puzzle that the police haven't been able to figure out," I say as I get up from my chair. "Betsey, thanks again for meeting with me. I'll let you know if I hear any news from the police."

"For sure, Andrew. I'll get back to you with some answers on Cassandra," Betsey says as we walk to her door.

In the state car I call Patricia, but her phone goes straight to voicemail.

Chapter 36 PATRICIA

Patricia sits in her friend's apartment and sees that another call has come in. Ever since reading the journal, she's been avoiding any contact with Andrew because she feels that she needs more time. Time to think of her next move and how she can help find out who killed Kay.

After reading the journal, Patricia feels very connected to Kay, and she got a glimpse of another side of Andrew. She thinks Kay's words are a possible map to her murderer. She carries the journal in her camera bag so no one can find it.

Confused about where to start, Patricia opens the journal again. From a fold in the back of the journal something falls out. It's Dr. Sol's business card. Patricia remembered a visit Kay had with Dr. Sol from one of the journal entries.

"Maybe I'll start with Dr. Sol. At this point going into Dutch Point is a little too dangerous," Patricia says to herself.

Chapter 37 ANDREW

I am supposed to have a protected day to input narratives. I guess that's not going to happen because I was assigned a new case. It's coded with a seventy-two-hour response, so I have a couple of days and don't need to go out immediately.

Stephanie and I are on the fence during the case conference about whether to remove Trevan.

"I spoke with Renee from the hospital earlier this morning. She said Trevan was doing much better and has gained several ounces. It's possible that he will be ready for discharge by the end of the week depending on what we plan to do regarding placement," I report to Stephanie during our conference.

"You said Madeline's whereabouts are still unknown and the visits with Mr. Donnelly have been going well," Stephanie says as she types notes from our conference into the computer.

"Yeah, I have not heard from Madeline and have exhausted all my searches for her. And according to Renee, visits between Mr. Donnelly and Trevan are going well. I plan to be at the next visit," I say and jot down a note to call Renee. "Since Mr. Buford Donnelly came forward, we had to look into him as a possible resource and possibly having the child discharged to him."

"We're going to be transferring the case to ongoing services anyway. Have the neglect petitions filed against Madeline. I mean, she did abandon her son. Also speak with the assistant attorney general about filing a motion for a paternity on Mr. Donnelly," Stephanie says, giving me a few more directives on the case. "Set up a legal consult with the principal attorney. I'll speak with

Tracey about the case because I still think there is a possibility that Trevan could be removed."

As I walk back to my desk after my meeting with Stephanie, my cell phone vibrates in my pocket. The number is unfamiliar.

"Andrew speaking."

" Hey, Andrew. It's Betsey."

"Hey, Betsey. I didn't recognize the number. What's up?"

"I wanted to get back to you about some of the questions you had about Cassandra. It looks like Cassandra wasn't registered at Kinsella or any other school in the Hartford system this year. The last known address was in Dutch Point, and the guardian's name listed is a maternal aunt named Persephone," Betsey says and gives me the address to the aunt's house.

"Thanks so much, Betsey. I'm sure this will be helpful."

"Good luck, Andrew. And again, keep me posted," Betsey says and then hangs up.

As I am about to sit down at my desk, I hear someone call me from behind.

"Hey, Andrew, how are you?" the female voice asks.

It's Claudia; she's back to work.

"Hey, Claudia, I'm well. How about yourself?" I ask, giving her a hug.

"Had some bad headaches for a couple days after the incident. I'm doing much better now," Claudia says with a smile.

"I'm so sorry I wasn't there with you," I say with a hand on her shoulder.

"You don't have to apologize. I was stupid to go inside without calling the police or some sort of backup."

That was the same thing I was thinking.

"Well, if you ever need someone to go into the field with you, let me know," I say as she walks away.

"Sure, Andrew, I'll let you know."

*   *   *

I drive the state car into Dutch Point. The project is located off of Norwich Street in the Sheldon/Charter Oak neighborhood. I haven't been back to this neighborhood since Kay's death. My supervisor graciously assigned cases from here to other workers.

I move slowly maneuvering through an obstacle course of potholes. I pass the building where Kay's body was found. A weird feeling comes over me. Maybe it isn't the smartest idea to return so soon, but today I have a mission.

My mind takes me back in time. I can remember seeing Kay's body lying on the floor with the blood-soaked sheet covering her. It all seems so familiar to me, but maybe that is because of the constant repeating of the scene in my head and conversations with Dr. Sol. Sometimes I feel like I was there at the moment she was killed. It must be the guilt in me for not being there to protect her. The pressure begins to build in my chest. The idea of coming here was probably a mistake. I focus my thoughts on the task at hand. The apartment number Betsey gave was for building one, unit six.

Over the years I have had many investigations in Dutch Point. It has always been a hotbed of gang and drug activity. I remember one time coming in with a colleague to remove a child. The entire community seemed to turn on us, and we stayed locked up in the car. That was a very scary night.

Inside the housing project children run around the buildings and the dirt patch of a lawn. Others ride their bikes right in front of my car without looking. I almost hit one of the boys. I can see many of the units are boarded up as a result of some sort of fire. There has been talk for years of demolishing these buildings and starting from scratch, creating a community with more owner-occupied residences. They also plan to keep several units for some of the older residents.

As the children play, I look at the picture of Cassandra and hope that she will run by my car, but I have no luck. I get to building one and see that it was one of the burned buildings.

Now what do I do?

I sit in my car and just look around. This is what Kay was walking herself into. She probably never saw the danger that was lurking over her shoulder. I pick up my cell phone and try to reach Patricia again, but she still doesn't pick up. I slowly turn the state car around and drive down Norwich Street heading to my new case.

Chapter 38 CASSANDRA

Cassandra sits with her head against the backseat of Gordo's Honda Civic as they head home from the Berlin Turnpike.

It was like he couldn't wait to get me back in the bed.

Cassandra rubs her stomach with one hand while the other massages her temple. She was feeling pain in her abdomen from the assault. Cassandra was put back into the rotation not only for the money that she lost with Iris but also as punishment for her disobedience. The guy she was with today wanted an older girl he could be rough with.

"No restriction today on marks, bruises, or tears," Gordo said to Cassandra's rapist as they stood in the doorway of the motel room while Cassandra sat on the edge of the bed listening.

"You'll learn for the next time," Gordo said to Cassandra as he closed the door of the motel room with a smile on his face.

"Yeah, you little bitch. You heard him," the rapist said and stood in front of Cassandra who was still sitting down.

Without warning, the rapist smacked Cassandra on her face and knocked her backward on the bed. He then forced her down in the bed, ripping her shirt open.

Cassandra looks out the window and watches the cars pass. She wishes that she was in one of them heading in the opposite direction. She wanted to get as far out of Hartford as possible. A state car passes, and she sees a worker on his cell phone. Cassandra wishes now that she told DCF what happened when they came out last year to ask about the sexual abuse she reported to Miss Kay.

*   *   *

It was less than twenty-four hours after Cassandra told Miss Kay about the abuse that DCF was at her aunt's door.

"Why are you at my house?" Persephone asked Mindy, the female DCF worker who stood in her living room.

Cassandra listened from the top of the stairs to their conversation.

"I went to the school to attempt to interview Cassandra about the allegations, but she already came home. If you don't mind, I would like to interview Cassandra one on one today," Mindy said.

"What allegations?" Persephone asked.

"An anonymous reporter called our hotline with allegations of sexual abuse toward your niece Cassandra," Mindy explained.

"Sexual abuse? That can't be true. Oh my god, not my Cassandra," Persephone yelled out in tears.

Cassandra stood nervously at the top of the stairs. She knew Persephone was crying loud enough for her to hear and to be prepared.

"I should have never told Miss Kay" Cassandra said to herself.

Cassandra knew what she had to do to make this all go away, but she was not sure if that was going to be enough to save her from getting beaten. Cassandra had been coached over the years not to reveal what went on in the home. Cassandra knew what to say and how to say it. She heard the worker walking toward the stairs. Cassandra rushed back to her room and grabbed her sketchpad from her dresser. Minutes later Mindy walked upstairs to her room unaccompanied.

"Hi, Cassandra, my name is Mindy. I'm an investigator from DCF. Do you mind if I sit here?" Mindy asked, pointing to the chair next to the bed.

What, you gonna sit on the floor?

"Whatever," Cassandra said without looking up from her pad.

"Do you know what DCF is?" Mindy asked with a smile and pulled some laptop device out of her bag.

"Yeah," Cassandra said as she sat on her bed and doodled Mindy's face in her sketchpad. "What's that?" Cassandra asked.

"Oh, this is a AlphaSmart. I'll be able to type our conversation into it and then transfer it to my computer when I get back to the office," Mindy said, turning it on. "So, Cassandra, who lives here in the home with you?" Mindy asked and then began typing on the little machine on her lap.

"Just me and my aunt," Cassandra said as she began to sketch Mindy's face.

"Do you have any contact with your mother?" Mindy asked as she typed.

"Why you want to know that?" Cassandra asked, looking up from the pad.

"It's just one of my questions, honey," Mindy said without looking up from the AlphaSmart.

"My name ain't honey, and no, I don't see her. Are you done?" Cassandra asked with an attitude.

"No, I actually have several more questions," Mindy said finally looking up. "Does anyone here use or sell drugs?"

"No."

"Does your aunt use any form of physical discipline, and if so, can you explain it?" Mindy asked as she typed.

Does my aunt use physical discipline? Let me see. Yes. Also my uncle Gordo rapes me and beats me whenever he feels.

"No, my aunt does not use physical discipline," Cassandra said.

"Cassandra, what do you call your private areas," Mindy asked, embarrassed by her own question.

"What are you talking about?" Cassandra asked. She could see that Mindy was not comfortable with the new line of questions she introduced.

"Well, everyone has private parts, but people have different names for them. What do you call yours?" Mindy asked.

"You mean what do I call my pussy and titties?" Cassandra giggled, making Mindy more uncomfortable.

"Well, if that's what you call them, that's what I needed to know," Mindy said, looking back down to type. "Has someone ever asked to touch you on your titties or your pussy?" Mindy asked, almost afraid to say the names of the private parts Cassandra used.

Cassandra knew where this was going. "No, and no to the next question you're going to ask, and no to the next question after that," Cassandra said and then closed the sketchpad.

"So, Cassandra, why would the teacher call our hotline reporting that you made a disclosure of sexual abuse to her?"

"You guys ever think that maybe the teacher misunderstood what was said? No one has ever touched me inappropriately in any way that I didn't like," Cassandra answered calmly. *Please help me. Please see that I'm lying.* Cassandra knew if she told Mindy the truth right now, she could possibly be taken out of her living hell.

Her uncle Gordo and aunt Persephone had also told her the horror stories of going into foster care. "You think you won't be raped in foster care? It happens even more there, dummy," Persephone and Gordo had told her in the past.

The interview was fairly quick, mostly due to Cassandra's responses and partially due to the worker's lack of experience with sexual abuse cases and victims. The worker returned downstairs to complete her interview with Persephone.

Cassandra watched through her bedroom window as Mindy got into her car and drove out of Dutch Point. Cassandra heard a low rumble coming up the stairs. It was Persephone.

"You stupid little bitch, you almost ruined everything," Persephone screamed as she smacked Cassandra off the bed.

"It wasn't me. I never said anything," Cassandra shouted as Persephone kicked her in the chest back to the ground.

Cassandra was beaten for another ten minutes by Persephone after Mindy left the home. Later that night Gordo returned home and beat her some more. Cassandra was kept out of school for the remainder of the year and didn't return. After the investigation was over, she was sent out of the state to stay with relatives in New York.

*   *   *

Cassandra knows that her life could have changed forever if she told DCF what had happened to her. Maybe she could have been reunited with her mother and placed in witness protection because that is what they do on television.

"I wish they had taken me," Cassandra says under her breath.

"What, you talking to yourself again, dummy?" Gordo asks as he parks the car.

Chapter 39 DETECTIVE DUPRI

The prints for the Love Lane John Doe were run through the Automated Fingerprint Identification System, and a positive identification was returned for the victim. After searching the department's in-house computer system, Detective Dupri found one incident in which the victim came up as a suspect a couple of years ago with the Juvenile Investigative Division. JID uncovered that he was a person of interest in a high-profile sexual assault and murder in the mid-1990s in the state of California. She now has a stronger motive for his murder as well as a name—Holter.

The notes in Detective Dupri's file show that JID and DCF both were conducting investigations on Holter around allegations of sexual abuse of a nine-year-old male named Alexander. Alexander disclosed during an interview with a DCF worker that Holter "put his thing in his mouth" at a motel thought to be located at the time on the Berlin Turnpike. The victim was taken to St. Francis Hospital where forensic interviews of sexually abused children are conducted through the Child Advocacy Center. While there, Alexander recanted his disclosure. A medical examination was conducted, and the results came back as normal. From Detective Dupri's experience of working sexual assault cases, she knows the police have only a seventy-two-hour window to gather physical evidence to help support a sexual abuse case.

The DCF worker and the JID detective also attempted to have Alexander identify the motel in which he was allegedly assaulted. Alexander couldn't remember which one it was, stating that he only remembered seeing a Hooters restaurant on the ride back into Hartford. The investigation stalled when DCF and JID tried to get information about how Alexander's family knew Holter. The family no longer wanted to cooperate, and the mother asked that the investigation be closed. There were numerous notes by DCF and the JID detective that the family feared for their lives. JID went forward with the arrest warrant based on the disclosure from the initial interview with DCF. The judge wouldn't sign the warrant because of Alexander's recantation. The police investigation was closed. Needless to say, Holter denied the allegations from the beginning. Detective Dupri's conversation with the JID detective revealed that the investigators believed Holder did it; they had no way to prove it, however, without the boy's disclosure. The record did note that DCF was going to keep the case open for further assessment of the family.

Detective Dupri closes the old file and then opens hers, which is labeled "John Doe." She makes note of the victim's name in her file. Holter was living in one of the shelters in Hartford at the time of the assault. JID interviewed several residents and staff at the shelter but turned up with nothing. Detective Dupri decides to start with Alexander, the sexual assault victim, and his family to see if they can shed any light on Holter's past and his untimely death.

Chapter 40 ANDREW

I take a sip of water before Dr. Sol begins my hypnotherapy session. I remember when he first suggested using hypnosis in our sessions. I thought he was kidding. My image of hypnosis has always been a group of people being called on the stage by a master hypnotist, and the hypnotist making a handful of his victims do some crazy things.

I once saw a hypnotist make a group of participants crawl on the floor like babies. He had another person bark like a dog whenever he said the magic word. The hypnosis I was thinking of was for entertainment purposes, which uses similar techniques of suggestion in order to elicit changes in the behavior and emotions of individuals they may work with. The difference is Dr. Sol's sessions are guided, and he is trained to help rid his client of certain fears, phobias, anxieties, and many other mental health or medical concerns.

We began the sessions to help me work through issues of anxiety with my job and then moved to working with issues of loss. There are times when I wake up and don't remember anything. The sessions have shown me that no matter how much I try to bury things in my mind, they are somewhere waiting to be found. With a little focus, suggestions, and guidance, everything can be found.

Recently, Dr. Sol has been taking me back to the day Kay was murdered. He says by doing this it will take the knife of guilt out of my hand and begin to help me move on. The only issue has been my mind blocking me from moving forward. I think I just don't want to remember that day. As I lie with my eyes closed, Dr. Sol begins his deepening method that will relax my body and lead me to the induction phase and later a full trance.

"Andrew, close your eyes and try to relax your entire body. Start at the top of your head and work your way down to your toes," Dr. Sol says, almost whispering.

I follow his directions and lie limp, relaxing every muscle in my body.

"I'm going to count from fifty to one. Every time I count down to the next number, you will fall deeper, and your body will feel lighter," Dr. Sol says.

After several minutes I feel warm, and my body and mind are very relaxed.

"Today we are going to go back to Dutch Point. Last time we were in front of the open door of the building where Kay was found. What do you see, Andrew, as you stand in front of the building?" Dr. Sol asks.

"Kay is there on the ground under a sheet. There is blood, a lot of blood," I say as my mind's eye begins to move forward, quickly passing through the emotion that I have carried.

"Go on. What else do you see?" Dr. Sol asks.

"I try to go to her, but the police won't let me through. I feel like things are fading now." I know this is where I usually stop and get blocked.

"Hold this thought, Andrew. I will count down from five to one. Every time I count down, you will fall deeper, and you will feel more relaxed. Five, four, three, two, one." Dr. Sol slowly counts down. "Andrew, do you trust me?" he asks, leaning in close to my ear.

"Yes," I say.

"Today I can help push you further in your mind than you have ever been. You have to trust me though. Do you want to push yourself, Andrew?" Dr. Sol asks.

"Yes."

"So, we shall go forward. Every time you feel like the picture or thoughts are fading, those thoughts will bring you deeper into your trance," Dr. Sol repeats. "Walk past the officers, Andrew. Go inside the building," Dr. Sol says moving further into my mind.

"Kay is not there anymore," I say seeing the building and the surroundings clearly.

"Let's see if we can find Kay, Andrew. Are you in the building yet?" Dr. Sol asks.

"Yes. I'm standing in an empty room near the front door. It doesn't look like anyone lives there. The unit is empty," I say as my mind moves me through the scene.

"Andrew, fall deeper into your trance. Feel your body float into the air. Familiarize yourself with your surroundings, Andrew," Dr. Sol says.

"All of a sudden, I feel like I'm flying. My feet lift off the floor, and I am looking down at my hands and feet as I float in the air," I say. I follow Dr. Sol's suggestion and float around the unit. "I'm at the window and see cars on the street. I can't see any people," I say.

"Do you see Kay?" Dr. Sol asks.

"No, I don't see her. Where is she?" I ask.

"Look out the window, Andrew. Look in both directions. Don't you see her walking in a hurry toward you?" Dr. Sol suggests.

"I see her. There she is. She's looking over her shoulder. She's walking right toward me," I say, feeling my heart beat faster. "Wait, no, Kay, don't come this way. My mouth won't open. She's not going to be able to hear me. I'm trying to open my mouth with my hands, but it won't open. Kay can't come in here. She's going to be killed," I say as I begin to panic.

"Andrew, allow your body to relax. With every bit of anxiety, feel your body relax. You will fall deeper in your trance. Allow the anxiety to pass through you," Dr. Sol suggests. "Look around the room, Andrew. Is there someone else in the unit?" Dr. Sol asks.

"My head moves from side to side, looking around the room. I float through the unit, looking in every room. As I go through a door, I enter into a room that is the same as the one I left. I can't see anyone. Kay must be getting closer. I have to warn her," I say going back to the window in my mind.

"Look at the door, Andrew. Kay is at the door," Dr. Sol says.

"I move my eyes to the door and see Kay. I want to go to her, but I am stuck. I am floating above her," I say as I feel my pulse increase.

"Look behind her, Andrew. Do you see the figure behind her? Who is it, Andrew? Who do you see?" Dr. Sol suggests, moving me through the scene.

"There is someone, but I can't see a face," I say, still trying to get closer to her but unable to move.

"What are you feeling right now, Andrew?" Dr. Sol asks.

"I feel angry, helpless," I say as tears roll down the side of my face.

"Andrew, look at the face behind Kay. That face is familiar. That face is yours, Andrew," Dr. Sol suggests.

"A light passed through the room. I can see the face. It's mine. Why am I there? Am I there to save her? Where is the murderer?" I ask.

"Look down at your hand, Andrew. Why do you have a knife in your hand, Andrew?" Dr. Sol asks.

"Why am I holding a knife? What's going on?" I ask, trying to fight against the images in my mind and the voice and anger that were driving me. I begin to yell, trying to open my eyes. "No, it's not right, it's not right."

"Andrew, try to relax. I will get you out of there. Trust me, Andrew. I will help you. I will make this all better. Kay is no longer there, Andrew. Look, you are no longer in Dutch Point. You are in a garden, a warm garden," Dr. Sol suggests to me.

My body begins to calm, but I am still breathing heavily and my heart is racing.

"Sit in the garden, Andrew, and watch the wind blow the branches of the trees. Listen to the water running in the stream next to you. Smell the nectar in the air, Andrew. Relax your body. Trust me, Andrew. I am here to help you. You will not feel this pain anymore. I am here to help you," Dr. Sol repeats as my heart rate slows and my body relaxes. "I will count from ten to one, Andrew, and you will wake up relaxed, calm, and fully aware."

At one, he orders me to open my eyes. My eyelids feel heavy. My face is covered with tears.

"I feel confused. I don't understand. That felt too real," I say as I look at Dr. Sol who is leaning toward me in his chair.

Dr. Sol puts his hand on my shoulder and asks, "Was it real?"

Chapter 41   CASSANDRA

Cassandra sits with her sketchpad in her lap and looks out her window into Dutch Point. With her eyes closed, she pulls from her memory every detail from the shape of the eyes, the color of the hair, to the wrinkles on the face. With her finger, Cassandra spreads the lead from the pencil across the sketch, adding shadows and depth. The scene of a horrible crime is complete, and a snapshot from her mind is now on paper.

Cassandra fans her fingers through the pages of her sketchpad and stops at one of Miss Kay. This was the face she wanted to remember, not the images that have haunted her mind. Cassandra rubs the angel necklace around her neck. She closes the sketchpad and secures it in a box under her bed.

Chapter 42 ANDREW

A couple of hours ago a thunderstorm passed over the city and the rain was coming down hard. Only a few people are at this week's group. I thought I was going to be able to spend time with Patricia, but I can't get a hold of her. Tonight's group is less dramatic than last week's. We speak of some of the things we miss the most about our deceased loved ones.

"For me, it is Kay's smile, her touch, her optimism. Nowadays people don't seem to think before they speak. Kay was the type of person that filtered her words and thought before she spoke in order not to hurt or offend the next person. At the same time, she was very honest and defended her opinions."

"My husband was the same," Stacey says with a smile on her face.

"Kay always tried to pull me up whenever I was down. I now know that it was my sadness and stubbornness that was too heavy for her to hold up at times," I say as I look around the circle.

"It's about having people in your life that care about you, Andrew. What you can do is show your love for those around you and still keep Kay in your prayers," Estrella says with encouragement.

"I'm starting to believe again. I pray for Kay and will pray for you guys in the room. I sit here and think that without my friend Patricia's encouragement to participate in the group, I wouldn't be here."

"Patricia really sounds like a special person," Estrella says.

"Yes, she is."

So why isn't she answering your calls?

"Not now," I say under my breath.

"What was that, Andrew?" Estrella asks, thinking I was speaking to her.

"The time is now is what I said. The time is now." I smile quickly and change the subject.

After the group, I spend I couple of minutes speaking with Estrella. "I took your advice and began to clean out the house. I wasn't prepared for how emotional it was. It was so liberating and turned a page to a new chapter in my life."

"Cleaning the house was the first step. Meeting Patricia was step two. You can take as many steps as you like, my love," Estrella says with a smile as I walk her to her car.

"Coming to this group has been one of the best decisions I've made in a long time. I'll see you next week," I say to Estrella and then walk to my car in the parking lot.

Inside my car I decide to try to reach Patricia again. The phone rings for several seconds, and she finally picks up.

"Hey, Patricia, it's Andrew. Where've you been?"

"I'm so sorry, Andrew. I got a new photo job that I've been working on and been so busy. I'll give you a call as soon as I'm done," Patricia says with her beautiful accent.

"That would be great. I'll be waiting for your call," I say and then hang up.

"I thought she wanted to get rid of me already," I say to myself.

Are you sure that's not on her mind?

*　　　*　　　*

I have a little time before my visit to the hospital to meet with Mr. Donnelly. At my work computer, I open up Link. I type in Cassandra's full name in the search field. Over twenty individuals with the same name pop up. I narrow the search by looking at the dates of birth and then find her under two separate cases. Her aunt Persephone had a case open one year ago, and the other one was open under her mother's name, Delia. I review the mother's case first.

The narratives show that Cassandra's mother was a participant under the maternal grandmother's case. The investigation that was conducted by DCF over twelve years ago was about allegations of sexual abuse by one of the maternal grandmother's boyfriends. Delia and Persephone disclosed that the boyfriend sexually abused them over many years while they lived in Puerto Rico and in Hartford. It was also believed at the time that Persephone's and Delia's fifteen-year-old brother Broga, also known as Gordo, was also sexually abused. There were never any disclosures of sexual or physical abuse by Broga, but there were some troubling behaviors of fire setting and aggression toward his sisters.

Delia was twelve years old when she gave birth to Cassandra while the family was residing out of state. There was no note of the father's name, but given the history of sexual abuse, there were suspicions that it could have been the maternal grandmother's boyfriend that impregnated Delia. Before the investigation could end, the family relocated and fell off the radar. It was not until last year's investigation with Persephone that they resurfaced again. I open Persephone's case from last year.

"What is this? Kay was the reporter?" I say to myself.

It's not that much of a surprise that Kay called in a report to DCF. She was a teacher and a mandated reporter by the state. I guess I am more shocked that she didn't speak with me about the case.

Persephone's report may have been assigned to an investigator in my unit, which investigates all sexual abuse cases. I do a quick assignment check and see that it was assigned to Mindy.

"Why did she get assigned to the case?" I ask myself. Mindy does not normally investigate sexual abuse cases.

The date of the report tells me everything. At that time last year my unit was bombarded with cases, and many of them were removals. So I understand why Mindy was assigned to the case. Her unit and several others were covering our case overflow. I can't believe how close I am to this case and possibly to Kay's murderer. The guilt begins to swell in my chest from my lack of attention to Kay during a time that she needed me the most. Tears fill my eyes.

The report notes that Kay was working in the afterschool program. I feel so stupid that I wasn't there for Kay. I could have easily gone into Link, just like I'm doing now, and seen everything. The narrative shows that Cassandra told Kay that she would not speak with DCF or the police if we came out. Mindy interviewed Cassandra and she recanted everything.

There was clearly no need for the investigator to speak with Cassandra again about the sexual abuse. Because Kay was a mandated reporter and already had gathered minimal facts, Mindy only needed to notify the Hartford Police Department and contact the Child Advocacy Center at St. Francis Hospital to arrange a forensic interview. Since Cassandra recanted, the CAC would not accept the case for an interview and it didn't look like the HPD did anything.

I exit out of Link and sit staring at the screen with tears rolling down my face. My wife's life was a couple of keystrokes away from me seeing that she was working after school and even going into Dutch Point. I'm convinced that Cassandra must know something about Kay's murder. Now all I have to do is find her.

Chapter 43 BUFORD & MADELINE

Buford Donnelly is buzzed into the Neonatal Intensive Care Unit to visit his son Trevan. He is told by one of the nurses that Renee will not be in until later and there is no covering social worker at the time. The certified nurse assistant, or CNA, behind the nurses' station has him wait as she pages the supervising nurse, Judith Monroe. Buford looks at the time on his cell phone and sees that Andrew is running late. He stands at the nurses' station with a gift bag and a camera. Nurse Monroe, a fifty-year-old short Caucasian female, departs the nursery with her attention divided between carrying the box of items in her hand and giving a directive to one of the nurses inside the nursery.

"After you change her, check the NG tube and give the morning feeding," Nurse Monroe tells the nurse as she walks down the hall toward Buford.

As she walks past the nurses' station, she is stopped by the CNA.

"Excuse me, Nurse Monroe," the CNA calls in a high squeaky voice in order to get Nurse Monroe's attention.

"Yes, Ceanna?" Nurse Monroe stops and looks at Ceanna, annoyed by her distraction.

"I have Mr.—I'm sorry, sir, what was your name again?" Ceanna asks, looking toward Buford.

"Buford Donnelly."

"Okay, and how can I help you, Mr. Donnelly?" Nurse Monroe asks as if Buford is wasting her time. Nurse Monroe then places the box in her hand on the nurses' station counter.

"I am here to see my son Trevan. Renee, the hospital social worker, told me to stop at the nurses' station before I entered the nursery."

"Do you have the log back there?" Nurse Monroe asks Ceanna.

"Yes, it's right here," Ceanna says and hands Nurse Monroe the log.

"We have him noted as Baby Williams," Nurse Monroe says as she sees a notation that the child is DCF-involved. "So where is your DCF worker?" Nurse Monroe asks in a matter-of-fact way.

"My worker should be here soon. Since I learned that this was my son, I was given permission by DCF to see him unsupervised. Renee was aware of this. Plus I have been here several times during the week with no problems," Buford patiently explains.

"Well, I personally feel that DCF should be here, even though you just learned that this was your son," Nurse Monroe says to Buford as she hands the log back to Ceanna. Turning to Ceanna, Nurse Monroe says, "I will have to check Renee's office for any note stating that it was fine for him to visit alone. In the meantime, you can bring him to the nursery." She then picks up the box on the counter.

"Like I said, my worker will be here soon," Buford says to Nurse Monroe.

"Ceanna, you will have to stay with him while he is in the nursery," Nurse Monroe says as she walks down the hallway in the opposite direction.

Buford carries his camera and a stuffed animal inside the gift bag. The nursery is nearly full with six infants. He looks around and sees one child on a respirator and another crying in a very high pitch.

"Trevan was moved since my last visit," Buford says.

"Yes, sometimes they move the cribs depending on children being discharged or new ones coming in," Ceanna says.

Buford stands over Trevan's crib and rubs his stomach with his fingers. "Have the withdrawals decreased?" Buford asks Ceanna.

"I'm sorry, but you'll have to ask one of the nurses. We can wait for her to get off the phone," Ceanna says, pointing to the nurse on the opposite side of the room. "Is this your first child?" Ceanna asks while she checks Trevan's diaper.

"This is my first son. I have an older adult daughter in the area," Buford says as he turns on his camera.

The nurse on the far end of the room hangs up the phone and walks toward Ceanna.

"Ceanna, we have to prepare for the twins that will be coming down any minute," the nurse says.

"I'm sorry, Mr. Donnelly. I'm sure you'll be okay for a couple of minutes by yourself," Ceanna says before she exits the room and heads down the hall.

Buford slides a chair over and then takes a couple of pictures of Trevan sleeping.

*   *   *

"Now wait for me near the Collins Street exit with the car running," Madeline commands Troy as she gets out of the car. She enters the hospital through the main entrance.

Earlier in the morning Madeline spoke with Buford, who told her that he was going to meet with the DCF worker during his visit with Trevan. In the past weeks he has been suggesting that she make contact with DCF, but she continues to avoid that thought.

Since the delivery Madeline has been able to remain underground. Madeline found out through sources that the guy she stabbed in the basement weeks before is looking for her. Without any money, Madeline knows that she can't go far and will not be able to hide forever. This is her last chance to be with her son Trevan.

Madeline and Troy followed Buford the entire morning to make sure of the exact time he would be at the hospital. Madeline takes the elevator to the third floor and then walks up the stairs to the fourth floor where the NICU is located. Madeline is well groomed, with her hair and makeup done, and she wears a dress borrowed from Towanda's daughter. Madeline takes her cell phone from her oversized purse and calls Buford.

*   *   *

Buford sits in a rocking chair next to the crib. He thinks about how he didn't see that Maddy was using. He knew that she smoked some weed but didn't know she jumped to heroin. In the past year Buford has tried his hardest to help Madeline by giving her money and a place to stay when she needed it. Buford thinks he should have noticed an addict more than anyone, as he is a recovering cocaine addict and has been clean for over ten years. Trevan sleeps with the occasional twitch. Buford realizes that he looks nothing like his son. He is still wondering where Trevan's hazel eyes come from, considering that neither he nor Madeline has eyes that color. Buford's cell rings in his pocket. It's Maddy.

*　　　*　　　*

Madeline stands on the far end of the fourth floor.

"Buford honey, I need your help. I need to see you right away." Madeline speaks fast and with concern in her voice.

"Maddy baby, calm down. What's wrong? Where are you?" Buford asks, rising from his chair.

"I'm here in the hospital. I'm downstairs near the back entrance near Au Bon Pain. Come now, Buford," Madeline says, trying to hold back her laugh.

"Baby, I can't leave right now. I'm with Trevan, and I have DCF coming to see me any moment," Buford says.

"Trevan won't be going anywhere. He will be there after you speak with me. Please, Buford, hurry up. I'll be waiting for you," Madeline says and hangs up the phone.

How fast will you be, Buford?

Just as the thought passes through her head, Buford comes running out of the nursery to the elevators.

"Perfect," Madeline says.

*　　　*　　　*

Madeline looks down the hallway, watching as Buford leaves the unit and heads to the elevators. She comes around the corner and strides to the door he exited. Madeline is buzzed in with no problem. As Madeline walks toward the nurses' station, Ceanna hangs up the phone.

"How are you doing? Who are you here to see today?" Ceanna asks.

213

Madeline hesitates for a second but then says with a smile, "Baby Williams."

"Oh, your father is visiting with your brother right now. I'll walk you down," Ceanna says as she leaves the nurses' station.

Madeline's stomach muscles clench to hold back her laugh.

This couldn't have worked any better.

"It's so hard to see the babies come into the NICU. They're withdrawing from some crazy drugs, dealing with respiratory issues, or suffering severe abuse due to their parents' neglect. They should really put their mothers in jail or take their babies," Ceanna says as they enter the nursery.

"Yeah, they really should. That's why my father and I are here for my brother." Madeline looks over to Ceanna, wishing she could knock her out but instead nods her head in agreement.

"I'm not sure where your father is. Maybe he stepped away to go to the restroom. Make yourself at home. I'm sure he'll be back soon," Ceanna says, walking to the phone on the opposite side of the nursery.

*　　*　　*

Buford stands at the back exit of the hospital in front of Au Bon Pain looking for Maddy but doesn't see her anywhere. All he can think is that she is in trouble again and needs his help. So much is running through his mind, from the conversation with the DCF worker about her drug use and past arrest for possession and prostitution to his suspicions about whether he is really Trevan's father. In spite of his shock about all the information that he learned, he still acknowledged himself as the father. Now he is there again to help her out of a bad situation. Buford tries calling Madeline's cell phone but can't get a signal. He goes outside to the garage to try again.

*　　*　　*

Madeline stands over the crib looking down at her son for the first time since the delivery. She can't believe how small he is and how pretty his hair looks. "You look just like your father," Madeline says as she begins to cry.

Madeline remembers that when she was eleven years old, she would take care of her newborn brother, Michael, while her mother was out prostituting.

214

DCF came out to speak with her about her mother's drug use one time. Madeline was parentified at a very young age. Back in those days, Madeline was supposed to clean the house, take care of her brother, and prepare her own dinner after school.

Madeline's life has been on a sketchy path for a long time. She recalls the day her aunt picked her up and brought her to the bus station to go and stay with her grandmother down South. Madeline knew something bad had happened to her mother but didn't get much detail until months later. She learned that her mother was severely beaten by one of her johns and later died in the hospital. Madeline's then two-year-old brother, Michael, witnessed the beating and was left behind crying on the floor next to their dead mother. A neighbor heard Michael crying, and when the neighbor came to check on him, her mother's body was found.

DCF came and removed her brother and placed him in foster care. Madeline's aunt Hattie was able to get to her before DCF or the police and sent her out of town. DCF wasn't aware of the family in Mississippi, and her aunt Hattie wasn't cooperative. Madeline stayed in Mississippi for years. She dropped out of high school and got caught up with the heavier drugs like heroin. It was Madeline's desire to find her brother Michael that led her back to Hartford. She didn't know many people, and she again connected with the wrong crowd and found herself walking in her mother's path of prostitution.

Madeline's friend Towanda, Troy's mother, was the one that introduced her to Buford. Towanda told her that he had money and a house and in the past had taken care of other girls.

"You're prettier than the other ones he's had," Towanda told Madeline.

So Madeline devised a plan to have Buford take care of her because she had nothing. Madeline succeeded in having him believe that Trevan is his son when in actuality Troy is the father. Madeline knows that Troy, who is only fifteen years old, is not ready to be a father. As painful as it was for her to leave her son after the delivery, Madeline knew that Trevan had a chance with Buford and his family. Now Madeline stands over the crib, posing as her son's older sister and about to do the unthinkable.

Ceanna picks up the phone that is ringing on the other side of the room

215

and then quickly hangs up. The twins are on the floor, and they need all available bodies.

"I have an emergency, and they need all available bodies on the other side of the floor. Your father should be back soon," Ceanna says as she walks to the door of the nursery.

I hope to be gone before he returns.

At the doorway Ceanna turns again and asks, "I forgot to ask your name."

Thrown off guard but playing the role, Madeline thinks how she always wanted to be named Bianca. "Bianca Donnelly. I'm the oldest," Madeline says with a smile.

With everyone out of the room, Madeline feels her palms begin to sweat. She knows that she has no time to waste. She quickly peeks out of the nursery and watches the nurses wheel the twins into a side room on the far end of the unit.

"This is my only chance," Madeline says out loud.

She grabs a couple of bottles of formula from under the crib and then a blanket to wrap Trevan in. Slowly she picks him up, trying not to wake him, and then places him in her oversized bag. Cautiously, Madeline peeks out the door. She sees that it's clear, and she anxiously walks down the hallway toward the door. Unexpectedly, Ceanna enters from a side room and heads her way.

I can't get caught. I can't get caught.

Madeline takes a deep breath and begins to walk a little faster with her head down.

"Did your father get back already?" Ceanna asks as they pass each other.

"I figured I'd go look for him," Madeline replies, still walking toward the exit.

Once out of the NICU, Madeline rushes to the stairs. She can hear her cell ringing in her back pocket. She pulls it out, hoping it isn't Troy calling with some bad news.

"Shit, it's Buford," Madeline says in anger.

She hesitates to pick up the phone. Then realizes that in order not to mess up her perfectly executed reunification, she has to speak to him one last time.

"Hey, honey, where you at?" Madeline asks breathlessly as she rushes down the stairs.

"Maddy, where the hell are you? I'm right where you said you would be," Buford says in anger.

"Wait right where you are, honey. I'll be right back. I went to the bathroom," Madeline says, picking up her pace.

"The bathroom? Are you at the one in the main lobby? I'm coming to you," Buford says frustrated.

"No, baby. Trust me. I'll be right there. Don't move, okay?" Madeline yells over the phone.

I'm almost there. I'm almost there.

Madeline quickly approaches the second floor. Suddenly, a gray-haired man in a white jacket comes out of the door and into the stairwell.

Shit.

Madeline continues to push forward and passes the man.

Trevan begins to cry inside her bag.

"Is that a baby?" Buford asks, barely getting out his last words before the line disconnects.

"Miss, do you have a baby?" the gray-haired man asks as Madeline rushes for the door on the first floor.

Without hesitation, Madeline grabs the straps of her purse tightly and runs down the final flight of stairs. In full panic, she turns out of the stairwell to the Collins Street exit where Troy is supposed to be waiting.

"All security to all hospital exits," Madeline hears over the hospital intercom.

The side exit reads "Emergency Exit Only." Now in full sprint, Madeline disregards the sign and pushes the door open. The alarm blares on the outside speakers as she rushes to Troy's passenger side door. Troy reaches over and pops open the door.

"Go, go, go," Madeline shouts.

Madeline sits back in the seat with her bag in her lap as Troy speeds down the street.

Troy turns to Madeline with a puzzled look and asks, "What's going on?"

Unzipping the bag, Madeline slowly picks up Trevan, who stopped crying during her hundred-yard sprint. She turns to Troy, then turns back, and vomits on the passenger side floor.

Chapter 44 ANDREW

Patricia and I decide to meet at Bushnell Park in downtown Hartford. I park my state car and walk across Trumble Street toward the park. I can see Patricia taking pictures of the carousel as I approach.

"You can't go anywhere without your camera," I say as I kiss Patricia on the cheek.

"I saw these beautiful wooden horses in the carousel and had to shoot them. Plus you're twenty minutes late," Patricia says and bumps me with her shoulder.

"I'm sorry. I had to stop and get some gas," I say with a smile. We begin walking hand in hand. "You want to take a ride on the carousel? It's only a buck."

"Maybe later. Let's just walk. It's been a long time since I saw you last," Patricia says, pulling me close to her side. "I love how open the park feels. There are so many beautiful statues. I took an awesome shot of the statue of the goddess Nike over there." She points in the direction of the statue.

"Goddess Nike? I didn't even know it was here," I say laughing. "I bet you the average person walking in Hartford has no clue that they are walking through history. For instance, this park is the first municipal park in the United States. And look over there. That's the Arch, Soldiers and Sailors Memorial. It was dedicated in 1886 and honors the four thousand Hartford residents who fought in the Civil War. One hundred and twenty-eight were freed slaves. I just learned that last week," I say as we walk toward the arch.

"Let me take a picture of you under it," Patricia says and pushes me foward.

"Hurry up. I don't want to get hit by a car," I say as I run in the middle of the street for a quick shot. "You got me?" I ask with my hand spread above my head.

"I got you," Patricia says.

"This feels so good walking with you out here. I have my own history in this city. Some of it is from very happy times and others very sad," I say as we continue down the sidewalk.

"Well, I hope this is a happy time," Patricia says smiling.

"Over there they have Monday night jazz in the summer," I say, pointing to the open field and stage to our left.

"There must be a lot of people out here," Patricia says.

"Yeah, thousands," I say as we reach the Corning Fountain on the east side of the park.

"Wow, this is beautiful." Patricia walks around the thirty-foot marble fountain. "Look at the detail in the Indians' faces and headdress. Do you know what tribe this is?" Patricia asks.

"They are this city's first people, the Saukiog Indians," I say as I sit on one of the wooden benches next to the fountain.

"I always admired the American Indians for their strength and fierce fighting against the European settlers. In Brazil we have a very large indigenous population. They are still finding tribes in the Amazon that have had no contact with the outside world," Patricia says while taking several shots of the statue.

"Are you serious? They are still finding tribes?" I ask with amazement.

"Yes. Some of the tribes and activists in Brazil have fought for years with the Brazilian government to preserve the land and culture of the indigenous people," Patricia says as she walks back toward me.

"America has a very sad history of treatment of our native peoples. Many of our Native Americans are still on the reservations that they were sent to when their land was taken from them."

"Reservations? How sad is that?" Patricia says as she sits next to me.

"For example, here in Connecticut there were many small tribes. The diseases brought over by the Europeans devastated them. We only have two federally recognized tribes in our state: the Mashantucket Pequot Nation and the Mohegan Tribe. Both of them have been fortunate enough to benefit from the construction of casinos on their reserved land," I say moving closer to her on the bench.

We sit for several minutes in silence. I close my eyes and hear the cars driving by behind us. A dog barks in the distance. A gust of wind rustles through the trees next to us. I try to absorb the moment. I feel Patricia begin to caress my hand.

"That feels good," I say, taking in a deep breath and opening my eyes.

"My touch or the silence?" Patricia asks, looking down at my hand.

"Both." I lift her head up with my fingers under her chin. "You look a little down. You okay, Patricia?"

"I've just been thinking about Andrew," Patricia says with a sad look in her eyes.

"I've been thinking about you too," I say, moving closer to her.

"How are your sessions going with Dr. Sol?" Patricia asks, still caressing my hand.

"They're going fine. You thinking about coming to a session?" I jokingly ask as my mind flashes to the last hypnotherapy session. I want to tell her about it but don't want to freak her out. "It looks like you have something on your mind, Patricia. Are you okay?"

"I don't know, Andrew. I'm worried. I'm worried about you at your job," Patricia says, looking directly at me.

"Kay would say that all the time." I look ahead into the field. "You know what? There are times when I feel like I'm in danger. I get scared sometimes, but I understand that it's the nature of my job. I know that people are unpredictable. When you really look at it though, I could've been worried about you being at the park alone. Look how crazy people are on the road driving in their cars. One can worry about many things," I say, slowly pulling my hand from hers.

"I'm sorry, Andrew. I'm sure you must discuss things like that with Dr. Sol. You asked what was on my mind so I told you," Patricia says and reaches for my hand again.

"It feels good to have someone worry about me. I feel appreciated. Plus Dr. Sol doesn't know everything about my life," I say, accepting her hand in mine.

"Do you know much about Dr. Sol?" Patricia asks.

"I know from the framed doctorate on his wall that he went to Stanford University. I know he worked for many years in California, but that's it. I can't explain it. I trust him. I feel like he's helping me understand what my purpose is," I say. "I don't know, something still seems to be bothering you. You sure you're okay?" I ask again, becoming a little worried myself.

Before she can answer, my work cell rings.

"DCF, Andrew speaking."

"Andrew, you have to get to the hospital as soon as possible. Someone abducted Trevan from the nursery," Renee says in an urgent tone.

"What? Are you serious?"

"Yes, Andrew. You need to hurry up. The police are already here questioning the staff. Buford told one of the detectives you were supposed to be here. I have to go, Andrew. Just get here soon." Renee hangs up the phone.

"Shit, shit, shit," I say, nearly throwing my cell onto the ground.

"Andrew, is everything okay?" Patricia stands from the bench and tries to calm me.

"I have to go, Patricia. Someone stole a baby on my case from the hospital. Shit. I was supposed to be there with the father. Shit."

You're a dumbass, Andrew. You didn't fuck up this much when Kay was around. Now that I think about it yeah, you did. You must like this new chick.

"Shut the fuck up. You don't know what you're talking about," I say to the voice in my head.

"Andrew, calm down, it's okay. Just go. Go."

"I'm sorry, Patricia," I say, accepting her strong embrace.

I run full speed across the park to my car.

Chapter 45 PATRICIA

Patricia stands and watches Andrew run across the park. The guilt of taking the journal begins to take its toll. Patricia remembers that Kay was also trying to talk with Andrew about something before she was murdered. Maybe there is more to Dr. Sol, or maybe the concerns about the information that was found were a big overreaction. Patricia puts her camera in her bag and heads back to the carousel for a ride.

Chapter 46 ANDREW

I speed down Collins Street toward the parking garage at St. Francis Hospital. Police cruisers and news trucks are parked all around the hospital.

"How could I have been so stupid?" I say to myself as I park the car. I rush out of the car and head to the back entrance.

"Sorry, sir, can I see your ID?" a Hartford police officer asks before I enter the building.

There are officers at every entrance and exit of the hospital. I show my badge and am given access. I arrive on the NICU floor and see at least five officers and four detectives questioning hospital staff. I show my badge one more time and am allowed to enter the NICU. Inside, I make eye contact with Renee who is speaking with one of her colleagues. Renee immediately walks toward me with a troubled look in her eyes and pulls me into an empty room.

"Andrew, where the hell were you? You said you would be here with Mr. Donnelly."

I was only supposed to meet with Patricia briefly in the park. I really don't have an excuse for being late.

It's only a matter of time before they figure it all out.

"I had another case to follow up with, Renee. I didn't think I was going to be that long," I lie.

"Another case, Andrew? You told me the other day you would be on time,"

"Are you blaming this on me, Renee? There's no way we could have predicted someone abducting a baby from the hospital."

"It's not me who's going to be blaming you, Andrew. It's going to be the police, the hospital, and DCF administration asking questions. My ass is just as deep in this as yours," Renee fires back as she paces in front of the door.

You're gonna let this bitch talk to you like that, Andrew? It's only a matter of time, Andrew. It's only a matter of time.

The guilt begins to build in my chest. The voice in my head speaks freely with no interference. Maybe the voice is right. It's only a matter of time before they figure it out.

"Shit, Andrew, I haven't even been here long. I can't lose my job now," Renee says with tears in her eyes.

"It's going to be okay, Renee. Do they have any idea who took the baby?"

"Buford Donnelly was here meeting with his son Trevan. Nurse Monroe allowed him in the nursery with one of the CNAs. For some reason, Buford left the NICU. I guess they thought he went to the bathroom. Ceanna, the CNA, says Buford's daughter Bianca came to visit Trevan while her father was away from the nursery. The last thing Ceanna recalled was seeing Bianca pass her in the hallway of the NICU. Bianca said she was going to look for her father."

"Bianca? Buford's daughter's name is Kendra."

"So who the hell was in the nursery?"

Chapter 47 BUFORD

Buford sits with one of the JID detectives reviewing the surveillance footage from the main lobby. The tape is paused on a clear picture of the face of the woman who abducted Trevan.

"Is this your daughter Bianca, sir?" the detective asks, pointing to the monitor.

Buford looks at the screen with a glazed look on his face and can't believe what he sees on the tape. After a long pause he answers, "No, sir, I don't have a daughter named Bianca," Buford says, realizing he has been played.

"Do you know who this is?" the detective asks.

Buford takes a deep breath through his mouth, and then says her name. "That's Madeline Williams, the mother of Trevan," Buford says sadly, putting his hand over his face.

"According to Renee, the hospital social worker, the mother was DCF-involved. Renee says Madeline wasn't supposed to even be here. Did you tell Madeline that you were coming today?" the detective asks while turning off the monitor.

"Yes, detective, you're correct. She was not supposed to have contact," Buford says, shaking his head silently. "Madeline must have had all of this planned from day one."

"Why you think that, sir?" the detective asks, taking his palm-size pad from his shirt pocket.

"Several weeks back Madeline came to my house. She told me that she had had our baby. Yeah, those were her words—'our baby.' Madeline mentioned being in some big trouble with DCF. 'All you have to do, Buford honey, is go sign an acknowledgment of paternity,' " Buford says, shaking his head from side to side and growing angry with himself.

"I don't mean to be rude, sir, but did you think that Trevan was probably not your son?" the detective asks politely.

Buford looks up with a smile on his face. "Detective, I know I'm an old man. Call me a sucker for allowing a warm body to lie in the bed next to me at night. I know she could've had someone much younger. But I truly believed and still do believe that Trevan is my son," Buford says, looking the detective in the eyes.

"When was the last time you spoke with Madeline?" the detective asks, sitting on the edge of the desk.

"Madeline called me today during the visit. She told me that she was downstairs and needed to speak with me in a hurry. I knew she couldn't come inside the hospital so I went to look for her. Plus it sounded important," Buford says as he looks out the window of the office.

"Did she say what she wanted to talk with you about? What was so important that couldn't wait?" the detective asks, looking up from his pad.

"We both know that she didn't want to talk about anything. She was preparing to take the baby, and I took the bait," Buford says and then bangs his fist on the desk in front of him.

"Mr. Donnelly, I know this all can be upsetting. What I'd like to do is have you come down to the station for further questioning," the detective says, closing his pad and placing it back in his shirt pocket.

"Am I going to be arrested? I had no idea she was going to do this," Buford says, looking at the detective.

"No, sir, you're not being arrested. Like I said, we have some more questions that we need to ask. We want you to put your information in the form of a written statement. That's it," the detective explains as he walks to the door to get the officer standing in the hallway. "Officer Jones will transport you to the station. I'll be there shortly," the detective says as he leaves the room.

Chapter 48 ANDREW

I speak briefly with one of the detectives as I exit the room with Renee.

"I was supposed to be here to supervise the visit," I explain to the female detective.

"So you weren't here when the baby was abducted?" the female detective asks, holding her pad open to write.

"No, I wasn't," I say.

"Well, we're all set with you. We want to try to get to everyone that was here at the time of the kidnapping." The female detective walks to one of the nurses standing at the counter.

That's it? No other questions? Maybe I came down too hard on myself.

My work cell rings in my pocket. It's Stephanie.

"Hey, Andrew. We need you back here at the office. Administration called for an emergency meeting."

You're not out of the dark yet.

*   *   *

"Andrew, we really don't have time to speak. All I can tell you is they're going to have a lot of questions," Stephanie says as we enter the office of Area Director Greg Black.

Two chairs are unoccupied on the far end of the large wooden conference table. I can feel the tension in the air and all eyes in the room watching me as I sit. Around the table there are many high-level administrators. At the head of the table, Area Director Black sits with the four program directors, two on each side of him. The principal attorney, my program supervisor, and my supervisor sit close to me. Across the table are a couple of people I have never seen. I suspect that they are from Central Office, possibly from human resources or personnel.

"Andrew, what is the update on the abduction and police investigation?" the area director asks, breaking the tension.

I quickly circle the table with my eyes. There is not a single friendly face in the room. I take a deep breath before I speak.

"The father, Buford Donnelly, was visiting Trevan at St. Francis Hospital today. While he was in the visit with his son, the mother, Madeline Williams, called asking that he come downstairs to speak with her. I guess she had something important to tell him. So Buford went downstairs to look for her, but she wasn't there."

Program Director Beatrice Jones quickly interrupts me.

"What do you mean you guess she had something important to tell him? This woman abandoned her son in the hospital weeks ago. She already asked for him to go acknowledge himself as the father. What was so important to ask him?" She speaks in a stern tone, setting the atmosphere of the meeting.

If people thought my program supervisor, Tracey, was a hard-ass, they would consider her Strawberry Shortcake compared to Beatrice Jones. Tracey has had investigators transferred because of their assessment skills and quality of their work. Beatrice, on the other hand, has been successful in having workers terminated. I think I would rather be sitting in front of Tracey right now.

"I'm not sure what Madeline had to ask. Buford wasn't able to find her. While he was downstairs looking for her, somehow Madeline was able to enter the NICU," I say and again am interrupted by Beatrice.

"This woman abandoned her son at this hospital. Are you telling me that there was no one there that noticed her? Where were you, Andrew? Your narrative notes that you were supposed to be meeting Mr. Donnelly at the hospital for the visit," Beatrice asks, reading from my investigation protocol.

Tell her, Andrew. Where were you?

"I was on my way to the hospital. Buford arrived there before me," I say, trying to calm my nerves.

"Well, that's obvious, Andrew. Mr. Donnelly had enough time to visit with his son, receive a call from Madeline, and walk downstairs to look for her. This is all before you even get to the hospital. Is that correct?" Beatrice fires at me.

"That's correct," I say, gritting my teeth to control my anger.

"So, Andrew, what happened next?" Area Director Black asks, briefly breaking the tension.

I pause for a second to try to regain my composure. The voice in my head keeps laughing at me.

Why don't you really let her know how you feel, Andrew? Like I said, they will find out everything in the end.

"Madeline told one of the CNAs that she was Buford's eldest daughter. So the CNA allowed her to enter the nursery. Renee, the hospital social worker, informed me that there was an emergency on the floor while Madeline was in the nursery. They believe that during this commotion Madeline abducted the baby, putting him in the bag she carried," I say calmly.

"In your protocol you write that you have never had any contact with the mother. In one of your case conference notes with Stephanie, you suggested that DCF use this *alleged* father, Mr. Donnelly, as a resource. Why would we do that? Was a paternity test done?" Beatrice asks, not letting up on her interrogation.

"You're right. No, I haven't been able to meet with the mother. If she passed me in the hospital today, I wouldn't have known who she was. We have a mother that abandoned her son just as you kindly pointed out. What we are trained to do in a situation of possible removal is attempt to look for family resources. So Madeline notifies the *alleged* father, and he voluntarily acknowledged himself as the father. Stephanie and I discussed the option of utilizing Buford as a resource. The decision whether to use him wasn't finalized," I say, allowing my frustration with the line of questions to show.

"According to your narrative, you had a conversation with Mr. Donnelly. You write that he told you that he acknowledged paternity and signed the proper paperwork. Is that correct?" the principal attorney asks.

"Yes, that's correct," I say and turn my head to the newly loaded gun in the room.

"The hospitals and other health care facilities have clear instructions and guidelines around the process of voluntary acknowledgment of paternity.

These facilities need to make the proper forms available to nonmarried parents who wish to go this route. This approach makes it easier for those who cannot afford a paternity test. The instructions clearly state that the forms have to be signed in the hospital or other health care facility in the presence of a witness from that facility. They also have to be signed while the mother is still a patient and within five days of the birth of the child. The issue we have is the mother left soon after she gave birth. And the alleged father showed up a week later to sign for paternity," the principal attorney explains to the group.

This isn't looking good for me, and it is about to get worse. It is clear that Beatrice was assigned as executioner for the day.

"Andrew, were you aware of Madeline's case history?" Beatrice asks, staring me down with her death rays.

"In my brief review I knew that this was her first child and her first case with the department."

Beatrice cuts me off once again.

"Were you aware of Madeline showing up as a participant on any other case with DCF?" Beatrice asks.

I sense she is leading me to the slaughter. "No, I am not aware of her being a participant on any other cases," I say, preparing for the guillotine to drop.

"Clearly you didn't look hard enough. From the simple person check I conducted in Link, Madeline pops up as a participant on the case of her mother, Mary Williams. It amazes me that you didn't look up the history on this family," Beatrice says agitated, flipping through the papers in front of her. "Madeline's mother was beaten to death ten years ago in the presence of her two-year-old son, Michael. I guess you weren't aware of that either. We removed Michael, and he was later adopted. During that investigation ten years ago, Madeline mysteriously disappeared. You didn't know this, Andrew?" Beatrice asks, shaking her head side to side.

"No, I didn't know this," I say, accepting my mistake.

"Part of it could be my fault. I should have reviewed the history for him," Stephanie speaks up.

I turn to Stephanie, thanking her with a quick smile.

"Well, it looks like we need new training in investigations on the proper protocol on assigning and investigating cases," Beatrice says, looking at Area Director Black.

Andrew, it's clear where this is all going. Just come back with me. I can help you get past some of this. Shut her up.

"Andrew, we all can understand the strain and stress you have been under this past year. Sometimes stress can make us behave in ways that are not normal. Sometimes with stress we may miss things that we normally wouldn't," one of the administrators from Central Office says.

"What are you talking about, stress and strain?" I ask, sitting erect in my chair and agitated by his comments.

"Well, Andrew, the concern is there have been many issues revolving around you lately," he says.

"Issues? What issues are you referring to?" I ask, but I already know where he's going with his remarks.

"Issues like your presence or lack of one during a very serious incident with a colleague. Issues like the current incident with the abduction and kidnapping of a child on your case. Central Office has to take all of these incidents into consideration. Especially when it involves the safety of our clients and staff," the administrator says calmly.

"Where are you going with this?" I ask, feeling my body temperature rising.

"All of us in this room think it's great that you have seen a counselor with the Employee Assistance Program. It's even better that you're seeing your own private psychotherapist now. We all have our own personal issues to deal with," the administrator says as he reads from a file in front of him. "We all can understand the murder of a loved one can cause a lot of stress and distraction in one's life," the administrator says, closing the file.

His words set me off.

"What the fuck are you talking about?" I yell, pushing the table as I stand from my chair. "You don't know what I've been through. What happened to my wife has nothing to fucking do with why I'm sitting here," I say, pointing at him angrily with my finger. "Yes, I've made some poor judgment calls. But maybe you can say the same for Beatrice over there, with her fast-ass teenage daughter. Maybe we can look at Director Black. Yeah, good old married

Director Black who hits on his secretary. Yeah, word gets around, people," I say, watching Beatrice and Area Director Black move uncomfortably in their chairs. "We all know that Claudia should've called the police and never entered the house. Regarding Madeline, this child wasn't in our care. The baby was still in the hospital, not in a foster home. So I'll admit to my faults here. But when you bring in personal issues, that's when I draw the line," I say, pushing the chair from behind me and then leaving the room.

Now that's the Andrew I know.

*   *   *

I jump into my car and just drive. I don't know where I'm going and don't really care. I felt railroaded but also know that I'm to blame. The frustration continues to build in me as I squeeze the steering wheel. How can one thing in your life be going so well and the other side crumbles? I try calling Dr. Sol several times while I am driving, but my calls go straight to his voicemail.

I get off the highway near the Hartford police station and park my car near the boathouse on the riverfront. I walk to the ramp that leads to the pedestrian bridge over Interstate 91 North. At the top I sit in the middle of the bridge and just cry. I cry for Kay, for me, for so many things. I look down at the speeding cars and think it should all just end right now.

Chapter 49   MADELINE

Madeline rolls out of the bed as her john throws her a twenty-dollar bill. She grabs the money as she wipes her mouth with her hand.

"Remember to buy my Colt 45 with that money. You can take your ten bucks out of that," the john says as Madeline leaves the room.

Madeline crosses the hallway to the adjacent bedroom and unlocks the door. Trevan lies motionless in the middle of a stained mattress wrapped in a UConn Huskies sweatshirt.

"Just as I left you," Madeline says as she kneels next to the mattress and places her hand on Trevan's chest. "Still breathing."

Madeline stands and puts on her oversized jacket and a hat that was on the floor. She looks at herself in the cracked mirror and sees a once happy girl. Taking Trevan from the hospital will forever change the path of both their lives. Madeline knows that she doesn't have much time to get her drugs. She leaves the room while Trevan is still sleeping.

"You'll be safe in there till I get back, baby," Madeline says as she locks the door behind her.

The hallway is dimly lit from the television in the living room. Madeline passes through the cluttered living room unnoticed. One of the guys who is renting a room in the house is having sex with a much younger girl on the sofa. The young girl was able to bring some formula and diapers from her aunt's home, helping out with supplies for the baby.

Madeline walks out the front door. A patrol car jets down Vine Street as she pauses on the front porch. She has been extremely cautious since taking Trevan from the hospital. She does most of her moving by night. Almost twenty-four hours since her last hit, she can feel a shooting pain in her muscles and bones. Madeline walks toward Mather Street at a steady pace with her eyes scanning her surroundings. On the corner she can't believe who she sees getting out of the car of one of her johns. Madeline tries to pass her before she is recognized. Then Madeline hears her named call from behind.

"Maddy, is that you? I thought I saw you from the car," the voice says talking fast.

It is Donna. Donna walks over in her high heels and short miniskirt and gives Madeline a strong embrace. As tough as the past couple of weeks have been going, Madeline thinks it is nice to see her old friend. Madeline thinks about the first time they met.

*   *   *

It was the summer that Madeline's mother put her in the YMCA day camp. The only person she knew that year was her cousin Derek. When she and Derek were younger, there were times when it felt good to be a kid. It was so much different then. Now they were both drug addicts who roamed the streets. While Madeline attended the camp, she made many new friends.

At the camp there was a boy named Edgar that everyone loved to tease. The other kids said he acted like a girl. Every single day someone called him a faggot or told him that he acted like a girl. It didn't seem like it bothered Edgar. It even looked like Edgar loved the attention. He loved to dance and sing like his favorite artist, Donna Summers.

"One day I'm gonna have long legs and big breasts. No one will know the difference. All the boys will like me then," Edgar said twirling around.

Madeline and Edgar laughed and became best friends, playing together the entire summer. After the camp ended, Edgar moved over the river to East Hartford. Madeline was sent to Mississippi soon after that and lost contact with Edgar. It was when Madeline returned to Hartford the previous year that she and Edgar reconnected. He had changed his name to Donna and looked more beautiful than some of the girls on the street. They ran into each other on the streets trying to get the same johns.

*   *   *

"Twenty dollars for five minutes. That ain't bad, girl." Donna says putting on some lipstick.

Madeline shakes her head and thinks that she undervalued herself. She walks with her legs shaking and face twitching as her body fights for her next hit. They turn onto Mather Street.

"Girl, I heard some crazy shit the other day. Some crazy-ass bitch stole her baby from the hospital. The news said they think she's in Hartford still. I hope they give a reward because I'd turn her ass in. Fuck that, we should both find the baby and make us some money. Shit." Donna laughs.

Madeline begins to get paranoid and looks up and down the block thinking that someone spotted her. Madeline knows the hospital had to realize by now that she took Trevan. A silver Ford Explorer honks as it pulls up to the curb. Donna digs in her purse and pulls out a strip of condoms.

"Protect yourself or wreck yourself," Donna says, giving Madeline a handful of condoms.

Donna jumps into the Explorer and rides down the street. Madeline stands frozen for a second and then makes her way across the empty lot. She walks down an alley between two buildings and knocks at a back window. Almost instantly the window cracks a couple of inches.

"Who?" a male voice asks from inside.

"It's me, Jo Jo," Madeline says and then slips the money inside the window.

A couple of seconds later her prize is delivered. Madeline snatches her drugs and goes to the dumpster behind the building to light up.

*   *   *

Nearly an hour after leaving the house, Madeline returns to check on Trevan. When she enters the hallway, she can see that something is wrong. Someone broke into the room. Panicked, she rushes down the hallway and sees that Trevan is no longer on the bed. Madeline runs out of the hallway and screams and knocks on doors. The young Hispanic girl who was having sex earlier walks out of one of the back rooms with Trevan in her arms.

"Oh, God, I thought someone took you. I'm sorry, baby. I will never leave you again. I'm sorry, baby," Madeline says as she takes Trevan from the girl's arms.

"We heard him crying but couldn't open the door. Reggie kicked in the door," the girl explains. "He drank about four ounces of milk and then fell back to sleep."

Madeline walks down the hall to her room. She closes the now broken door behind her.

"You gonna pay to get the door fixed, girl," a male voice calls out from behind the fractured door.

Madeline sits on the mattress and cries with her sleeping son in her arms. She knows that she can't stay at the house long. She has to leave quickly but doesn't have many options, especially with a baby and the entire city looking for her. There is a street close by with several abandoned buildings. She'll go there tonight, giving her time to think of her next move.

Chapter 50 GLEN

Sigourney Square Park is swarming with its regulars stopping for their midday fix. Glen, aka "Eight Ball" or "Eight," is playing a chess game on one of the concrete tables with an old-timer from the neighborhood.

"Checkmate, Eight. How many times I gotta beat you, boy?" the old-timer laughs and takes a swig of his Colt 45 wrapped in a brown paper bag.

A couple of kids play on the monkey bars in the park. Alizè sits with her backpack on and draws in her coloring book. Keith, a tall, skinny Caucasian fellow, shuffles across Collins Street into the park. He holds a newspaper under his arm as he approaches Glen's crew. The crew members are huddled in a circle and freestyling.

"You and me can never be on the same page at the same time 'cause you got green eggs and ham and I got the holy Koran," Chase, one of the crew members, freestyles.

The other crew members wave their hands in the air, high-fiving one another. Keith paces from side to side in front of the concrete table, waiting for Glen to finish his game.

"Nigga, you distracting me. Go walk over there with that face-twitching shit," Glen says and waves Keith away.

In a low-toned stutter, Keith breaks Glen's concentration on his game. "Yo-yo, Eight, you-you got a dime bag?" Keith asks and then pulls out a couple of crumpled dollar bills and some change.

"Checkmate again, fool," the old-timer says to Glen.

Frustrated, Glen stands up and begins yelling at Keith. "Nigga, don't you see I'm busy? Crackhead ass." Glen grabs the money from his hand. He notices that it's only a couple of dollars and some spare change. "What I look like, a coffee shop, nigga? How you gonna ask for a dime bag with this shit?" Glen says as he walks toward Keith in a threatening manner.

"Look at this, nigga. Give me that," Chase says and grabs the newspaper from under Keith's arm.

Keith is forced backward by Glen's approach. He holds his frail hands in front of his face and stumbles over his own feet to the ground. The crew burst out laughing. Keith tries to raise his voice to speak over them.

"You-you know I'm goo-good for it, Eight," Keith says, standing up with his hands shielding his face.

Glen turns around and walks back toward the concrete table to grab his Colt 45. "You see that little girl over there with the book bag? She has your shit." Glen points over to Alizè. "Ask her for the little white rock candy in her bag," Glen directs Keith who is already striding away before Glen can finish talking. "Nigga, if you try to run with the whole bag, you gonna feel some hot lead in your ass," Glen shouts to Keith.

They all laugh hysterically.

Before Glen can sit to get beaten again by the old-timer, Chase rushes over and lays the front page of the *Hartford Courant* on the table. "Look at this shit. That's the bitch that shanked you, son," Chase says as he looks up at Glen.

A blown-up picture from a grainy piece of surveillance shows Madeline running through the hospital emergency exit with a bag over her shoulder. The headline reads: "DCF Fails to Protect Another Child."

Glen stares at the picture with his hand on his healing wound. "That's her. You know what you gotta do."

Chapter 51 ANDREW

I stagger into the office with a hangover from the previous night. I walk onto the investigations floor to more stares and whispers as I pass. I know the word has gotten out by now about the abduction and my outburst in the meeting the day before. At my desk I spin my chair around and see a copy of the *Hartford Courant*. On the front page the headline reads: "DCF Fails to Protect Another Child."

I pick up the paper and then look around the investigations floor. Suddenly I get no eye contact from anyone. I feel like cursing out everyone and asking who put the paper on my chair. Instead I sit in the chair and throw the paper on my desk. A red light glows steadily on my phone, which means the voicemail is full. I spin my chair toward the wall and put my hand over my face. I feel like crying, like punching the wall. I can't focus on anything. I'm not sure how much longer I can do this. This job. This life. This world.

They are going to slowly take you apart, Andrew. Wait and see.

My desk is stacked with cases that haven't gotten my attention in days. My computer was left on from the day before. I scroll through my e-mail, barely able to keep my eyes open. I think taking the pills this morning was a very bad choice. I feel nauseous.

I received an e-mail from the office assistant regarding my Department of Social Services check.

"Andrew, here is the information you requested on Persephone," the office assistant wrote.

At DCF we do DSS checks in order to determine what services, such as food stamps and cash assistance, a family is receiving. This is also a good way of tracking families we can't find. Many times our system has old addresses.

240

Sometimes the wrong address is also given at the time a report is made. Usually families keep their information up to date with DSS because it's a difference of receiving or not receiving benefits.

"Persephone didn't move too far from her old address," I say to myself and print out the e-mail with the address on it. Persephone moved across from Dutch Point to one of the buildings on Norwich Street.

My office line rings. It's Stephanie and she wants to meet.

I haven't spoken with Stephanie since the meeting with administration. I enter her office still a little pissed off. I feel like I could fall asleep if I closed my eyes. I slowly guide myself down to the chair and sit.

"Andrew, I'm so sorry about yesterday. I knew it was going to be bad. I never saw that coming from them though."

"You don't need to apologize. It wasn't your fault that we had the meeting," I say, struggling to keep my eyes open.

"I tried calling you while you were at the hospital, but you weren't picking up your cell phone. I wanted to try to give you a heads-up that Central Office and administration were reviewing the case record," Stephanie explains as her voice echoes in my head.

I sit speechless and a little numbed out from my pills. "It's okay, Stephanie. That's the process," I mumble, barely able to get all of the words out of my mouth.

I massage my temples with my fingers. I can feel that I'm breathing much faster now. The room is spinning, and my body is getting weak.

"Are you okay?" Her voice is faint in the distance.

My eyes open and shut slowly.

*   *   *

There are voices speaking excitedly around me. I'm lying down and rather comfortable. With great effort I squint my eyes. Peter and my mother stand at the foot of my bed. I lift my head briefly from the pillow to look at them and sink back down.

"Andrew, baby, you're awake." My mother rushes to my side.

"Hey, guy, you got me scared over here," Peter says embracing me.

"How long have I been asleep?" I ask.

"You've been out for almost eight hours, man," Peter says as he stands next to my mother who is sitting on the edge of the bed.

"Baby, I thought I lost you." Tears slowly flow down my mother's face as she hugs me tightly.

My family knew little about my binge drinking and dependency on prescription drugs. I'm sure they know everything now. I was stupid to even try to come into work as I had done so many times before. They ask nothing about how I got to the hospital.

"I hope you get better, baby," my mother says, wiping the tears from her eyes with a tissue.

"You know I'm here for you, bro," Peter says, putting his hand on my shoulder. "Hey, guy, you got a visitor," Peter says calling my attention to the door.

Standing in the doorway is Patricia. She holds a bouquet of flowers and tears fall from her beautiful brown eyes.

My mother kisses me on my cheek. She and Peter exit the room to leave Patricia and me alone.

"Are those for me," I ask as Patricia gives my mother a hug before she passes her.

"Yes. These tears are for you," Patricia says, walking to my side and giving me a long and strong embrace.

"I didn't know what to think. We were praying for you to wake up, Andrew," Patricia says.

"Well, I'm still here. I hope I didn't disappoint you by waking," I say with a smile as she sits on the bed next to me. "I'm happy to see you," I say, rubbing her hand. "I can feel the love around me," I say and begin to cry.

"You are a lucky man," Patricia says and hugs me again.

I worked so hard to hide my emotions, drowning them in the drugs and alcohol. It's when I'm clear minded that I see what I have. Patricia lies quietly next to me with her head on my shoulder.

*   *   *

After the fainting incident, my supervisor suggested that I take some time off. All my cases were distributed to the other unit members to handle while

I'm gone. Madeline and the baby haven't been found, and they think she is getting help from someone.

My mother hung around for a day or so after my discharge from the hospital. She has already returned to White Plains. She also told Peter and me that she may relocate to the Hartford area to be closer to us. Peter and Patricia both have stopped by since I've been home. They also call every couple of hours to check up on me.

I lay in my bed staring at the ceiling and wondering how my life got to this point. I tried to fight against my sadness and anger as I tried to cope with the loss of Kay. I came into the field of social work to help those like me. I find myself trying to win an endless battle to save every family that I encounter. Instead, I feel like I'm falling into an emotional pit of self-pity. I attempted to cure myself by trying to destroy my demons. I thought my work was leading me to salvation. I'm starting to feel that it's my work that has taken so much from me. The loss of my Kay was the loss of my heart. My introduction to Patricia was the beginning of my healing.

I grab the remote and turn on the television to the news. After a report of another shooting in the city the previous night, a clip from a news conference with the governor is shown. One of the reporters asks the governor why he vetoed a recent bill the legislature was trying to pass. The governor's response to a different question gets my attention.

"Governor, do you have any comments on the continued fumbling of care and services by budget-squeezed DCF. Specifically, the recent child abduction during an open investigation?" the reporter asks.

The governor looks directly into the camera, pointing his finger as he makes his statement. "There are no excuses. No excuses for the lack of care or services that our children and families should receive in this state. Regarding the recent abduction, my office has been in very close contact with the Hartford Police Department, and they have a suspect that they are actively seeking. I have personally been in contact with the commissioner from DCF, and all I will say is appropriate actions will be taken. Heads will roll."

A slap to the face from the highest level. Congratulations.

It's amazing how they continue to forget that the child wasn't taken out of a foster home. The abduction is no longer internal; it is now political.

Chapter 52 MADELINE

The nights are getting cooler. Madeline's supplies are getting sparse. For the past couple of days Madeline has been off the streets. She has been hiding out in an abandoned building on Pliny Street in the city's North End. A couple of buildings away from Madeline is My Sister's Place, a shelter that helps victims of domestic violence and homeless and unemployed women find a safe haven. If Madeline wasn't on the run, DCF could have helped her get into a substance abuse program or possibly into My Sister's Place. Instead, Madeline sits in a cold, rat-infested building trying to figure out where she will go next and how she will get her next high.

With her face all over the newspaper and television news, Madeline is afraid to present herself in the open. She knows DCF and the police are pursuing her. She is scared that the bald-headed guy is trying to track her down. If only she had a little money, she would leave the city and try to start a new life with her son. Even Troy is no longer picking up her calls. Troy said she was crazy to take the baby from the hospital. Madeline has no one who will help her. There was only one option left. It also looked like the best one for both her and Trevan.

Chapter 53 CASSANDRA

Cassandra lies on her bed with her eyes closed rubbing the angel necklace Miss Kay gave her. She imagines being in a big backyard with her parents having a BBQ. She can see herself running around, playing, laughing, and having fun. Cassandra wonders why she was sold like a piece of candy. She asks herself why her uncle and total strangers raped her. She lies there remembering Miss Kay, how nice Miss Kay was to her, and how Miss Kay wanted to help her.

The last time she saw Miss Kay's face still haunts her. Just like the abuse she suffers from Gordo and the others, she now has the memory of seeing the murder of Miss Kay playing in her mind. Madeline tries to erase this one horrible memory. As she does this, she finds herself erasing Miss Kay and all the happy times they had together. She can remember the night Miss Kay came to her home to speak with her aunt. Cassandra was so surprised to see her, especially after she called DCF. Miss Kay was only trying to give her support to the family, but Persephone got upset and began yelling. After Gordo arrived, things got worse. He too began yelling at Miss Kay.

"There was no reason to call DCF. You know it was bullshit, lady," Gordo said.

"I don't think it was bullshit. I believe something happened to her. I also believe that you guys threatened her not to tell," Miss Kay said.

Cassandra remembers listening from the stairs that night. She heard that Gordo and Persephone just didn't get it. They didn't understand that they were wrong.

Miss Kay then left the house. Gordo followed behind her and continued to yell at her outside. Cassandra ran down the stairs and snuck out the

245

back door. Cassandra watched from a distance as Gordo followed Miss Kay around the building and out of view. Cassandra ran around the building in the opposite direction. She noticed that Miss Kay was walking in a different direction back to the school.

It was when Cassandra got around the corner that she saw what happened.

Out of all the nights in Dutch Point, how could she have been the only one out there at that time? Cassandra thought as she hid behind the building. It all happened so quickly. Cassandra stood with her eyes wide and tearing. She couldn't believe the horror playing in front of her.

The only person that seemed to care about her was lying in a pool of blood. She wanted to go to Miss Kay, but she knew she couldn't. He was still there. She also didn't want to get hurt herself. Cassandra ran crying to the bodega down the street.

"Call the police! He killed her! Call the police," Cassandra screamed to the attendant behind the counter.

This loss added another secret to the many that seemed to fill Cassandra's small heart. She is the one person who can identify Miss Kay's murderer. She can't imagine the consequences if she ever told.

*   *   *

All of a sudden Cassandra hears several voices. One is familiar to her and the other she hasn't heard in a long time.

"Mom?" Cassandra says as she opens her bedroom door and then stands at the top of the stairs to listen.

"Cassandra, come downstairs to your mother," Cassandra's mother Delia yells out.

"Leave my fucking house. Cassandra ain't coming down," Persephone says.

"That's my fucking daughter. I can see her if I want. Cassandra, come down," Delia shouts very loudly again.

"If you don't leave, I'm gonna call the police. You're fucking crazy," Persephone says as she argues with Delia.

"I'm crazy? No, you're crazy," Delia fires back.

Cassandra stands at the top of the stairs crying. She wonders why her life can't be normal.

For several minutes, Persephone and Delia argue at the front door.

"You made me fucking sign custody over to you. You just wanted the welfare check," Delia says, pacing side to side in front of the door and pointing her finger at Persephone.

"Why don't you just leave and get your crack? You fucking crackhead," Persephone says as a crowd begins to build outside.

What Cassandra hears next surprises her and makes her sick at the same time.

"Go ahead. Call the police. I'll fucking tell them Gordo fucked me and got me pregnant when I was twelve years old, bitch. Call, motherfucker. Call 'cause all of you fuckers tried to hide this shit. I ain't hiding it no more," Delia yells and waves her hands in Persephone's face.

Cassandra runs downstairs to her mother with no resistance from Persephone.

"Mommy," Cassandra says, running into her mother's arms.

"Baby, I knew you were here. I'm so sorry, baby. I'm so sorry," Delia says as they cry in each other's arms.

"Come the fuck inside," Persephone says, pulling them into the apartment. "What the hell y'all looking at? Go the hell home," Persephone yells to the bystanders.

Chapter 54 PATRICIA

P atricia sits in her friend's apartment with her laptop open. She pulls out
Dr. Sol's business card and then conducts a Google search.

So who were you before you came to Hartford?

Patricia remembers from the journal that Kay mentioned the Golden Gate
Bridge and Stanford University. She types "Dr. Sol + Stanford + California"
in the search engine. Millions of hits pop up with these search words. Patricia
double-clicks the first one. To her surprise, it is an article from *The Stanford
Review* archives from the 1990s.

The article highlighted Dr. Sol as one of the alumnus making great
achievements in the community and in the fields of psychology and
hypnotherapy. He taught in the Psychology Department at the university for
over ten years. He served as a consultant and evaluator for California state
agencies. The article reported that after a decade of service to the university and
the community, Dr. Sol left California because of controversy and tragedy.

Controversy and tragedy?

Patricia attempts to locate more information. After a couple of minutes
of searching, she finds another article from a local newspaper. The headline
reads: "Murder of a Professor's Son." The article reported that Dr. Sol's seven-
year-old son was kidnapped and later found murdered. Further review of the
article reveals that his son was sexually abused and sodomized.

"Maybe his work with the prison population is what led to his son's murder,"
Patricia reads in a comment on the Web site on which she viewed the article.

Prison population?

"Maybe this is what Kay wanted to talk with Andrew about," Patricia
says out loud.

Chapter 55   ANDREW

I look over my shoulder and see that I'm not being followed. The moon is high in the sky and projects its light on the street in front of me. We had split up afterward, and I hoped he had dumped the car far outside of the city. The state car was parked back in the lot unnoticed.

Steady, steady.

My car keys shake in my hand. I take a deep breath in and a long exhale. My heart beats at an incredibly fast rate. The adrenaline rushes through my veins. Inside the car I dig at the bottom of my bag and find nothing but loose change.

"Where is it? Where is it? Shit!"

Check under the seat.

My hand grabs freely under the driver's seat, but nothing is there except crumbs. I turn to the passenger seat and find the empty bottle. On the floor next to the bottle, my fingertips can feel a couple of pills. I pick them up and hold them in the palm of my hand. I take the bottle of Jack Daniels from the backseat and pop the pills in my mouth.

What a perfect mix.

I drive down Hamilton Street toward Zion and then turn and park on the side of the street. With my seat pulled back, I close my eyes. Nirvana's song "Lithium" plays through my speakers as I wait for the tempo of my heart to slow down.

*   *   *

"Andrew! Andrew!"

My body rocks back and forth.

Patricia?

I turn and see Patricia lying in the bed with me.

"When you invite someone over, you're not supposed to be asleep before they get here," she says as she wipes the sweat off my forehead.

When did I invite you over?

"Looks like you were having a bad dream. You're soaked with sweat."

I sit up and lean my back against the headboard. "Bad dream? I don't know. I just remember you calling my name," I say, wiping my face with my hands. I reach over to touch her hand. "How long have you been here?".

"I was out with some friends at a bar when you left your voicemail. You said you would leave the door unlocked for me. I got here kind of late. You were knocked out when I arrived." She picks up her bag from the floor.

I look to my side and see an empty bottle turned over. I haven't been out of the house for days.

"While you were sleeping, you kept saying, 'You're no different than the rest of them.' What does that mean?" she asks.

" 'You're no different than the rest of them'? I'm not sure. I gotta go to the bathroom. I'll be right back," I say and give her a kiss.

In the bathroom I splash some water on my face. I look at my face in the mirror and see the bags under my eyes. I sit on the edge of the tub and close my eyes. "You're no different than the rest of them." Why was I saying that? Images begin to flash in my mind. I remember now.

*   *   *

Holter's car was parked waiting for us just as we planned. I exited the car and folded the paper with the assignment written at the top. I knocked on the passenger side window and then took a quick look back to my vehicle. Holter reached across the seat and opened the door.

"I got a special way of opening that door," Holter said with a smile."Is the boy with you?" he asked excitedly.

"Yeah, he's here," I said with disgust as I thought another one of them would be off the streets soon. "You're no different than the rest of them," I said.

"What are you talking about?" Holter said with a nervous laugh.

Suddenly the driver side door opened. Dr. Sol pulled Holter out of the car by his neck. I saw that Dr. Sol was enraged as he slashed and stabbed Holter with the knife that he held.

"Dr. Sol, what are you doing? You were supposed to be in the car," I said as I ran to the driver side of the car.

I saw that Dr. Sol was swift and enraged. Holter had large punctures to his chest and abdomen. I had never seen Dr. Sol that way. Holter's body lay motionless in the street. Dr. Sol knelt beside the body, pulled Holter's pants down, and then cut off his penis.

"What the hell are you doing?" I asked Dr. Sol as I felt the onset of panic.

"What are you talking about? This is part of the cause. This was a special one you've helped me track. I knew you were the perfect one for this job," Dr. Sol said as he calmly stood up.

"What do you mean 'special one' and 'tracking for a long time'?" I asked confused.

"We don't have time to discuss this, Andrew. We have to get rid of the body fast while the streets are quiet," Dr. Sol said and then began to direct me. "Drag the body under the tree over there. I'll dump the car outside of the city," Dr. Sol said and then moved quickly into Holter's car and drove down Love Lane.

Now all I had to do was return the state car to the state lot. I'd been successful with taking the cars from the state lot for the past several months. Dr. Sol and I had to alter our plans when administration changed the policy on how the cars would be signed out. What I'd been able to do was take the keys from other units. That way I had access to two cars with none linking back to me. Since it was the weekend, no one would miss it.

After I dumped the body as far from the street as I could, I rushed back to my car. As I got into my car, I saw someone jumping out of an SUV on Vine Street. I quickly sped out in the opposite direction before being seen. I looked over my shoulder and saw that I was not being followed. The moon was high in the sky and projected its light on the street in front of me. I hoped he had dumped the car far outside of the city. The state car was parked back in the lot unnoticed.

I open my eyes and hope that I didn't reveal too much while Patricia was present. All I can think is I have to end this with Dr. Sol. Things are getting too risky. The last assignment brought "The Cause" to a new dimension, one I am sure I don't want to continue. Maybe Patricia was right when she asked if I felt like I was in danger. I'm starting to feel this way for others and for myself.

When I enter the room, Patricia is holding her bag and sitting on the edge of the bed with her head down.

"Are you okay?" I ask, approaching her with concern.

Patricia pulls me down to the bed next to her. "Andrew, I have something to tell you."

Shit, she's just not that into me. She's leaving for Brazil tomorrow.

Patricia reaches into her bag and pulls out some sort of book. "This belongs to you," she says and hands it to me.

"What are you talking about," I say confused as I take the book.

"It's Kay's," Patricia says with tears in her eyes.

"Okay, so what's wrong?" I ask, still trying to figure out what's going on.

I look down at the book and don't recognize it as being one of Kay's books.

"It's Kay's journal, Andrew. I found it while we were cleaning the room," Patricia says, putting her head down.

"I don't understand, Patricia," I say and look down at the book and the angel embedded into its leather cover.

"I found it at the back of Kay's drawer while you were taking a shower. I thought I could help you, so I took it. I read Kay's journal."

"You found Kay's journal? And took it from my house and read it? Why didn't you tell me that day?" I ask as I stand from the bed.

"I'm so sorry, Andrew. I thought that maybe she wrote something in her journal that could help find her murderer," Patricia says, reaching for my hand.

"I didn't even know it was there, Patricia. I can't believe you stole from my house," I say, raising my voice in frustration.

"Kay was worried about you, Andrew. She felt that you were in danger."

"Patricia, I can't believe you did this. I trusted you," I say, pulling away from her.

"Please, Andrew, I know it was stupid. Trust me, I was only trying to help," Patricia says, reaching again for my hands. "Before she died she was working on something. She didn't feel right about Dr. Sol. Look at these papers. Look at what I discovered," Patricia says as she takes some papers from her bag and tries to hand them to me.

"I don't want to hear anymore, Patricia. I don't want any papers," I say frustrated and then walk into the living room.

I can't believe the feeling I am having. My mind is so confused. I really liked her.

"Andrew, please, just hear me out," Patricia says, following behind me.

Nothing is forever, Andrew. I could have told you this wasn't going to last.

In the distance I can hear my work cell phone ringing. I find it in my coat on the sofa. I pick up the phone and see that the number is private. I look at the phone and back to Patricia.

"I'm sorry, Patricia. You're going to have to leave," I say coldly, handing her the jacket that was on the sofa.

Patricia freezes in the middle of the living room and looks at me. I can tell she wants to cry. She holds back her tears and takes the jacket from my hand.

"I'm sorry, Andrew." Patricia places the papers that she was trying to give me earlier on the sofa and walks out the door.

My cell phone continues to ring in my hand.

"DCF, Andrew," I answer my cell as I close the door behind Patricia.

"Is this Andrew Edwards?" the female voice asks.

"Yes. Who's this?"

"If you want Trevan, you need to come to this address," the female voice says.

I quickly scramble to find a pen and piece of paper. "Is this Madeline? Where are you?" I say, shuffling through my bag for a pen.

"Just come to this address. Trevan will be waiting. Hurry," the female voice says and gives me the address where Trevan can be found.

I hang up the phone, still very upset with Patricia. I change my focus to what was just said to me on the phone. If the person is telling the truth, this can change my life.

*   *   *

I slowly drive onto Pliny Street, looking at the numbers on the houses in front of me. I suspect the person on the phone was Madeline. She said I would see three vacant multifamily homes toward the middle of the street. The one Trevan will be in is the one in the middle. In the past couple of days there has been a lot of press coverage on this abduction. I have also been getting a lot of heat from DCF. I have no hesitation to come to the building. Some could question my judgment for not calling the police or administration. I look at this as an opportunity for redemption.

I exit my car and make my way down the driveway. I was directed to go through the back of the building and up to the second floor. As I walk to the back, I can see the majority of the windows and doors are boarded up. I notice that the back door is broken open. Inside, the stairs have a strong smell of urine and are littered with liquor bottles and bags of garbage and clothes. I cautiously make my way up the stairs and enter the unit through the kitchen.

The room was stripped of all copper piping for the gas. The plastered walls and hardwood floor were falling apart from the water damage. The only noise I hear is from the cars driving by and some kids playing in the street.

Was she going to keep her word?

I enter an open room adjacent to the kitchen. I notice something on the floor wrapped in a cover. I rush and see that it is Trevan. He is sleeping. My heart jumps with excitement. In between the folds of the cover is a piece of paper. I open it up and read it.

You were the only one I could turn to. Please help my son find a better life.
Maddy

I pick Trevan up and rush to the back door. I know I didn't have much time.

"Thank you," I shout, not knowing if Madeline is still in the building.

I place Trevan in the car seat. I take one last look to a window on the second floor. I think I see something move. Possibly it is Madeline. With no time to lose, I pick up my cell phone and head to St. Francis Hospital.

*   *   *

Renee stands at the entrance of the emergency department with several other hospital personnel. As soon as the car is parked, they are able to secure Trevan and bring him inside for an assessment.

"Well done, Andrew. I'll see you inside," Renee says, leaning into my rolled down window.

I park the state car and make my way into the emergency department. I pick up my phone to call Stephanie to tell her the good news.

"Stephanie, I found Trevan. I just brought him to St. Francis to be checked," I say with excitement.

"You what? Did the police arrest anyone? Where did you find him?" Stephanie asks excitedly.

"I'm going to follow up with the police after I leave here. Can I let the hospital know that we have a ninety-six-hour hold this time?" I ask as I walk into the emergency department.

"You definitely have it. Just take care of business and then call me back. I'll give administration an update. Good job, Andrew."

After a thorough assessment of Trevan, a decision is made jointly by DCF and the hospital to admit him for the night for further monitoring.

Stephanie assumed that the police were with me when I found the Trevan. I knew the police were going to have many questions. My second call was to the Hartford Police station. I was transferred to a Juvinile Investigations Detective. Minutes after my conversation with the detective several units arrived to the hospital. They request that I follow them back to the police station for questioning.

*   *   *

After over three hours of questioning and a visit to the location where Trevan was found, I was finally released. At one point during the questioning,

255

I though I was going to be arrested. The detective told me that I was stupid from not contacting the police on such a high profile case. I gave them the telephone number Madeline called me from and the note she left at the scene. They currently had crusiers searching for Madeline.

I decide to go to the office to begin the order of temporary custody paperwork for the case. All eyes look toward me as I enter the investigation floor. With my heart filled with pride, I hold my head high and walk to my desk. I see several colleagues nod their heads with approval.

"Good job, Andrew," a female colleague says.

I have just a couple of more things to take care of.

Chapter 56 DETECTIVE DUPRI

D etective Dupri exits her car on Forest Street located in the Asylum Hill neighborhood. The neighborhood was formerly known as Nook Farm, and it features some of the city's greatest landmarks. On the opposite side of the street stands Hartford Public High School, the second oldest secondary school in the nation. Further down the street is the Mark Twain House and Museum and the Harriet Beecher Stowe House and Library.

Detective Dupri walks dozens of feet above water. Hundreds of pedestrians and drivers travel along this street every day, and few probably realize that below them flows a river. In the 1600s, Dutch explorers named it the Little River. It was later renamed the Park River after the completion of Bushnell Park in the 1860s. The river was plagued by years of pollution and flooding. It became a hazard for the city, which forced it to be rerouted underground. The river now stays hidden like so many of the stories of Detective Dupri's deceased victims. Today Detective Dupri has hope. She has hope that the information that she received will lead her to the mouth of the river. With the right information gathered, she could expose what was unknown and unseen.

Detective Dupri walks to the front door of the building. She presses the button and waits to be buzzed in. Earlier in the day, she called the mother of one of Holter's sexual abuse victims. The mother was willing to have a conversation about Holter's old sexual abuse case.

A preadolescent male answers the door.

"Hi, is your mother home?"

"Yes." The boy turns around and walks down the hallway.

"What's your name," Detective Dupri asks as they get to the apartment's door.

"Alexander," the boy says and walks into the unit.

Detective Dupri recognizes the name from the file as the victim on the case. Alexander leads her to the kitchen where his mother is preparing a meal.

"Hi, I'm Paula, Have a seat. Just trying to get dinner prepared," the woman says as she covers her pots and pans on the stove.

"Detective Sandy Dupri. We spoke earlier. Paula, thanks for taking the time to speak with me today. Like I said over the phone, this is not a new investigation. I just have a couple of questions for you and possibly for your son," Detective Dupri explains.

"Well, like I said over the phone, I don't want to press any charges. Alex has moved on, and he is doing much better now," Paula says, drying her hands with the rag on her shoulder.

"As I mentioned over the phone, I'm a homicide detective. The purpose of my making contact with you was because Holter was killed a couple of weeks ago."

"So someone actually killed that bastard. You see that little boy in there? He went through hell," Paula says, nodding her head with approval at the news of the murder. "With all these shootings on the news, I must have missed that one," Paula says as she stands to get a glass. "You want some juice?"

"No, thank you. We were only recently able to identify my victim as Holter," Detective Dupri says.

"Your victim? He deserved everything that he had coming to him. He's no victim. My son is the victim," Paula says, sitting back down with her glass of juice. "So, this bastard is dead. He can't hurt anybody else. What you here for? You think I killed him?" Paula asks.

"No, Paula I don't believe you killed him. I only want to talk."

"For the record I wish I was the one that killed him. What do you want from me?"

"I was reviewing the old case that DCF and JID conducted. It said you were drug involved back then."

Paula immediately cuts her off. "I've been clean for years. You can't hold that shit against me now," Paula says in anger.

"I'm not here about your past drug use. I was just reading from the notes. Let me finish."

"Okay. Go on."

"The JID investigation mentioned that you were having one your friends from Dutch Point watch your son when you got high."

Paula cuts her off again. "That's bullshit. What it probably doesn't say is at that time I lost by brother. Yeah, he was a King. My mother died a month later of a heart attack. I think she was heartbroken for my brother. I knew after that shit I had to change. DCF helped me get into a program to get clean. I've been good ever since," Paula explains.

"So when did Alex's disclosure of sexual abuse come out?"

"I was about midway in my program. Alex told his teacher that some guy touched him," Paula says with tears in her eyes. "DCF went to the school and interviewed Alex. DCF had me take Alex to the hospital for an interview," Paula says wiping her tears.

"So when did you start receiving the threats?"

"Soon after DCF's involvement, the harassing phone calls began. The guy said if my son or I said anything to DCF and the police, we would be killed." Paula begins to cry a little harder.

"I'm sorry to hear that, Paula. I'm not here to get you nervous again," Detective Dupri says, trying to comfort her.

"After I heard we would be killed, I stopped talking. Yeah, Alex changed his story and said nothing happened. After the investigations were closed, the calls stopped," Paula says, wiping her nose with the rag on her shoulder.

"Did you have any idea who the person was that was making the threats?"

"I had my suspicions. I didn't want to say anything. I wasn't trying to die."

"But do you have an idea of who it could have been? Do you think it was Holter?"

"I'm really not sure. Persephone, the girl that babysat Alex back then, had a brother named Gordo. I thought it was possibly Gordo calling. I can't be sure though," Paula says, sipping her juice.

"Have you seen Persephone or Gordo lately?" Detective Dupri asks as she takes some notes.

"I rarely go back into Dutch Point. I've got a lot of friends back there. I just try to stay away from the negativity now. The only thing Alex told me was he was at some motel out of the city. Alex said when they were at the motel, there was another girl there taking pictures." Paula stands to check the food that is cooking.

"Do you remember her name?"

"To be honest, no. I'm sure Alex remembers. He says she was cute," Paula says, turning down the temperature under the pots. "Alex baby, come here," Paula calls out.

Alexander walks in to the kitchen slowly. He was listening to the entire conversation from the hallway. He sits at the table with his head down and arms crossed against his chest.

"There is no more monster, baby. He's now gone, okay?" Paula comforts Alexander by rubbing his back.

"Do you mind if I call you Alex?"

"Sure," Alex says, wiping the tears with his shirtsleeve.

"Alex, you're not in trouble for anything today. If you don't want to speak with me, you can get up and go to the other room if you like. Okay?"

"Okay," Alex says with his head down.

"I am here because I am trying to get a better understanding about who this guy Holter was. I want to know if you remember any of the other children that were at your babysitter Persephone's home."

Alexander takes a deep breath and begins to speak. "There was this older girl named Cassandra," Alex says with his head still down.

"Who was she? Did she live there or was she being babysat?" Detective Dupri asks in a soft tone.

"I think it was Persephone's niece."

"Thank you for that information, Alex. You're doing a great job," Detective Dupri reassures him. "What kind of things did you do at Persephone's house?"

"On my first day at the house, Persephone told me that I had to take a picture. She said it was like the ones we take at school. Cassandra led me to a room upstairs. Cassandra's uncle Gordo was there waiting. Gordo said I could play with the toys and promised that he would get me my favorite ice cream after the pictures."

"Anything else?"

"Every once in a while I had to go upstairs to Gordo's room and take new pictures. After a while Gordo began to tell me to take my clothes off. Gordo gave me all the ice cream I wanted after that," Alex says, looking to his mother.

Alex goes on for almost an hour giving details about the different encounters with Holter and others. He says Cassandra was always there in the background taking pictures.

"Alex, I think you were brave to come forward to talk. I have a better picture about who Holter was. Paula, do you remember where Persephone was living?"

"Persephone doesn't live in Dutch Point anymore. I think she moved across the street to Norwich Street," Paula says walking Detective Dupri to the door.

Chapter 57 — CHASE

After receiving a lead from one of the area dealers, Chase and one of the other crew members drive slowly down Garden Street. They look closely down the driveways and at every passerby. They turn onto Pliny Street and continue looking down the driveways and into the windows of some of the vacant buildings. Just when Chase is beginning to think this is a big waste of time, he sees Madeline walking straight toward them. The car accelerates in her direction.

Chase can see that Madeline noticed them. He watches from the passenger seat as she immediately turns and jets in the opposite direction.

"Move! Move!" Chase directs the driver.

Chase can see Madeline dipping down a driveway and running for her life. Chase jumps out of the car in pursuit on foot. Madeline cuts through several yards. He is about twenty yards behind her but catching up quickly. Chase enters Old North Cemetery, one of Hartford's oldest cemeteries, right behind Madeline. They both run atop the graves of some of city's most famous residents. Chase high steps through the uncut grass and brush. Like a cheetah after its prey, Chase is able to trip Madeline's feet from under her. He watches as she falls face-first into the grass.

"Get your ass up, girl." Chase pulls her up by her hair.

"No, no, let me go." Madeline tries to break from his grip but is punched in the face.

Chase pulls her back to the street, but Madeline continues to fight.

"I told you to stop, bitch," Chase says, knocking Madeline unconscious with several blows to the back of the head.

The car pulls up beside Chase. He opens the back door and throws Madeline on the floor. He then runs to the passenger side, and the car speeds away.

Chapter 58 CASSANDRA

Cassandra stands in the kitchen making a sandwich. She smiles as she remembers the night that she spent with her mother Delia. All the stories that Madeline has been told about Delia were ways for her uncle and aunt to continue to manipulate her. Yes, her mother was an addict. During their conversation, Delia told Cassandra she has been trying to get help. Cassandra believed every word Delia told her.

"I'm sorry, Cassandra, that you had to find out about your father this way," Delia said while they were eating.

Cassandra now has the hope that one day she will return to Delia's care. Cassandra knows that the life that she has lived was not normal. To find out that her uncle Gordo is her biological father burns her soul and scrambles her mind.

This couldn't be how a real father was supposed to treat his child. Never mind a brother treating his sister or a stranger treating another stranger.

Cassandra has a goal of a new life with her mother. Cassandra feels in her heart that she will fight to make that happen. She will no longer let anyone get in the way of her dreams.

As Cassandra finishes making her sandwich, Gordo walks into the unit from the back door. She hasn't seen him since Delia's visit. She suspects that he was told that one of his secrets was out. Her aunt Persephone is at the grocery store, and she is home by herself—a rare occasion.

She glances to the living room and watches Gordo take the camera battery out of the charger and then place it in his bag. Cassandra walks to the refrigerator as Gordo enters the kitchen.

Cassandra watches as Gordo walks to counter and takes the sandwich that she just made. He turns around and begins eating it. She looks at him defenseless, angered, and sickened. She thinks that he has taken so much that she will never recover.

"I got another client. Be ready in thirty minutes," Gordo says with his mouth full.

Cassandra rubs the angel necklace, holding on to the hope of a new life with her mother "No. I'm not going," Cassandra says confidently.

Gordo quickly turns with his eyebrows raised. "What did you say?"

Cassandra knows he heard her the first time. She knows there is no turning back now. "I said I'm not going."

"Listen, you little bitch, you ain't gonna lose no more money for me. Now get your ass ready," Gordo says angrily with pieces of the sandwich flying out of his mouth.

Cassandra knows how violent Gordo can become. She also knows he always carries a gun. Cassandra sees that she is close to the back door. She calculates the plan in her head to run if necessary. "I don't want to do this anymore," Cassandra says firmly.

Gordo walks toward her with his hand raised. Just as she begins moving in the opposite direction, a knock comes from the front door. Cassandra isn't expecting anyone.

Persephone would never knock on the door.

Gordo throws the half-eaten sandwich onto the couch. He points for Cassandra to move out of sight. He moves slowly to answer the door.

Chapter 59 ANDREW

At the corner of Stonington and Norwich streets, a group of crows picks at a carcass of a cat. Black clouds cover the sky over Dutch Point and Colt Park. The once vibrant onion-shaped dome of the Colt factory towers above the streets like a silent guardian watching over the now desolate and desperate landscape. I turn left onto Norwich Street. A group of young men stand in front of the bodega with their car stereo system blasting the latest rap music. All of them are dressed in the uniform of the streets: a variation of army fatigue jackets, baseball caps, cornrows, sagging blue jeans, and Timberland boots.

"Monica, what up with tonight, girl?" one of the guys calls to the three girls walking on the opposite side of the street.

My car slowly passes by. I can see that all the eyeliner and form-fitting clothes hide three little girls no older than thirteen. Two of the girls fight for the guy's attention while the other pushes a stroller. A handful of kids play football in the middle of the street. Another group of kids is in the grass, jumping on a dirty mattress pretending its a trampoline. Watching the kids brings me back to my own childhood playing in the neighborhood with friends.

A tap dance begins to play on the roof of my car. As the rain builds in intensity, the street and apartments melt and merge together on my windshield like a ghetto gumbo. I pull over to check the address and notice that it is further down the street. I drive along a bit. To my left stands a brick tenement common to the neighborhood. A red Honda Civic is parked in front of the building. Before jumping from the car, I grab my hat. I make my way across the street into the building. The rain begins to come down harder.

The front stairs are littered with broken glass. Tobacco is scattered across the ground, the leftovers from someone making a blunt. The security system is completely nonfunctional. The bottom glass panel to the door is kicked out, and the lock is missing. From the main lobby of the building, I can hear music blasting from one of the units on the first floor. The bass is so heavy that the walls vibrate. The only light in the staircase is coming from a cracked skylight.

The second floor has two units. I look for unit four. As I get closer to the door, I can hear a male voice yelling at someone inside.

I'm here for Kay.

I look down and see that I still have my work ID on. I begin to take it off but think I'll keep it on just in case I have to use it. I move closer to the door and knock. I can hear over the blasting music that the male voice stops yelling. After several seconds, the door is cracked open. A short, chubby Hispanic male looks me up and down.

"What you want?" the Hispanic male asks with an attitude.

"My name is Andrew Edwards. I'm looking for Persephone." I double-check that my ID is turned so he can see DCF written on it.

"She ain't home," he says and then begins to close the door.

Before he can shut it, I see a young girl in the background move into my line of sight. It is Cassandra.

She's wearing Kay's necklace.

"Cassandra!" I call out to her as her eyes widen.

In a flash the door swings open. The chubby guy lunges at my neck and pushes me into the wall. I am completely shocked by his attack. I shield my body from the barrage of punches. This is the last thing I expected. I'm not sure who he thinks I am. He has me by my neck, very tightly. I can see Cassandra in the doorway, yelling over the music from the first floor.

"Let him go! Let him go!" Cassandra shouts.

"Get the gun! It's in my bag. Get the gun!" Gordo directs Cassandra as he squeezes my neck with his arm.

This guy is going to kill me.

Adrenaline shoots through my body. I'm able to break loose before my back is against the wall. We trade several punches. I'm much taller than he is. His short stocky body moves around me, wrestling me to the ground. He strikes me on my head.

"Get the fucking gun!" he yells out to Cassandra.

I stand with him on my back still choking me almost unconscious. That's when I see Cassandra in the doorway again. This time she has a gun in her hands.

"Shoot him! Shoot him!" the guy commands Cassandra.

"No! Don't shoot," I say, ramming the guy backward into the wall.

I can't die like this.

I was only trying to find out who killed my wife. Now I am possibly seconds away from being killed, yards away from where Kay was murdered. Cassandra holds the gun firmly and tries to take aim.

How much bigger does she need the target?

"Shoot him!"

He squeezes my neck and forces my head up.

Shit, not in the face. Not like this.

I hear one loud pop. Then the air leaves my lungs.

Fuck, I've been shot.

My neck is released. My body crashes to the floor like a demolished building. I feel almost paralyzed as I lie there. Everything begins to move in slow motion. The voices are muffled in my ears. I can see the guy rush back into the unit.

"Give me the gun!" the guy commands Cassandra, holding out his hand.

I struggle to keep my eyes open. I watch as Cassandra begins to back up. She now has the gun pointed at him.

"Don't fucking move, Gordo!" Cassandra yells out over the music that is still playing.

Gordo. That's her uncle.

Gordo stands still with his hands in the air. "What you gonna do, shoot me?" Gordo laughs, mocking Cassandra. Gordo puts his hands down and begins to walk toward Cassandra. "Give me the fucking gun," Gordo says more firmly.

"I said move back. Move the fuck back!" Cassandra yells with the gun shaking in her grip.

Gordo continues toward her and then takes a lunge at her. I hear two loud pops. As I'm losing consciousness, I see Cassandra drop the gun and stride toward me.

"Mr. Edwards? Mr. Edwards?"

Everything fades to black.

Chapter 60 MADELINE

The basement floor feels cold and damp as Madeline regains consciousness. She pulls her knees tight against her chest and she sits up, her eyes darting with fear. A dark trickle of blood seeps from the corner of her mouth. Whether it is from fear, her need for drugs or the trauma to her head, her arm and legs start shaking violently. Madeline hears a familiar voice. It is the bald-headed guy that she stabbed. The guy that caught her in the cemetery called him Glen. Glen leans down and pulls her up by her hair.

"What, bitch? You didn't think I would find you?" Glen says, smacking her back down to the ground.

There are four other guys standing behind Glen.

"So this time we gonna do this shit right." Glen laughs as he unstraps his belt. "Hold her down," Glen directs the other guys.

Madeline tries fighting as they rip off her clothes. Every move is met with a punch to her face or other body part. They have her completely naked and restrained on the ground. Glen stands over her and unbuttons his pants.

"I will be the first to ride this train." Glen laughs at the guys beside him.

"No. Let me go! Let me go!" Madeline yells as she struggles to get up.

"Turn her on her stomach," Glen says.

Glen ravishes Madeline viciously from behind.

"No! No!" Madeline screams out.

"Yeah, bitch, now what?" Glen says as he penetrates her.

Every stroke feels like knives cutting her insides. After several minutes, she can no longer scream. Her vagina and anus throb. One by one, they all take turns raping her.

"Yeah, son. Get it. Get it." The guys laugh.

Madeline cries and blood drains out of her body. She thinks if she was caught days earlier, she would have had her son with her. Who knows what they would have done to them. Madeline lies weeping on the stained floor. The last guy drops the broomstick that he used to penetrate her.

"How you like me now, bitch?" the guy says, throwing the broomstick toward Madeline's head.

Glen returns to the basement. He leans down to her, pressing his finger into the side of her head. "This better teach you to never steal from me again. Now you know how it feels to be stabbed, bitch." Glen laughs as he and the rest of the guys leave her on the basement floor.

"Fuck!" Madeline screams out, holding what is left of her ripped shirt between her legs.

Madeline is left in the basement alone and hemorrhaging. She must make it out if she wants to survive.

Chapter 61   DETECTIVE DUPRI

Detective Dupri can't believe her luck. She receives a call for two gunshot victims. One is deceased, and the other is in critical condition. The local news stations are already setting up shop outside the unit as Detective Dupri arrives. She pulls her unmarked vehicle in the back of the building. She walks into the unit from the back. There are several officers already at the location. She is the first homicide detective on the scene.

"Hey, Sandy. EMS is working on the critical in the hallway. The other victim is facedown on the living room floor. We have a call into JID. The shooter is a kid. She admitted to shooting both of them. Her name is Cassandra," the African American officer says, providing Detective Dupri with an update.

"Who's that with her?" Detective Dupri asks the officer.

"It's her mother," the officer says.

"Hey, Kim. Let me have a minute with her," Detective Dupri says to the female officer adjusting Cassandra's handcuffs.

"It's Cassandra, right?" Detective Dupri asks.

"Yes." Cassandra cries with her head on her mother's shoulder.

"You guys don't understand. My daughter is the victim. Not that motherfucker," Delia yells in tears, holding Cassandra in her arms.

"I understand your concerns. You have to understand that someone was killed today. We also have another person critically injured. From your daughter's own confession, she was the one that shot them. That is a crime," Detective Dupri explains.

"That fucker was raping her. He was selling her to have sex with other men. You should be going after Persephone not Cassandra. What the fuck?" Delia cries harder.

"Cassandra, we're going to take you down to the station. There will be another detective there to ask you some questions," Detective Dupri says.

"I'm all set with her," Detective Dupri says to the female officer.

"No. Don't take her," Delia screams, holding on to Cassandra.

"Miss, if you don't let go, we're going to arrest you for interference," the female officer says firmly.

"Ma, it's okay. Everything will be okay now," Cassandra says calmly to her mother who is still crying.

The officer walks Cassandra to her cruiser through the back of the building.

Chapter 62 ANDREW

I can feel my body moving. My mind flashes scattered scenes. I feel like I'm lying at an angle. It's dark, and voices are all around me. Suddenly there is light. Water is falling on my face. I hear more voices, people asking questions.

"What happened in there? Is that DCF worker Andrew Edwards?" a voice asks.

Yes, I'm Andrew Edwards, I think but can't speak. The water has stopped falling. Now there are bright lights shining in my eyes. The air is getting thin. I can't keep my eyes open. Something is put over my mouth.

"He's going out again. Give him some oxygen," an accented voice says.

My body and mind suddenly feel at peace. I feel weightless. No pain, no confusion. It is like I am floating in the air. I look down and can see myself in an ambulance. I'm bleeding and have an oxygen mask on my face. The paramedics are working hard to keep me alive. I then remember what happened. I was shot. In a matter of seconds all the memories of my life pass before me. A strong jolt passes through my body and then another one. I was no longer outside of my body. The ambulance has stopped. I'm taken out and rolled into the hospital.

"He's losing a lot of blood," a male voice says.

I continue to go in and out of consciousness.

"One after another. I can't believe they found that lady on the street bleeding and naked like that. Crazy," a female voice says.

"I think this guy is worse. He's losing a lot of blood," the male voice says as I'm wheeled down a hallway.

There are beeping noises and urgent voices. I close my eyes and take a deep breath. I'm at peace.

Chapter 63 MADELINE

Madeline slowly crawls up the basement stairs to the door. She holds her shirt between her legs and uses every bit of strength to push open the heavy door. She loses her balance and falls to the ground outside. Madeline slowly rises to her feet. Her blood-soaked hands leave a handprint on the side of the building. She's feeling lightheaded. Madeline's naked body is covered with blood. The shirt between her legs is drenched with her blood. The blood seems to be gushing out of her body. Madeline staggers toward the street and falls in the grass in the front yard. She manages to look up. There are no cars or pedestrians on the street. She drags her body with her one free hand to the street. She hopes to end the pain.

Madeline manages to use every ounce of energy that is left. She rolls to her back and looks up to the sky. Rain begins to fall on her body. The earth is cleaning her and preparing her to return to God. She loses consciousness.

"Miss! Miss! Wake up. Jorge, she's alive. Help me get her in the car." Madeline can hear a female voice call out.

Madeline is rushed to Hartford Hospital in critical condition. The surgeons try to stop the bleeding but fear that she has lost too much blood. They suspect a vicious sexual assault. Madeline lays thinking of Trevan. She prays that he is safe and will have a good life. Madeline thinks of her brother Michael. She wonders how he looks, if he grew up to be a good boy. Madeline closes her eyes with the image of her mother in her mind. She prays to meet her in the next life. There is a beeping noise and urgent voices. She closes her eyes and takes a deep breath. She is at peace.

Chapter 64 ANDREW

Nearly a week after being admitted to the hospital, I'm discharged. The surgeons said the bullet went through the upper part of my chest. They said it missed major organs and arteries. I lost a large amount of blood. I owe my life to the paramedics because they were able to stop me from bleeding out.

After Patricia heard about the shooting, she rushed to my side. No words of the past were spoken. There was only support for the day. My mother, brother, and many colleagues visited me, leaving flowers and well-wishes.

As I leave the hospital, I thank all the nurses for helping me during my stay. I smile and wave as Peter wheels me off the floor.

The entire time I was in the hospital I couldn't get Cassandra's face out of my mind. The anger in her eyes seemed to radiate through me as she held the gun pointed at me. Cassandra's hesitation to pull the trigger was only because I was in front of Gordo. I was fortunate that I wasn't the one who died that day.

As I recover from my wounds, I know I still have to speak with Cassandra about Kay. I find out that Cassandra is being held at the adolescent female detention center on Washington Street in Hartford. Since the shooting, Cassandra's aunt Persephone has disappeared, abandoning their apartment. While I was in the hospital, Delia, Cassandra's mother, sent a card and flowers. In the card she said Cassandra was so sorry about the shooting. Delia wrote that Kay meant so much to Cassandra. I know one way to see Cassandra is for Delia to give me permission. I locate Delia's number and speak with her. She is willing to speak with me in person.

I arrive at the building off of Park Street and knock on the first-floor door.

"Hello, Mr. Edwards. You're looking much better," Delia says and holds the door open for me.

"Thanks. I have to take it day by day," I say as I walk into her one-bedroom unit.

"Excuse the mess. I just moved into the place. I haven't been able to unpack everything," Delia says as we walk to her partially furnished dining room.

"Nice place. It's much cleaner than my place." I smile and sit at the dining room table.

"Mr. Edwards, I have to tell you that Cassandra is so sorry for shooting you. She really didn't mean to do it." Delia begins to tear up.

"I know that Cassandra wasn't trying to shoot me. She was put in a very difficult situation."

"My family has so many secrets. I'm sure you were able to read it in your DCF paperwork. I recently found the courage to speak about my sexual abuse by my brother. Now Cassandra is in jail for killing him. It all doesn't make sense. It's like I've been living in one big nightmare," Delia says, wiping her tears.

We sit and converse for several minutes.

"I have something Cassandra wanted me to show you. I'll be right back." Delia excuses herself and then walks out of the room.

She returns with a sketchpad in her hands. "My daughter is an artist," Delia says with joy as she opens the pages of the pad. She turns the pages of the pad and admires Cassandra's talent for sketching. She stops at a beautiful sketch of Kay.

My eyes begin to water.

"She said Kay was like an angel to her."

"She was an angel for me too," I say as Delia turns the pad toward me. "The detail that Cassandra was able to capture is amazing. Everything is so perfect, from the shape of her eyes to the shadowing on her face," I say with a smile.

I wish that I can jump through the page and grab Kay in my arms. I know I only have her trapped in my memories.

"Cassandra told me that the day you came to the door and told Gordo your name, she knew who you were. Cassandra said she thought Miss Kay, her angel, had sent someone to save her," Delia says.

I never imagined that I would be sitting at a table crying my heart out with the mother of a person who shot me. I cry for many reasons, mostly for not having Kay. I cry for the void that her loss left in my heart. To think I could have saved Kay or prevented her murder if I had just listened crushes my soul. I knew Kay was special when I met her. I see that her generosity and love touched others besides me.

I flip through the pages of the sketchpad, admiring Cassandra's many drawings. Some of them are of faces, others are of objects and flowers. As the pages pass, I see a face that surprises me. I quickly return to the page. I'm shocked.

Why did she sketch this face?

Delia observed my reaction.

"Are you okay?" Delia asks.

"Do you know who this person is?" I ask, turning the pad toward Delia.

"No, I have no idea who that is. Cassandra enjoyed sketching everyone. It's probably one of her teachers," Delia said, taking a closer look at the sketch.

It's surely not one of her teachers.

"Delia, as I mentioned over the phone, I want to know if you would give me permission to speak with Cassandra in detention."

"Mr. Edwards, I am sure she would be happy to see you. You can definitely go see her. I think your problem may be her attorney not me," Delia says.

"Well, thanks again for your time."

"I think Cassandra would like for you to have this," Delia rips the page with the sketch of Kay out of the pad.

"Thank you. That means a lot to me."

Delia also allows me to take the sketch of the face that I asked about.

After being buzzed into the lobby area of the detention center, I wait for the counselor to come pick me up. I get many stares from the staff as I am escorted to an office on the second floor. I know they are looking because of all the news coverage from the incident with Madeline to the recent shooting in Dutch Point.

I spoke with Cassandra's attorney about visiting his client. I told him that it wasn't about the shooting. As tragic as it was for me, I understood where she was coming from. He was very resistant about me meeting with her, but he spoke with Cassandra, and she said she was willing to speak with me.

When I enter the room, Cassandra is in the corner with her head down, sketching on a sheet of paper. Her attorney is sitting next to her, talking on his cell phone. He quickly hangs up.

"Hi, Attorney Collins. My name is Andrew. We spoke on the phone the other day." I introduce myself and then sit on the opposite side of the table.

"Yes, Mr. Edwards. This is Cassandra." Attorney Collins turns to Cassandra.

"Hello, Cassandra." I turn to Cassandra, who looks up from her drawing.

"I'm so sorry." Cassandra begins to cry, covering her mouth with her hands.

"It's okay, Cassandra. I know you didn't mean to hurt me. I know what you were going through," I say and reach my hand across the table.

"Miss Kay was such a nice person. I miss her so much," Cassandra says, wiping her tears from her cheeks.

"I know Cassandra. I miss her too," I say in a soft comforting tone.

"I forged a permission slip to get into the program because of all the fun things my friends were saying they were doing." A little smile appears on Cassandra's face as she recalls the memory.

"I have my own history of forged permission slips," I say and smile at her. "How long was Kay walking you and the other children into Dutch Point?"

"It was for a while. I'm not sure how long," Cassandra says. "I worried about her walking us into Dutch Point. I live there. I know how dangerous it was for me. She looked like she came from the suburbs. I don't know if she ever saw a project before." Cassandra smiles.

"Yeah, I worried about her also. And I don't think she had ever been in a project before."

"The funny thing is after she started walking us home, we all felt safer. I always felt safe around her," Cassandra says, looking down to her angel sketch.

"I knew Kay was only trying to help you guys. She loved working there. Kay probably never imagined that she was putting her life in danger."

Attorney Collins takes an envelope out of his bag.

"This belongs to you." Attorney Collins slides the envelope across the table.

I open the envelope and see that it was the angel necklace that I gave to Kay. I look up and see that Cassandra still has tears in her eyes.

"This is yours now," I say and slide the necklace back across the table. "It meant a lot to Kay. If she gave it to you, she must have cared about you," I say, smiling.

"Thank you so much. I told Miss Kay how much I loved it," Cassandra says, rubbing the angel pendant with her fingers.

I open the folder that I came with and take out one of Cassandra's sketches. "Cassandra, while I was visiting your mother, she showed me several of your sketches. There was one that caught my eye. Who is this?" I ask as I slide the sketch toward her.

I immediately see that her demeanor changes. She pulls back when she sees the face.

"Are you okay?" I ask as she takes her sketch and looks at the face closely.

"I've seen him in Dutch Point before," Cassandra says, looking up at me.

"What?" I ask, surprised by her remarks. "Was he there the night Kay was killed?" I ask confused.

"Cassandra, you don't have to answer that question," Attorney Collins advises her. "Mr. Edwards, this interview is over," Attorney Collins says, rising from his chair.

"No, wait. Cassandra do you know something about Kay's murder?" I ask, pushing the subject.

"No, you wait, Mr. Edwards. This is not how I thought the interview was going to go. I'm sorry, but we are done," Attorney Collins repeats more firmly. "Let's go, Cassandra," Attorney Collins says as Cassandra stands.

"I'm sorry about Miss Kay," Cassandra says, handing me the sketch that is now folded.

Attorney Collins and Cassandra exit the room. I turn to put the folded sketch back into the folder on the table. I unfold the sketch and have my answer. Cassandra quickly wrote on the bottom of the sketch before she left the room. What I read is all I needed to know.

*   *   *

I stand anxiously inside the elevator and wait for the door to open. I take an express ride to the nineteenth floor. The time is seven o'clock, long past business hours. The elevator door opens. I rush toward his office.

"Hi, Mr. Edwards. Wait! Dr. Sol has a client inside. You can't go in!" the secretary says getting up from her chair as I whisk past her.

"Dr. Sol, we need to speak," I stress as I barge into the middle of his session.

"What's going on?" a frail Caucasian female asks nervously, turning to Dr. Sol.

"I'm sorry, Dr. Sol. I told him you were in a session," the secretary says apologetically.

"No. We need to speak now," I insist, standing a couple of feet in front of Dr. Sol.

"Angela, I think we came to a good area to end for today. How about you go with the secretary and schedule a makeup?" Dr. Sol calmly says to Angela, who is still visibly shaken by my interruption.

Dr. Sol walks Angela out the door. He tells the secretary that she can leave for the night after she was done. He closes the door behind them.

"Andrew, how can I help you?" Dr. Sol asks, unfazed by my urgency.

"How can you help me? You can start by telling me why the hell you were

281

in Dutch Point on the night Kay was murdered!" I say, holding Cassandra's sketch in front of his face.

"Andrew. What is this? Is this a joke?" Dr. Sol asks calmly, taking the sketch from my hand. He sits behind his desk and examines the sketch.

"A joke? Do you think I'm fucking kidding with you? Why the hell were you in Dutch Point the night Kay was murdered?" I demand an answer, banging on his desk with my fist.

You know why he was there. He's just toying with you.

"Andrew, you really need to calm down. Listen to what you're asking. You tell me how it could be possible that I was there," Dr. Sol says inverting my question.

His words briefly defuse my inquiry.

"How the hell could Cassandra draw this sketch of you if you weren't there? Fucking tell me the truth, so help me God," I say, pushing the papers off his desk.

"The truth. So you want to know the truth, Andrew?" Dr. Sol asks without emotion, leaning back in his chair.

He's playing with you, Andrew. He knows the truth.

"Stop fucking sitting there all calm like nothing is happening! I read Kay's journal. She came here to speak with you. Why didn't you tell me?"

"Andrew, I thought it was best that you didn't know that Kay came to see me," Dr. Sol says. " I did it for-

I cut him off in midsentence. "Best I didn't know? What, was it some fucking secret?" I shout, gesturing with my hands.

See, Andrew. He's fucking around with you. If you don't get it out of him, he won't give you the answer.

"Shut the fuck up. Stop talking. Just let me think," I say to myself, rubbing my face with my hands.

Think? How much more do you need to know, Andrew?

Dr. Sol calmly sits in his chair and studies me as I argue with myself. I can feel my other side emerging as the anger and frustration build.

"You really don't know, do you?" Dr. Sol asks with his hands folded in front of him.

"What the hell are you talking about?" I yell and then kick his little table to the floor.

"You know that feeling you have right now, Andrew? The anger, the confusion, the voice in your head, the dreams? That is power when it's under control. Power when it's focused and molded can't be stopped," Dr. Sol says as he squeezes his fist in front of him.

"What the fuck are you talking about? What does this have to do with Kay?"

"It has everything to do with Kay," Dr. Sol says calmly. "I waited for a very long time for you, Andrew. Through our hypnotherapy sessions, I was able to unlock your past. It only took a couple of sessions for me to know that I found the perfect soldier for the cause," Dr. Sol explains.

"This doesn't make any sense," I say, my confusion and anger rising by the second.

"You feel that anger you have right now, Andrew? I was able to harness that anger. Your past created it, and I found the source. I channeled it to help us clean the streets," Dr. Sol says, smiling at his own words.

"You were using me for some fucking game?"

"It was no game, Andrew. You wanted it just as much as I did," Dr. Sol says.

I never understood the voices in my head. Why there were certain things I just didn't remember.

"Andrew, the answers to some of your questions were right in front of you. It amazes me how someone as smart as you couldn't figure it out," Dr. Sol says, still sitting in his chair.

"Figure it out. Figure what out? You're just trying to confuse me. That's it." I say leaning forward and pushing the desk back toward Dr. Sol.

"You're only confusing yourself. You've tricked your mind not to understand," Dr. Sol says.

"Understand what?" I ask, trying to wrap my mind around his words.

"Understand that you suffer from dissociative amnesia and dissociative identity disorder."

"Dissociative amnesia? Identity disorder? I'm not fucking crazy!" I shout, with both hands planted on the front of his desk, ready to jump on him.

"You're right, Andrew. You're not crazy. You're just no different than many of the clients that you work with. What did your stepfather do to make you so angry, Andrew? Think about it. It holds the key to everything," Dr. Sol says as he leans back in his chair, examining my reaction to his questions.

"My stepfather? The key?" I say, rubbing my head.

You know what the pervert did to you, Andrew. It was the touching, the sucking, and fondling. That's when you met me, Andrew. You pushed yourself so far away from reality, you created your own world. We hid in the cocoon, Andrew. It protected us for a while.

"No, that's not right. Nothing happened to me," I say, squeezing my head with my hands.

"Andrew, those voices you hear in your head. That's you, Andrew. You created it," Dr. Sol says as he leans over to open the file cabinet next to his desk.

"No. What the fuck? No! That's not right," I say, moving to the chair.

"Andrew, as a child you had to create an escape to separate yourself from the abuse. You had to detach yourself from reality. Escape in your mind," Dr. Sol says as his voice echoes in my head.

"You see it so clearly with the children on your cases. You only missed it in yourself."

"No. No. It's not right," I say, rocking back and forth in my chair.

This time he is right.

"Please shut up! Just shut up," I shout to the voice speaking in my head.

"You blocked the memory. Sealed it in the back of your mind." As Dr. Sol speaks, images of my own abuse begin to flash in front of me.

"How come I didn't see this before?" I ask as I struggle to understand the gap in my memory.

"Some things aren't for you to see, Andrew. They are for others to find. The voices in your head were the fuel for the cause." Dr. Sol's voice bounces around in my head.

"It doesn't make sense. This is some trick," I say angrily, standing and then throwing the chair toward him.

"It's no trick, Andrew. You just have to remember. We did this together. Every single one of them deserved what they received," Dr. Sol says as the chair barely misses him. "This is what we've worked on, Andrew. This will help you remember," Dr. Sol says, spreading some papers across the desk.

"What are you talking about? What is this?" I ask, picking up one of the papers.

"They are our targets, Andrew," Dr. Sol says proudly, reading from one of the papers.

"Assignment one sodomized three little boys. He never spent a day in jail. That changed after we found him. Assignment four raped his ten-year-old daughter and impregnated her. He spent five years in jail only to rape again. We made sure he could never do it again. It goes on and on. Do you remember now?" Dr. Sol asks, holding one of the sheets of paper in front of me.

My mind flashes through the assignments. The faces. The blood.

"You are the perfect partner, Andrew. You give us access to the resources that we need to track our prey," Dr. Sol says calmly. "We all have our secrets, Andrew. Your deep-rooted anger was based on your stepfather and the abuse. The loss of my son is what drives me. Drives me to kill all these sick pedophiles out on the street. I knew I couldn't do it alone. That's why I know we were meant to do this together. The cause is our purpose, Andrew," Dr. Sol says proudly.

"Now I know why Kay wanted to know so much about you. I understand why Patricia asked about my sessions. They were both trying to warn me. I blocked them out. You made me block them. You were right. All of the pieces are in front of me," I say as my head throbs.

After Patricia departed a couple of days ago, I read through the paperwork she left behind.

"I know about your son. He was kidnapped, sodomized, and murdered. The guy we just killed, Holter, was your son's murderer," I say, making the connection.

"The police didn't have enough evidence to hold Holter. That anger just grew inside of me. It transformed me. Made me heartless. I resigned from Stanford and went into private practice. That way I could have more time to watch Holter. Then one day he disappeared. I knew from one of my buddies at the police station that Holter had connections to Connecticut. So I decided to leave California. I lost my son, my wife left me. I had nothing, all because of Holter. It was by divine intervention that you came into my life. You helped me track him down here in Hartford. I thank you for that," Dr. Sol explains.

"You still haven't explained what Kay had to do with all of this," I say, returning to the reason I was in his office.

"Kay? Andrew, did you not hear me? This cause was made for both of us. We couldn't allow anything to get in between our destiny. Kay just got in the way," Dr. Sol says, annoyed by my comments.

"Got in the way?" I rush behind the desk and strike him to the ground.

"Kay was getting too close, Andrew. You want to know what she told me when she came to see me? Kay said she went to the house of one of our assignments. Kay could have ruined everything we worked for," Dr. Sol says with his hands up in front of his face.

"Did you kill her? You motherfucker!" I yell, grabbing him by his shirt.

"I wasn't going to allow her to throw all of our work away," Dr. Sol says, smiling in my face.

"You motherfucker!" I shout, throwing him across his desk onto the floor.

"You want the truth, Andrew? You want the truth? I followed her everywhere she went after she visited me. You were right to be concerned about her going into Dutch Point. I just waited for the opportunity," Dr. Sol says, trying to stand.

"Opportunity?" I say, stomping him back down onto the floor with my foot.

"You were getting us so close to finding Holter. There was no way I was going to allow her to ruin our plan. To stop us before we found Holter," Dr. Sol says as I pick up the table, throwing it at him.

Dr. Sol sits on the floor trying to dodge my assault. His tie is askew and his face is damp with sweat. "Your hands were stained with her blood too, Andrew. You're connected to her murder more than you know," Dr. Sol laughs as he wipes blood from his mouth.

"What the hell are you talking about?" I ask, pausing in my attack.

"The night Kay was killed, you picked me up. Remember, Andrew? You picked me up!" Dr. Sol says, laughing harder.

"We discussed a new assignment," I say out loud to myself, remembering the night. "You used me for your cause? You used me as a tool in the murder of my wife?"

Suddenly, I realized my mind was clear for the first time in years. The voice in my head was gone. There was no mistake about what was going to happen next. Dr. Sol made sense of who I am. What I've become.

"For the past year I wept with sadness for Kay. I had a lifetime of many questions. Now I have answers," I say, looking at Dr. Sol as he rose to his feet, adjusting his tie and righting his chair.

"So, Andrew. You see, we're the same," Dr. Sol says, smiling as he wipes himself off.

I pull the gun from my waist. I point it at Dr. Sol.

"What the hell is this, Andrew?" Dr. Sol asks surprised, putting his hands up. "Andrew, there is so much more that we have to do. We've only gotten started," Dr. Sol says slowly, taking his hands down.

I aim the gun at his head.

Should I shoot his face off?

I then aim the gun at his heart.

Which shot will kill him faster?

I then aim back at his head. I stand there thinking of Kay, the love he took from me.

This is too easy. Dr. Sol deserves to suffer.

"Hey, I'm the only one that knows the real Andrew," Dr. Sol says with a large smile on his face.

"You're right." I smile and then pull the trigger.

Chapter 65 ANDREW

The deafening explosion from the gun echoes in my ears. My knees buckle. It feels like all of the air is being sucked out of my body. I step back and collapse into one of the leather chairs, my right arm dangling off the side. The gun is still in my hand. It's over. *Or is it?* The pain is still there. It feels like it's crushing me. Exhaustion sweeps through my body. I close my eyes and everything goes black. The dull thud from the gun slipping from my hand and hitting the carpeted floor snaps me out of the fog that consumes me. *How long have I been out?*

My head throbs. I lift my hands to my face, pushing my fingers into my forehead, trying to focus. I look out the window. The sky is dark. I look down at Dr. Sol. *Pig.* The office is wrecked. Overturned chairs, papers everywhere. Blood seeps into the carpet. I take a deep breath and exhale through my mouth. I reach down toward the gun, which is lying on a mass of scattered papers on the floor. Next to Dr. Sol's body lays the hard plastic case of his office phone.

For a moment I think about Patricia, about Cassandra, about what is, what was and what might have been. All I can remember is my mind repeating over and over and over "Kay. My Beautiful Kay." She is no longer with me in this life. By the decisions that I have made, she may not be with me in the next life either. I can no longer live a life with pain or with this irreplaceable void. I will only return to learn what I have neglected to realize.

You know what you have to do, Andrew.

On the other side of the city, the moon glints off the Colt building's blue onion dome. The night settles over Dutch Point. I think of the Hartford of today and a Hartford of the past. Hartford was a once rich city that housed

288

some of the world's greatest minds and innovators. I live in a Hartford that was transformed into one of the poorest cities in the nation. Our lives are full of unorganized thoughts, sorted confusion full of hidden secrets only to be revealed.

In a span of a week, I stand close to the edge of death. Some try hard to stand on top of their own Mount Olympus, trying to defeat the Titans. No matter how hard we try, we're reminded that we are all mortal. We're reminded that God is the one that gives life and at any moment can take it away.

I opened the closet. I faced my demons. I exposed my past. I lived a life of good and evil only to be manipulated and consumed by revenge and hate. I beat down the hands that surrounded me. I was left standing in a bottomless pit. The many people that I've helped over time were canceled out by the bad deeds and wrong decisions.

With the gun in my hand I think of the forever changing Dutch Point and the city of Hartford. It will hold the history of the greats and the stories of the forgotten. I will release myself from this pain. I will release myself from this day. I have no more thoughts. I stand from the chair and walk toward the window. I raise my right hand to my head. It...is...over.

I close my eyes and wait.

"This is 9-1-1. What's your emergency?"

Kareem R. Muhammad was born into a family with over forty years of experience in social work. Living and working in Hartford, Connecticut, for over ten years, he has been exposed to many dimensions of abuse and neglect as an investigative social worker for the Connecticut Department of Children and Families.